I0772243

No part of this publication may be reproduced, stored in a retrieval system, or transmitted in any form or by any means, electronic, mechanical, photocopying, recording, scanning, or otherwise, without the prior written permission of the publisher, except in the case of brief quotations within critical reviews and otherwise as permitted by copyright law.

NOTE: This is a work of fiction. Names, characters, places, and incidents are a product of the author's imagination. Any resemblance to real life is purely coincidental. All characters in this story are 18 or older.

Copyright © 2024, Willow Winters Publishing. All rights reserved.

One Kiss Isn't Enough

Willow Winters

WALL STREET JOURNAL & USA TODAY BESTSELLING AUTHOR

One is never enough,
which is why a romance collection filled with love
stories is perfection.

This collection contains all the kisses and feels (and
standalone short story romances).

STORIES INCLUDED:

A LITTLE BIT IN LOVE WITH YOU
THEN YOU KISSED ME
FALLING AT FIRST SIGHT
ALL I WANT IS A KISS
JUST A LITTLE CRUSH
PRETEND YOU LOVE ME
SEDUCTIVE
A KISS TO KEEP

Then You Kissed Me

CHAPTER 1

BRODY

'm not supposed to be here, in this bar, to flirt with a girl I don't even know... it's all I can think when I notice her.

Her curves are not why I'm here, although they're exactly why I'm standing in the middle of the bar, stopped in my tracks before I can even sit down. *She's not on my to-do list tonight.*

Even with the internal voice scolding every thought I have, I know the second I lay eyes on her, perched on a stool with a faraway look in her striking hazel eyes, that there's something about this girl that makes it harder to keep walking than it should be.

"You can seat yourself," a hostess, with a tight but

kind smile and three tall menus for the Blue Room wrapped in stamped black leather, tells me as she walks past at the pace of a woman who's busy as all hell in this crowded bar. "Thanks," I answer the back of her white dress as she heads off.

This place is made to look like a modern day speakeasy with the clean décor but darkened corners. And packed at that. Makes sense, I guess, since it's a college town. It's amazing there's even a seat open at the bar. Especially one next to a woman like the one in that tight red dress.

My good friend Griffin told me about this bar. He said it was a good place to think since it's always busy and the chatter and ambiance makes for decent white noise. He knows the shit I'm going through and a beer and good atmosphere will do wonders to take your mind off things you'd rather not deal with. Well according to him.

Taking a glance at the far end of the bar that separates the large space into two halves, I'm sure Griffin didn't have that blonde at the bar in mind when he said I should go clear my head. Sit down. Have a beer. Watch the game. Those were my marching orders.

Getting lost in her is exactly what I'd rather do than spend the night drinking alone, waiting on Griffin to be done his ... whatever the hell he had to do. Of all the people in here, she's the only one I really notice.

Although it's obvious she did that by design.

She's alone at the bar, even though her short, red dress is a show piece. The way the silky fabric rides up her thigh and she blushes when she notices... it does something to me. The mix of sultry and innocence. Like she's not sure how much she should give away. She's not used to doing this. This young girl on the hunt for a good time charade.

If nothing else, I know if I don't sit next to her, someone else will. If I don't take her home tonight some other asshole in this place damn sure will. The moment that realization hits me, I know there's no way in hell I'm going to let that happen.

Smirking, I watch her throw back the pink cocktail and make my way to her as she watches the crowd. I'm no knight in shining armor, but I know how to buy a girl a drink.

I've decided, after less than a minute of watching her, that she's on the prowl, but too damn cute and innocent to know what she's doing. Telling myself that's all this is, I drag out the bar stool and ask her if she needs another drink.

Her eyes hit me first then the blush in her cheeks rises all the way up to her temple. My blood simmers and travels lower. I was right, she's a shy little thing to be sitting alone, wearing a dress that's meant for a good time.

She keeps looking at me, her fingers fiddling with the rim of her empty glass. Even that small movement is sexy as hell. The smile is sweet and the fact that she's too busy eying me up to realize she hasn't answered makes me laugh.

That gruff sound that comes deep from my chest turns her cheeks to an even hotter shade of red. I might be man candy to some girls, but damn she doesn't hide it at all.

"Yes please, if you're offering," she finally answers, twirling the ends of her wavy hair around the tips of her fingers flirtatiously. Her voice is soft, and gentle, but with a playfulness that's undeniable. And her lips... fuck, my cock is already hardening.

Better than that, she can barely keep her gaze on me without smiling even harder.

She's fucking adorable. The perfect mix of sweet and sexy. Just knowing I get to her makes the black tee shirt that's already tight on my broad shoulders even tighter. I know I look blue collar; I can't hide that rough side of me. Dark jeans and a black tee shirt are about as dressed up as I ever get.

This girl looks like anything but that.

But the way she fidgets and keeps glancing at me like I'm man candy she hasn't tasted, lets me know she's as interested in me as I am in her.

Thank fuck. I'm not from around here, never went to college, and it's been a while since I've dated anyone.

She's not eye fucking me, she's eye glancing me because she's too bashful to outright stare at me. Everything about her makes me smile. She's too damn cute to be here alone.

Small talk is easy with her. This girl named Rose. It suits her with the red dress and delicate features of her slender neck. Throughout the night, all I can think about is kissing her there. Every time her hand slips down to my thigh. Playful and seemingly innocent but I know she knows what she's doing.

Every hour that passes, the place empties out more and more. She doesn't seem to notice or care. She's too busy asking me questions that are far too sweet and demure to elicit anything more than a laugh and more of those stolen touches. *What's my favorite color? What's my best friend's name? What's a joke I'd never tell my parents?*

Until she asks what brought me here since I'm not in college. Saying I came to visit a friend worked the first time, but she pries deeper so I hit her back with the same kind of question. The kind of question where there's a piece of it you don't want to exist.

"What brought you here tonight? In a red dress, sitting all alone?"

Her slender fingers slip on the straw in her glass of water and her gaze drops to the bar. At first, I think she's not going to answer, but she surprises me. Her bottom lip slips out from her teeth, grabbing all my attention to her kissable lips before Rose answers me, "I wanted to meet someone tonight."

"Is that right?"

"Yeah," she nods, the tension that was there for a split second when I asked her the question vanishes and her small hand lands on my thigh again, doing all sorts of things to me that the simplest of touches shouldn't be capable of doing. Thump, thump, my blood pumps harder as she brings her lips to the shell of my ear.

"I kind of want to go home with you tonight," her warm breath sends a shiver down my neck, past my shoulders and doesn't stop.

"You're tipsy," it's only a comment, but there's an invitation hidden in my tone. I give her the way out though, just in case it's only liquid courage. "I could take you home, drop you off if you want?"

"You're cute," Rose whispers around her drink as she peeks up at me with her thick lashes. My grin is easy. All of tonight has been easy. I haven't thought about a damn thing except what she has to say. When the lights turn on behind the bar, the music turns off and the check hits the table, I slap the cash down, tipping the bartender well.

I ask this sweet Rose as she climbs off the stool, standing next to me a head shorter and her gaze focused on the dip in my throat, "What do you want to do?"

She sets her finger right where she's looking, her touch gentle and her voice nearly lost in the air between us, "I want to kiss you right here."

That does it. Wrapping an arm around her waist, I pull her in close and revel in the feel of her soft body against mine as her heels hit the floor and she squeals in delight.

She doesn't let go of me, and in the cab she fucking tortures me, kissing me just below my ear on that tender spot I thought about kissing her.

"Not yet, my wild Rose," I half scold her in a whisper but as she pulls away, I capture her lips in mine. The kiss is searing, that first one in the back of the cab, with the taste of temptation and tequila mixing. My blood runs hot, my fingers inching up her thigh the way she did it to me all night. The only difference is I'm touching bare skin and the light, tender touch isn't enough.

Her gasp fills the cab when I pull away and when the cab driver looks back at us in the rearview, I keep my gaze forward, as if nothing at all is going on back here against his black leather seat.

As if I don't want to rip off her dress and push my

hand between her legs, and rock my palm against her clit.

"You're already hard," her whisper comes with a hint of awe as she grips me through my jeans. Fuck, my head falls back and I close my eyes when the cab driver tries to meet my gaze again, his eyebrows much higher up on his forehead.

"Wait just five more minutes, Rose."

"I don't want to wait." Her protest is adorable, but there's no way this driver is getting a show.

"You're killing me," I groan and decide I should satisfy her before I come undone and take her right here.

With my fingers spearing through her gorgeous blonde locks, I mold my lips against hers, stealing her surprise gasp and loving the soft moan of pleasure she gives me when I kiss her again. Her fingers play along the back of my neck, her tongue dancing with mine and I make sure to keep my hands right where they are on the small of her waist. One move, and I swear I won't be able to stop.

I've never been so relieved to hear a cab driver tell me "we're here" and hand over the cash.

Rose's cheeks are a gorgeous hue of pink that travels down to her chest.

Griffin's not here when I unlock the apartment door. She's in my arms, her legs wrapped around my waist, her ankles hooked behind me with her heels digging into my ass before I can even kick the door shut behind me.

This girl knows what she wants and I've never been so eager to give it to her, to satisfy every sordid thought I know she had back at the bar.

I don't bother turning on the lights to Griffin's bachelor apartment, barren of everything that makes a home a home considering his student budget.

She doesn't need to see any of this place, she doesn't want to either. All she wants is to get in bed and as I kick my shoes off, our lips still locked in place, I'm just fine with that.

Her ass fits perfectly in my palms, but this damn dress is in the way.

My desire to shred it is only tamed by the fact that I know this is all she has to wear when this is over and I sure as shit know Griffin doesn't have any chick's clothes here.

When I toss her on the bed, the faded light shining through the slits in the blinds and casting the most beautiful shadows along the curves of her neck and breasts, she takes in a deep inhale, arching her back like she's been deprived of breath all the while.

That's when I realize the heavy rising and falling of my own chest, and sharp need to be buried inside of her that overrides any other sane thought that might come to me.

My jeans are off, my shirt ripped over my head and tossed carelessly on the floor in seconds. Her dress and lace underwear are quick to join my pile of clothes.

"I love the way your hands feel," she moans as I cup her breast in my hand. Her chest is small but full and when I run the pad my thumb over her hardened peaks, her head falls back, her lips part just slightly and her eyes close. I let her lose herself in the pleasure I give her, skimming my hands over her body, kissing every inch of her until I find her hot and glistening between her thighs.

With my breathing finally calm again, and hers ragged as she lays under me, I pump my cock once in my hand to get her attention. Her eyes go wide and that seems to wake her up.

She doesn't say anything, but her gaze doesn't leave my length and she stills on the bed.

Fuck. That is not a good sign.

"You alright?" I ask her realizing something is very fucking wrong right now. Please don't back out. Please, for the love of all things holy, I need to be inside this woman more than I need to breathe.

Licking her lower lip, her body relaxes only slightly when she looks up at me and says, "You're... you're really big." I don't break her hazel stare.

"I'll go slow."

She nods and gets settled, the sheets rustling as she

lays down, far more aware than I think she's been all night.

Nestling my hips between her thighs, she spreads her legs wider for me. The first kiss I give her is in the crook of her neck, that spot I was dying to kiss before. With the head of my dick pressing against her warmth, I let the tip of my nose run up her neck and take my time kissing her again.

The warmth comes back to her body, every small touch bringing her closer and closer to the edge of writhing under me. I nip her lower lip and she kisses me desperately.

That's my cue to enter her in a swift but slow, deep stroke. I stare down at her as I push all of myself into her. Her nails dig into my back, her reddened lips, swollen from kissing me, making a beautiful little "o".

And her gaze stays on mine as her heart pounds in time with mine. I stay that way, letting her stretch and get adjusted until she finally breathes again. It takes longer than I thought it would, but every second is worth it.

The next stroke is faster, deeper and then harder. Working my way up to taking her like I want. The slapping sound due to her arousal and my pistoning hips stirs with her strangled moans of pleasure. She tilts her hips every time she comes and it lets me in deeper as her pussy flutters around my cock.

I want to come more times than I can count, but I

can't get enough of the feeling when she gets off. The sound of her crying out my name. The pleas she makes not to stop. Every little thing she does is mesmerizing.

When I finally have my release, it's four o clock in the morning and her breathing comes in chaotic pants, her body well spent and well fucked.

"Can I crash here?" her voice is a whispered wish, sleeping dragging her down deeper into the covers. As if I'd kick her out. *What kind of men is she used to?*

"Yeah, of course," I answer her, pulling the covers around us both. I'm rewarded with a small smile on her gorgeous face and a hum of satisfaction as she scoots closer to me. Apparently, she's a cuddler. A piece of me is more than satisfied with that side of her and the feel of her against me and the easy way she lets me hold her.

Her body molds to mine, her soft curves not leaving an inch of space between us in the bed. The bed protests with a groan at every small movement we make. The dim light that slips through the blinds, provided only by the street lights, lays against her soft skin, and begs me to kiss her again. Right there in the crook of her neck, just to see if she'll shiver again at my touch. If it wasn't for her steady breathing and the angelic look on her face as she sleeps, I'd wake her again and take her again. There's something about her that's addictive. Something that calls to a deeper side of me, telling me she needs it just as much as I do.

Lying beside the messy halo of her blonde locks, with the floral and fragrant, I drift off. Sleeping beside her lures me to sweet dreams of her soft moans as I take her again and again; I sleep better than I have in months.

I'm not prepared to wake up alone. Finding her side of the bed long gone and cold is a bit of a surprise to say the least. I want her again. I dreamed of the sounds she'd make early in the morning. Her legs wrapped around my waist as I pounded into her. Fuck, I can't wait to hear her cry out as her nails scraped down my back. There's no better way to start a morning than a good hard fuck. But the house is empty.

She didn't even leave me a note, my wild Rose.

That realization makes me laugh as I shake my head and pour myself a cup of coffee. She must've left before the sun was even up. I remember her asking if she could stay last night and I wonder if she's been kicked out before and didn't want to go through that again.

That's the first sign of unease I feel, but I shake it off, feeling confident that I'll see her again at the bar tonight.

It was a wild night and missing her only makes me want her more. Just like the red dress at the bar, she knew what she was doing. Playing hard to get.

I thought she was toying with me. I was so damn certain I'd see her again.

I only went to that bar to look for her. I only stayed in that town an extra week, waiting for her. Every day that passed, the disappointment grew deeper. I decided one day we'd meet again, and I'd make her ass pay for not saying good bye. I got a lot wrong in my life, but I've never been so grateful that I was right about running into Rose again. Even if it was four years later, in another town.

Even if she'd kept something from me that changed everything.

I thought I had life all figured out... and then she kissed me.

Falling At First Sight

PROLOGUE

AUTUMN

"It's his ass and you know it."

Magnolia has to cover her mouth as she laughs and haphazardly sets the wineglass down, doing her best not to lose any of the sweet wine with the motion. I'm awful glad I waited to take a sip until Renee said what she wanted to say. She's the comedic one in our group of four. Twirling a lock of auburn hair, she leans back, her wicked hazel eyes glinting. Renee is sharp and shameless.

But it's definitely not his ass. *At least not for me.* My comment remains unspoken because we're discussing Sharon's crush, after all.

"Renee, you know darn well I am not a butt lady. I couldn't care less about what's good on the backside."

"But he has a really nice ass," Renee insists, completely ignoring Sharon.

With the mason jar string lights hanging above us, Sharon's patio offers plenty of light, even as the southern sun sets in a beautiful hue of marigold and rose. Add in the wicker furniture, a touch of salt in the air plus the smell of fall surrounding us, and I'm all for Wine Down Wednesdays starting up again with this group of friends. It's been too long and I've missed them.

"What does Henry think of Mr. Morgan?" Sharon asks me and I instantly feel the telltale sign of a blush rising up my chest and making my cheeks flush.

My mother always told me I couldn't hide a thing from anyone. My face gives away the truth every time.

"What does my son think of your crush?" I respond with a question and quickly take a sip of my wine, then another, buying time. Sharon called dibs on Trent Morgan in before I had even walked my son into the preschool for his first day. That was almost a full year ago.

Now that school has started back up, I have to see that handsome face every day, my words stumbling and my laughs coming a little too often every time he talks to me.

He's off-limits. My son's teacher and my friend's

secret infatuation.

Truth be told, even if Sharon hadn't claimed Trent in our group of single ladies, I wouldn't have the guts to make a move.

Single mom and a little shy is what would be on my dating profile … if I had one. I'm rusty, to say the least, and haven't been on a date in over a year, other than horrible disasters which are "events that shall not be named," according to this particular group.

They're all still looking at me, waiting for an answer. Does my son like Trent Morgan?

Finally I shrug, setting my wineglass down and leaning back in my rocking chair. "You know all the kids love Mr. Morgan. He's the fun one who makes the best airplane sound effects."

All eyes are still on me as if they can tell exactly what I'm thinking, so I add a little comment: "They don't like him the same as you, though." Chuckles lessen the nerves racking me.

Little nerves that wish I'd make a move. Little nerves that pine from a distance just to see that smile again.

CHAPTER 1

TRENT

Any minute now. The exhale after my first sip of coffee, with just a touch of cream and a touch of sugar, is long and impatient. Any minute now she should walk through that door.

The doors open, catching my attention, but the person who enters isn't who I'm waiting for.

"Morning, Mr. Morgan!" Savannah sings out, not bothering to slow down in her race with her brother Liam as the sibling duo run to their designated room.

"Good morning, Savannah," I say, smiling broadly when they both get to Stacey, who's waiting for them in her section of the first floor. There are already two dozen children playing and laughing, getting their excitement out, and another half dozen to go. My class is the first one, closest to the front door, filled with a mix of kids who are four and five years old, and shared with Miss Sandy.

There's one student in particular whose absence forces my gaze to move back to the clock on the far wall. Any minute now and Henry will walk through those double glass doors. He'll probably press his hand to the painted print of his palm that we did last week to decorate for September. It forms a pattern of fall leaves and is taped to the lower half of the door.

That moment is what I'm waiting for. He'll let go of his mom's hand and she'll peer through the window, and those beautiful green eyes will meet mine.

With an asymmetric grin, fate gives me exactly what I ordered. Little Henry, with his dark, thick floppy curls falling in front of his forehead, races to the front door. It's not quite a mohawk that Autumn gives her son, since it's just a little higher on top. She told me it's because she loves his curls. His skin's a bit lighter than mine; a tawny brown. Henry's treasured Iron Man backpack hits the cement and the woman I've been waiting for bends down in her sundress to scoop it up for him.

With a simper on her lips, she moves her gaze from her son to me. Those green eyes spark, her smile widens and I can hear that feminine sigh that I know she just let slip from those full lips as she looks away.

The first thought I had about Autumn Holloway is far too inappropriate for this setting. As is my reaction every single time I see her.

Last year, she teased me, giving me mixed signals. Watching her gather Henry as they enter, I remember how I asked her out almost a year ago. She declined. Clearing her throat far too many times and that rosy hue that drives me wild staining her cheeks.

I gave her space, but every day since then she's given me that same shy smile paired with covert glances. Every. Single. Day. This year, the tension is even thicker and my longing for just a chance is even worse.

The front door opens, bringing in a refreshing fall breeze. "Mr. Morgan!" Henry yells although he's not paying me any attention at all as he races past me to the gate where Miss Sandy is already waiting for him.

"Miss Sandy!" he calls out with the same enthusiasm as I tell the five-year-old good morning and watch Sandra take him back. He's a happy kid and reminds me of my own son, Chase. Who just happens to be his best friend.

"Sorry I'm late," Autumn says, holding the backpack with both hands.

"No worries," I respond and hold out my hand for the backpack. I have to grin when she stares at my hand for a moment too long and then shakes her head with her eyes closed. She opens her eyes, her gorgeous green gaze finding mine before she passes over her son's backpack.

"Right, right." Her smile widens, beautiful and filling me with warmth as she stares back at me and says, "You'd think I'd remember this from last year." With the backpack now in my hand, I swallow thickly.

"No worries," I tell her again and inwardly scold myself. *Say something else. Damn.* This woman does something to me. I co-own the preschool and I don't want to push boundaries, but I want her.

I've never wanted a woman like I do Autumn. Her sweet blushes, her shy smiles, her luscious curves—I want it all.

As she signs her son in, I can't take my eyes off of her. That is, until her hand whips around, pen still between those fingers, to point at me and say something. She doesn't get a word out though other than "shit."

My disposable coffee cup was practically filled to the brim still and luckily only lukewarm since some of it splashed onto her forearm.

"I'm so sorry," she says, obviously in distress as she pushes out the words, frantically wiping up the mess with a stack of tissues she pulled from her purse. Mom-ready.

I almost say "no worries" yet again as I grab some paper towels, helping her clean up the mess that I could and should take care of by myself to put her at ease.

Almost. Almost but I don't.

Stopping myself, I wait until the chaos has left her beautiful gaze.

"Looks like you owe me a coffee date," is what comes out instead. The casual maybe-joke, sets a tension between us as I clean up what's left of the mess and shy Autumn pauses her movements to peek up at me.

I swear my pulse slows and every noise around us fades to nothing when I watch her reaction. The way her mouth parts slightly and then her teeth sink down into her pouty lips. The swallow that follows makes her neck seem that much more tempting to kiss.

"Mr. Morgan," she barely says my name in a breathy voice and then clears her throat, the nerves getting to her. *They get to me too, beautiful.*

"Are you asking me out on a date?" she half teases back and the two of us toss the soaked paper towels in the trash can.

"Yes," I answer her and that playfulness evaporates. "Just coffee," I tell her, holding my ground, and then I hold my breath.

Wide eyed, her gaze drops to my lips for just a moment. I'll be damned if this woman doesn't want me. "Please," I add for good measure, plastering a smirk on my lips. The smirk that always makes her shift in place from foot to foot.

"Just coffee?" she asks softly.

I can only nod, because I'd rather do that than lie.

As two more youngsters enter, breaking up the moment when one of them cries not to be left by her father, I worry I've lost her. And that she's going to politely decline.

Instead, she tucks her hair behind her ear and agrees to the date by saying, "I think coffee would be nice."

CHAPTER 2

AUTUMN

My phone is blowing up as it lays on my somewhat made queen bed. I never tuck in the sheets, but the off-white comforter with a gray paisley pattern is pulled over enough that when I tell my five-year-old son it's time to make his bed, he can't point a finger back at me.

Ting, ting. The phone chimes and buzzes again, and I'm quick to read the updates from Mags followed by the response from Renee. Magnolia's life could be a story line for a soap opera. Or a Lifetime movie maybe. I've thought it for years but especially now given what's going on in her love life.

I'm quick to reply and then silence it, but not before catching Sharon's comment. Just seeing her name on the screen produces guilty tumbles in the pit of my stomach.

What do you do when your friend and you like the same man? You don't touch him. You certainly don't go on a coffee date with him over the weekend.

I don't even see what Sharon replied or know what position she's taking on Magnolia's situation. All I know is that I said yes to coffee with a guy I know she likes.

"Ugh." The groan slips out as I pull my sundress down and then blow a few strands of curly, dark blond hair out of my face. Makeup is done, this dress is brand new and I love how it flows, but my goodness, I cannot get past this feeling of betrayal. No matter how excited I am.

"You look pretty, Mommy." Henry's voice catches me by surprise. The door creaks as my son pushes it open even more. "Pretty for date." His tone is mischievous.

My bottom lip drops and my mouth opens with shock for this little cutie staring back at me as he climbs onto my bed. His little fists grab a handful of bedding and I help him, scooting his bottom up until he's on the mattress.

"It's not a date, sweetie," I tell him and there's practically a scold in my tone. Maybe that's why he arches that little brow of his at me. It's nearly comical.

He's always had a mind of his own.

It's between a glance in the vanity mirror and a glance back at him that I see his true intentions. "Nope," I say and snag my phone just before he can reach it. The last time he got ahold of my phone, I had about 100 pictures of his mouth and up his nose in my camera roll.

Before he can protest or reach for it, I change the subject. Distraction is my best parenting weapon. I think it was Maggie who told me that if a kid wants something, offer them something else while taking what they want out of view. It has worked like a charm for years.

"Do you want Aunt Renee to come by and hang out this morning?" My voice takes on a bit of a sing-song quality as I set my phone down on the dresser. "She might have said something about ice cream sandwiches."

Now it's my son's turn for his mouth to drop in surprise. As he chants "Auntie Renee," my smile grows and all those nerves take a back seat. Until I check my phone again.

Aunt Renee spilled the beans in the chat. With a grimace, I read the texts.

When are you bringing my little man over so you can go on your coffee date, Autumn? She sent the text only a minute ago and the other two ladies in the chat pile on:

Ooh, a date?

With who?

My stomach drops when Renee answers Sharon's question regarding who this coffee date is with. *The hot preschool teacher with the nice butt.*

Sharon assumes wrong, typing back, *Mr. Harding?*

And frozen in my spot, I watch the horror story play out in real time with Renee correcting her: *Nope, she snagged Trent.*

Before my eyes close, I catch sight in my periphery of Henry jumping on my bed while chanting, "Date, date, date. You date Mr. Morgan. I date Renee!" His gleeful song is accompanied by the squeak of the bed frame and more vibrating in my hand from the phone.

Oh my God, kill me now.

CHAPTER 3

TRENT

Keeping it PG is how my buddy Harding would describe this coffee date. He's far more experienced than I am on the dating scene and if he was here now … he'd enjoy laughing at me.

Autumn and I snagged a coveted table on the patio outside a mom-and-pop coffee and cake shop. There's not a cloud in sight and the breeze is just right. So right that when it blows by, Autumn's dark brunette hair sweeps across her shoulders.

Yet this date is less like a date and more like small talk between two people who are both waiting in a doctor's office for a rectal exam. Yeah, Harding would laugh his ass off right about now.

"Our boys get along real well," I say and take a sip of my coffee, my thumb tapping rhythmically on the edge of the generic white ceramic mug. I don't know what it is about this woman, but I have no game whatsoever with her. Even less so this morning. Maybe I just need more coffee.

"I know, Henry talks about Chase all the time." She mimics the way the two boys say, "best buds for life," then lets out a small laugh. Very short and riddled with the same kind of nerves that won't settle in my gut.

I know she already knows that the boys get along. The two of them hit it off Henry's first day of preschool last year.

Even though I can't manage a conversation outside of the weather, the cinnamon cake on the table, and our boys, I still think it's going well because when that wind blows and she has to retuck her hair behind her ear, she smiles down into her latte that smells so sweet and then peeks up at me, all shy-like.

Maybe I'm not the only one affected.

"So you took over the preschool from your mom?" Autumn asks. The conversation is still steadily in the category of small talk.

"Don't tell her that," I joke with a huff of laughter. "She still says it's hers."

That gets a broader smile from Autumn. "I mean, her name is on it. So ... Ann's ABCs and123s Preschool."

"Well, she would kill me if I change the name." Again she smiles and lets out a small laugh. I know this small town likes to talk, but I have no idea what all she knows about my past. "I have my master's in education but I never thought I'd run a preschool. That was my mom's thing."

"A master's?" she asks and doesn't hide the surprise. "I almost went back for mine before I got the editor position."

"You like that? Working for the town paper?" I could see Autumn doing anything at all. She's personable and charming, but smart and driven. It doesn't take more than a handful of conversation to know that.

"Well, like you, I never thought I'd be an editor. I was always a math and science kind of girl, but I love it. I wouldn't change a thing."

It's easy to smile at her response. Everything between us is easy all of a sudden and I'm grateful for that.

"What were you going to do with your master's?" she says.

Shrugging, I admit, "Administration of some sort was the long-term goal. But when Chase was born and his mom passed, I wanted to be more hands on. I had to be, really. With my mom's vision going ... it just made sense to take over the preschool and be close to him."

Autumn's tone holds her condolences. "I'm so sorry to hear about her passing."

"Thank you," I reply automatically. It's been years since I said goodbye to my ex-wife, but my throat still gets dry whenever she comes up in conversation.

"Does Chase ever talk about her?" Her question catches me off guard but it's the genuine concern that resonates with me.

"Occasionally. He has some questions, but he's still so young and never knew her."

"It was cancer, right?"

"Yeah," I say and my voice is tighter than I'd like. I loved Candace and I wish things could have been different, but I know Chase and I make a duo she'd be proud of.

"I'm so sorry," she repeats, her voice gentle and comforting.

"What about Henry's dad?" I ask her to change subjects and move to lighter topics.

"We're on really good terms. We should have only ever been friends, to be honest."

"Just didn't work out between you two?" I already know that's what the town says. They were young, their son a blessing that came from a disastrous pair.

She shakes her head, setting down her mug and

pushing it away gently. "We actually broke up amicably before I found out I was pregnant. We tried to make it work but it we're much better off not being ..." she trails off and scrunches her face in distaste rather than finishing.

"And no boyfriend now?" I say, leaning forward. The way my voice lowers yet is still full of hope causes that blush to come out full force.

Shaking her head, she asks me the same, "And you don't have a girlfriend, Mr. Morgan?"

"Not yet I don't." I let the statement add to the brewing tension between us.

There's a moment of silence and then I say, "So, two single parents ... meeting up at a coffee shop on Saturday afternoon."

"Oh, the scandal," Autumn jokes mockingly with a broad smile.

"I'm just saying ... us single parents, we have to stick together."

"Is that right? Is that why you asked me out?" she asks and it's the first bit of flirtation, *real flirtation* from her since we sat down. The nerves have finally settled as another couple slips by and heads into the coffee shop with the telltale ding of the two bells above the door announcing their entry.

"I thought it was because you tipped over my coffee

but—" Covering the embarrassment on her face with both hands, her reaction stops me from finishing the thought.

"You're a cute mix of sweet and shy," I say and I don't know why the confession slips out of me, but it does.

She doesn't blush, though, like I thought she would. Her smile stays put and her eyes flash with something. Something that tells me it's okay to keep pushing her.

"You think I'm sweet?"

"I know you are, but what do you think of me?" I dare to ask.

"Handsome. I think you're just my type, Mr. Morgan. Tall, dark and handsome … I would put good money down that you're just about every woman's type."

A rough chuckle leaves me as I reply, "But I don't want to be out here with *any* woman. I only asked one to coffee."

Setting her mug down on the white rattan table, she wraps both her hands around the cup. "Speaking of which, mine is almost gone."

"Well, you have been clinging to it like it was going to save you from having to make conversation."

"Did not," she says, the beautiful smile never fading even with her rebuttal. "Although I'm glad I was able to get you a coffee. Since I did spill yours and all."

"Well … actually, I asked you out for coffee so I could

ask you out for dinner."

Her laugh in response is light and the sound is music to my ears. "You are something else, Trent."

"As are you, Autumn." An asymmetric smile pulls up on my lips. It doesn't escape me that she doesn't respond to the invitation. My pulse picks up and I swear there's a hard thump in my chest when she looks away for a moment.

"We could do tomorrow night?" I offer her. It's a holiday weekend and we have Monday off for Labor Day. Tomorrow is perfect for a real date.

"Tomorrow? So soon?" she asks as if it's a joke, but I think there's something real about her hesitation.

"Is there a rule against having a dinner date right after a coffee date?"

"There are lots of rules against that," she answers with all seriousness. Before she can deny me, I slip my hand over hers, which is still laying innocently on the table. There's a spark, a heat between us that's met with a small gasp from her lips. My dark umber against her fair skin. My thumb runs soothing circles, but all it does is stir up that heat, making it hotter and hotter.

"When I want something, I go after it. And I want you."

"Trent," she says and my name is a plea on her lips. She lets me lift her hand in mine and I take my time, letting my intentions be clear as I plant a single kiss on the inside of her wrist. The smell of her sweet perfume and the little sigh that slips from her, a sigh of coveted lust, does things to me that a coffee date never should.

I pull away easily enough, but Autumn still seems caught in a trance.

"Tomorrow night?" she asks after a moment, her voice low and full of the sexual tension that resonates in every inch of me.

I only nod and in response, she gives me a sweet smile and agrees, "Tomorrow night."

I leave her by her car with a small, chaste kiss. Tomorrow night, though … if I'm going to kiss her, it's not going to be on her cheek.

CHAPTER 4

AUTUMN

"I Have. A. Playdate. With. Chase." Henry smacks his hands with each word from the back seat of the car. "Mommy. Has. A. Date. With. Mr. Trent." My eyes roll hard as we sit at the red light on Main and Sixth Street. A row of cute houses is to my right and the coffee shop I sat at with Trent is to my left.

Even as I let out the frustrated breath, I stare longingly at the white rattan table we sat at. The table where his lips first touched me like I've been dreaming about. And everything inside me blazes. He may be my son's teacher ... but there's no doubt that Trent Morgan could teach me a thing or two.

Turning down the music as the red light changes to green, I question Henry to get his mind anywhere other than the date I have with his preschool teacher.

My phone pings and I wait until I'm at the next red light before I peek at it.

Sharon wants to know if I like him and how the date went.

Ugh. Those nerves from before rattle inside of me and I struggle to come up with another response. I know she knows I do like him and that the date was "just fine" because that's what I wrote in the group chat.

Not only was it "just fine," it was a low-key icebreaker that somehow turned scorching hot out of nowhere. I've been imagining all sorts of things for over a year but what I wanted to do to that man on top of that little table is downright deviant.

I'm surely not going to tell Sharon that. My plan is to drag my feet as long as I can until I know if there's really something there between Trent and me.

One kiss really. It's all in the kiss, isn't it? That's what they say, so … just one kiss. A real one. Not a peck on the cheek to say goodbye after a coffee date, but the type of kiss that slows down your whole world as you kick up one leg and turn to jello.

Nodding my head in agreement with … well with myself, I realize I've been ignoring Henry.

"Right, Mommy?" Henry says.

"Yes, that's right," I answer and immediately regret agreeing without knowing what I'm agreeing to.

"You like Mr. Morgan! Mommy likes Mr. Morgan!"

Ping. My phone goes off again as I roll up to the address Trent texted me.

I'm just curious! Sharon wrote and I know I need to write something back so I settle on a sort-of truth: *He asked me out tonight so we'll see!*

And with that response, my phone is turned on silent.

The inner voice in my head is anything but, though. With a heavy breath out, I lie to myself. I'm not a bad friend. She had a year. A full year. There has to be fine print in the dibs clause and if she was upset, she would have said so.

All the nerves that nag at me vanish the moment my gaze lifts to the dark blue front door of the raised ranch house. Standing there in the yard and staring straight back at me is the man I can't get off my mind.

In a crisp white button-down with the sleeves rolled up to his forearms and dark blue jeans, he looks impeccably handsome. That look in his eyes when our gazes meet, and the way his lips kick up into a crooked grin ... morphs his clean-cut look into that of a tempting devil.

It's only when his mother calls his name that I'm

snapped out of it and unbuckle my belt. As I gather Henry and his bag out of the car, I can barely hear their conversation.

"Is this your partner in crime, Chase? The one you've been telling me about?" Mrs. Emma Morgan's glasses slip down the bridge of her nose as she speaks, but even still the woman is a force. I used to think age didn't know her name; she could be Trent's sister if the whole town didn't know any better. She practically raised half of us.

The past few years may have added some lines around her eyes and as she smiles, some new wrinkles rest there too, but his mother is still the woman I remember.

Which makes it a little ... odd to show up and ask her to watch my son while I date hers.

"Mrs. Morgan, how are you?" I give her the largest smile I can and do my best to pretend that there isn't anything at all weird about this.

"Wonderful," she says and her gaze slips down to my dress. "Don't you look as pretty as a peach in June."

The smile on my face is genuine when I tell her thank you and then add, "And thank you for watching Henry."

"Trust me," she says and stands upright, watching Henry run off to the flower bed where Chase is currently stacking rocks and knocking them down with some Transformer or other plastic figure of some sort I'm sure cost twenty bucks or more. "It will be easier on me for

Chase to have a friend to keep him occupied."

"I really appreciate it."

"You don't have to keep thanking her," Trent says and slips a hand on my lower back as he adds, "She'd kill me if I let someone else watch him on her weekend with Chase."

His mother gestures with a hand before I can say anything and she writes us off with a wave as she says, "Enjoy your date."

There's this thing about a small town and how people talk. Word spreads and even the most innocent of things can turn scandalous.

That's probably why the only words I can think of right now are that it's not a date. But I know very well it is, so instead I stand there, watching the woman who used to watch me take a seat in a lawn chair and call out for us to have fun.

This is the specific time my friend group calls *the moment*. The one where you know you're really on a date and it's happening. So either you turn back, or you run full steam ahead.

"Your car or mine? I would immediately go to mine, but since it's not a date-date …"

"What?"

"You just muttered it's not a date-date," Trent says jokingly and with him next to me, standing there, I have to crane my head to look up at him. Even in these wedge sandals.

Standing there in the late summer warmth that's quickly fading into an early fall evening chill, I'm lost in his amber eyes for just a moment.

"If I had it my way, it'd be a date-date, you know?" he says, the confession sounding like it's something sinful.

The boys yelling out on behalf of the toy men in their hands breaks me from the spell Trent is so darn good at putting me under.

"Henry is already chanting that we're dating." I'm busy tucking my hair behind my ear when Trent replies, "That's my little man."

I can't deny it does something to me, listening to him talk about son like that. Little butterflies make my stomach flip and I can see a happily ever after with him. Already. I haven't even had my kiss yet.

As he asks me, yet again, whose car we're taking since I still have my keys in my hand, I come to a very real observation.

Dating a man you really want to hold on to for more than one night is completely terrifying.

CHAPTER 5

TRENT

With dim, candlelit lighting, modern furniture draped in plush velvet, and the other guests dressed to the nines, Blue Bay is the fanciest restaurant this town has to offer. And the only one I can imagine taking Autumn to tonight. Even if she did drive and refer to this evening as not a date-date, this is an official first date. And judging by her shyness and the quiet thank you as I push her chair in, Autumn is very much aware of that.

With the din of chatter and clink of silverware surrounding us, the waiter takes our drink order.

A glass of chardonnay for Autumn. I make a mental note of which wine she's having. If my father taught me anything before passing, it's that love is in the details. Small gifts that bring memories will go a long way. I intend to have that with the woman I share my life with.

I'm almost certain it's Autumn.

Every moment with her, the tension gets thicker.

Every moment without her, she's all I can think about.

"This is a really nice place," she says and her voice is gentle with more than a hint of gratitude as she lays the napkin across her lap.

"This is the only place I thought to take you tonight."

"Really?" She sounds surprised.

"You're a single mom and from what I can tell, a workaholic." I answer her with complete honesty. "When's the last time you treated yourself to a night out?"

"I have my friends. We do get-togethers ... but not like this."

"Exactly."

"So you want to spoil me?" She lays the question out as if it's a joke.

"Most definitely," I answer with as much charm as I can manage. The nerves are gone, the fears of ruining this with her nowhere in sight. It's just me and her and a date that is long overdue. "I really like you and I wanted to make sure I made that clear tonight."

There's a pause as the beat of my pulse and everything else slows when she looks back at me. Until she answers with five little words, "I really like you too."

The waiter is silent as he drops off our drinks, interrupting the moment, but it's pleasant enough and we place our dinner order.

The atmosphere mixes just right with the jack and Coke and her glass of chardonnay.

After a moment, Autumn seems to remember where the conversation was and picks it right back up. "As my son might say," she says and the words leave a beautiful smile on her lips as she sips the sweet-smelling wine that carries all the way across the table. "I kind of sort of, maybe, quite possibly, like you a lot."

"Is that flirtation I sense?" I tease her and she lets out a small hum of amusement as she nods her head.

"How am I doing? I may be a bit rusty."

"Well, this is a compliment I never thought I'd give, but I like you rusty."

Her shoulders shake with the laugh and her hair flows over her shoulders. In this moment, she's beautiful and I know I was right to wait for her to finally come around and give me a chance.

"Oh, aren't you just the charmer," she says but lays her hand on the table, palm up. I'm quick, but not too quick, to lay mine on top of hers and she threads her fingers through mine.

The conversation flows easily, a bit of laughter, a bit

more of deeper conversation.

The only interruption comes when she checks her phone and then peeks up at me.

"You don't get out much, do you?" I jokingly scold her for checking on the boys again. "My mom has some experience here, you know?"

"Oh, come on, just text her and ask how they're doing."

"They're fine. I'm sure."

"Please," she says as the waiter refills her water goblet.

"You could message her," I say just to tease her. "I'll send you her number."

"I'm not texting your mother while I'm on a date with you."

"Ooh, so you admit it? We're on a date?"

Bright red stains her cheeks but she doesn't waste any time flicking her cloth napkin at me and saying, "Just ask her, please."

"She already messaged ten minutes ago and said they're watching Batman and the two of them ate an entire bag of popcorn."

Her smile grows and she slips her phone back in her purse with a simple thank you.

Before I can tell her she doesn't need to worry, before I can remind her she's on a date, she tells me, "You're lucky you have your mom. I don't have much family and none of them live around here anymore."

"I know I am. She loves watching Chase."

Her eyes spark as if she's about to say something daring. "So, I'm just going to put the obvious out there … if we were to do this thing, really date I mean. I think we'd make a cute little family."

I take a moment to let it sink in that she's considering things I've considered. This may be our first date, but it's not like we didn't already know what we were getting into.

I voice aloud a thought I've had ever since she agreed to that coffee date. "People might think Chase and Henry are twins … not the identical kind, but because of their age."

With bright eyes and a soft smile, Autumn replies, "So that didn't scare you? Because if we do this, really do this … I don't want just a fling."

"Men aren't scared off by the thought of a family. I know what I want, and I'm not looking for a fling either."

She bites down on her plush bottom lip and all I can think is that I want to do that nibbling. With my cock hardening, I readjust in my seat and thankfully, I'm saved by the waiter.

"The rib eye," he says as I lay my napkin across my lap, "and scallops and medallions." Nodding toward our drinks, I answer him before he can ask the question, "Another for each of us, please."

Autumn looks giddy staring down at her plate with

a small hum of satisfaction. One thing I hadn't realized before tonight was how laid back and easily pleased Autumn is. She's all smiles all the time although there has to be something that gets to her.

"You look like a kid at Christmas," I say as she pops a roasted potato into her mouth the second the waiter is gone.

"I love good food." Autumn doesn't hesitate to cut into one of her scallops. "You're going to wish you got these," she taunts playfully, the chunk of caramelized scallop speared on her fork.

"I think I'm going to be just fine with my steak."

"It does look delicious," she says and eyes my meal like she may steal it if I don't eat fast enough.

"Where do you even put it away? You're a tiny little thing."

"All the way down to my toes," she says and the joke makes me grin. "So ... this is a date-date?"

"It's a date-date," I say, nodding in agreement.

All she does is smile at my answer and I comment, "You like to smile, don't you?

Her head tilts with a small nod. "Happiness is a choice."

"I want to be happy." I don't know why the words slipped out, but they do.

"You aren't now?" she asks with all seriousness, giving me her full attention.

"Happier," I say, amending my statement.

"What would make you happy?"

You. The word stays at the back of my throat and I shrug, taking a swig of my drink rather than answering. "Life is good, but I just want make sure it's everything it can be for Chase."

"I don't know a lot of single dads, and only a few single moms. But I know you're doing a good job. Chase is a sweet kid and he's happy."

"So is Henry."

A smile instantly blossoms on her lips and she tells me thank you.

"So ... since this is a date-date, can we agree to one thing?" she asks, changing the subject.

"What's that?"

"Can we can go slow?" she asks me.

"Slow?"

"I just think it's best, with the boys and all."

"Slow it is then."

And just like that, the serious tension is gone, but both of us know what the other wants.

One small problem, though: there's nothing about the two of us that I want to do slow.

CHAPTER 6

AUTUMN

"You're the one who said let's take it slow." Trent makes the comment as I catch my breath and lay my head back on the driver's side seat.

Dinner and another drink at the bar after, and then some more flirting and small touches, took most of the night. It's dark outside of the car. The moon is almost full, the stars on full display in the midnight blue sky.

Trent can't get the grin off his smug, handsome face.

"And yet ..." He lets the words hang in the air as he gestures to my house. I drove to my house after dinner. Not to his where his mother and both of our boys are.

Freudian slip is all I can say in defense.

"You just wanted to take me home. Admit it," he teases and with his rough chuckle I can't help but laugh.

He's not wrong, though. Not in the least.

Something changed at dinner. My heart won't stop thumping for this man.

I just hope it's as real for him as it feels for me. Every time he breaks our kiss, I remember something Renee likes to say that serves to answer that nagging little question: *You'll find out by morning.*

With a grin pulling at my mouth, I lean over the console and lay another kiss on his lips. Our hands don't stop roaming. Both of us feeling up the other and enjoying the kind of making out I thought was only for high school and puppy dog love.

I suppose romance has layers. And I happen to really enjoy all of Trent's layers. Every last little bit of every single one.

Very few cars have driven by but when they do, we've paused, caught our breath and teased the other for starting up the kiss again. It starts with a little touch, then inching closer ... I just can't get enough of him.

Ping. His phone goes off and this time I groan in protest, until I realize it's his mother.

He reads the text out loud. *They're both fast asleep so stay out however long you want. Go to a movie or something.*

"Are movies even playing this late?" I ask.

"She doesn't have to know all the details."

His words hang in the air. The pull between us only gets stronger as the seconds pass.

It's his turn to lean in and kiss me, which he does. His right hand on my thigh, his fingertips grazing against my bare skin and then higher, pushing up the hem of my dress.

I moan into his mouth as my left hand does the same to him, slipping up his collared shirt and finding his taut muscles beneath the fabric as our kiss deepens. He's got me every kind of hot and bothered.

It's only when a pair of headlights flashes and drifts by that the kiss is broken, leaving me breathless and more than that, wanting.

A million questions about how we're going to make this work and if it's going to last bombard my mind, but the only one I ask is, "You want to come in?"

CHAPTER 7

TRENT

Maybe it's because I've wanted her for over a year. Maybe it's because her hands roam freely down my body like I've dreamed about. Maybe it's because her kiss tastes like lust and sweet wine and everything I ever wanted.

Whatever the reason, the second we're through her front door, I pin Autumn to the wall, my lips never leaving hers, and my hands reaching below her dress.

The sudden gasp from her lips only fuels me to deepen our touch. Her small noises are the only sounds I can hear apart from the blood rushing in my ears and my heart pounding inside my chest.

"Trent," she moans my name against my lips, our warm breath mingling. I don't know how she has any time at all to speak. I want all of her, in every way, without any thing between us. Not even words.

My fingers inch up her thighs, the soft fabric taunting me until I reach the thin lace of her panties. Her smile against my lips is sultry and sinful, just like the words she whispers. "Tear it if you want."

Fuck. As if I couldn't get any harder for her.

The thin fabric shreds easily enough and I let it fall before pulling my shirt over my head. Her hands fumble with the buckle on my belt and I swear it feels like first love all over again.

Each of us wanting, needing, and desperate to take this to the next level.

With half our clothing a careless heap piled next to us, I make a move to lift her dress, but she stops me, breathing out heavily and taking in the cool air.

"Bedroom," she murmurs against my lips and I never knew I could hate a word so much. Not daring to put space between us, I lift her in my arms and take the stairs two at a time. The lust still clinging to every inch of us, I rid us of the remaining clothing before falling onto the bed with her beneath me. With my forearms braced beside her head, she seems so small beneath me.

The windows are opened just inches, the curtains

blowing with the cool evening breeze that dances along our bare skin.

Slipping my hand between her thighs, I run my middle finger up her slick seam, finding her hot and glistening with arousal. As I spread it over her clit, I leave gentle kisses along her neck and let her mewl and writhe under me.

I'm hard and eager, but I want this to be perfect.

It's not until she's begging me, whimpering both my name and the plea, that I stroke myself and rest the head of my dick against her sweet center.

I kiss her once, watching her lashes flutter down as her eyes close. Readying myself, I can barely push my head inside of her. Fuck, she feels like heaven, but the expression on her face tells me I'm the only one feeling this pleasure right now.

Pausing to give her time to adjust, I nibble her lip and wait for her expression to relax.

"It's been a while," she says, the confession leaving her in a whisper.

"I told you I'd go slow," I answer with all sincerity, but a worried smile and a huff leaves her.

"That's not quite what I mean," she says, her voice low and holding questions I don't have the answers to right now.

Her heart races against mine as I hover over her,

leaning down with a kiss to silence her.

With her lips still on mine, I thrust forward, as easy as possible. Her lips part as she holds her breath, feeling every inch of me until I'm buried to the hilt.

The mix of pleasure and pain stirs in her gasps and moans, edging closer to pleasure with every thrust. I take my time, pulling nearly all the way out then pushing myself deeper and harder each time. It doesn't take long before her nails are digging into my shoulders, her legs wrapped around my hips and her heel digging into my ass to fuel me on.

"Yes," she begs and I happily oblige. *Harder. Faster.* I fuck her into her mattress like I've dreamed of doing. Each time I get close to finding my own release, I slow, pressing myself as deep inside of her as I can. She loses herself, pleasure racking through her body and her back bowing in ecstasy.

She's so tight I can feel every bit of her orgasm as she pulses around me, screaming out my name. I don't give her time to come down from the sweet high. Instead I fuck her mercilessly, pistoning my hips and riding her harder. She angles her hips, taking it all and clinging to me as her head presses back into the mattress and she cries out in pleasure.

This is what I've dreamed of for so long, but even my dreams weren't this good. This is perfect.

When I finally let go, I bury my head in the crook of her neck, kissing her there and giving us both a moment to catch our breath.

Falling to the side, I lie there next to her and hold her close, recalling how our night unfolded. With my hand on the small of her waist, I run soothing circles over her soft skin with my thumb and kiss her hair.

Sleep could take us both, and as much as that would make me happy, life and responsibilities are calling.

I'm not the only one thinking it.

"Time to go pick up the boys," she says and her voice resonates two things. A longing to stay just like this. And a resignation that this night is over.

Peeking down at her, she's still vibrant and beautiful, but I know she loved getting away tonight. Her gaze is lost until she closes her eyes and she plants another kiss on my chest. She needs time to know I'm serious—hell, she needed a year just to let me take her out for coffee. I'll give her all the time in the world ... tomorrow. But right now?

"Not yet," I tell her, positioning myself on top of her again. The bed groans and her bottom lip drops open just slightly. "I'm not done with you yet. Spread your legs for me."

CHAPTER 8

AUTUMN

It's not a walk of shame. Not at all. There are no rumpled clothes or a hangover. Nope. My pencil skirt is practically pressed within an inch of its life and my blouse fits exactly like it did on the mannequin at Macy's. Yet as my heels click on the pavement and Henry runs up to the glass doors of the preschool building, it feels just like that.

There is not a single doubt in my mind that every soul over the age of eighteen in that building knows I hooked up with Trent Morgan two nights ago. Deandra's daughter volunteers in the newborn section; she's only sixteen and I bet she knows too.

The blush that won't go the heck away is writing out the details on my face. I'm sure of it.

Still, I make a beeline right for him when I open the door and Henry takes off toward Chase to show him the pinball keychain he hasn't stopped talking about all morning.

"Good morning, Henry," Trent calls out to Henry's back when he zips past him and right to his friend.

"Well ... it is a good morning, isn't it?" Trent's gaze flows down the length of my body, sending goosebumps over every inch of me. He's discreet and no one else heard, but still.

"Not here," I say, scolding him beneath my breath, although my smile seems to disagree with the sentiment. "I haven't told my friends yet."

There's only a hint of guilt in that confession.

"When are you going to tell them?"

"Soon?" My response is a question too. I need to rip this bandage off.

"Well, you better tell them before the rumor mill does." His warning is all too real in this small town. With a quick kiss, I tell him to have a good day and any nerves are gone, replaced by butterflies wreaking havoc in my chest.

The last person I expect to see when I turn around is Sharon. She doesn't have kids. There's not a reason in the world for her to be here. Well ... except for the fact that she's telling Maggie's little girl to have a good day and appears to be signing her in.

I bet Mags had something that had to be done and Sharon's just helping her out.

"You all right?" Trent asks at the same time Sharon peeks up and beams as she says, "Look at you two."

Pen still in hand from signing in Magnolia's daughter, she raises it in a friendly gesture.

"Have a good day, Sharon. Nothing to see here," Trent jokes to her before whispering to me, "You have a good day too." The way he says such innocent words sounds scandalous to the point that my ears burn.

With the heat of a blush still rising, the tap of the pen from Sharon gets my attention, but even more than that is the wide grin she's trying to contain.

I only get a couple steps in before she squeals in delight. "Oh my God," she mouths and I'm quick to pull her out of the building before embarrassment of my not-walk of shame fully takes over.

"You two look so cute together," she says and her statement is as easy as her walk.

The guilt that ate away at me seems to subside. "I really like him," I admit to her because it's the only thing I can think to say.

She speaks as we make our way to our cars in the parking lot. She parked right next to mine. "One, you can tell. The tension is thick."

A hint of a laugh escapes me, but the nerves are still there, waiting for her approval. Waiting for one of my best friends to tell me it's okay that I took the guy she had dibs on. Freaking please have mercy because I really, really want to be with him. "He's not some fling for me and I know you called dibs—" The excuses tumble out of me and I wish I could stop them.

Seriously, if I could pluck the words back, I would. I'm so embarrassed and sick to my stomach over this.

"Whoa, I was just joking," she says and both of Sharon's hands fly up. "I call dibs on every hot guy in this town. You know that ... don't you?" The look in her eyes reflects exactly what I feel. It's the fear over being a bad friend.

"I just felt bad because I should have told you guys, but I didn't want to if there wasn't a connection in case ... in case you really liked him."

"I was never going to go after Trent. Look ... I can prove it. I texted Renee last year sometime," she says and scrolls through her phone without missing a beat. After a moment she adds, "You can ask her, because I can't find it." Looking me dead in the eyes she confesses, "I told her the two of you were going to hook up and then a couple months later I got drunk and asked her what was taking you so long.

"You guys have always had tension and you look so cute together. We all wanted it to happen. But Renee said not to push. With, you know, kids involved and you working on your career. So I stayed out of it."

Leaning against my car, I let the truth of what she just said wash over me.

"So … you're not mad?"

"Heck no, but we need details. Wine Down Wednesday?" she says, opening up her car door. I check the time and note that I'm going to be late if I don't get moving.

"Yes, definitely."

Wednesdays are for girls' nights, but Fridays are date nights with Trent. That was decided on the ride home last night, with his hand in mine.

There's no reason not to choose happiness and go for what you want. My only goal is to not overthink it and let us fall into place. Which oddly enough, seems to be right where we are now and right where we're meant to be.

"Oh my God … and did you hear what happened with Magnolia?" Sharon easily moves the conversation into new territory as she says, "We need to bring her a bottle just for herself … or rather, two of them."

"That bad?" I ask, both of us still standing although our driver car doors are opened.

Sharon smirks. "If you ask me … that *good*."

A Little Bit In Love With You

CHAPTER 1

BRIANNA

I forgot how hot it is back home. Pulling my tank top out in the center of my chest offers a cool bit of air to filter down, but the relief is lost on me. Until I see Asher and tell him exactly how I feel, there's not a damn thing that's going to ease this anxiousness inside of me.

Nearly slipping in a pot hole I didn't see in the long gravel pave up to his parents' house, I let out a hiss of irritation. It's too darn hot for August in Beaufort South Carolina. The coastal sea island is supposed to keep this place from hitting the high 90s, but there isn't a breeze to be found.

My jean white jean shorts are a bit too tight since I

gained a little weight my first year of college. Freshman 10 and all that. I huff, feeling my cheeks redden in this heat as I turn the corner of the backroad surrounded by thin threes that don't offer any shade and the airplane hangar in the distance.

I haven't been back home for more than 48 hours and I'm already miserable. Although if Asher was answering his phone, if he would just talk to me, I know it would all be okay.

We didn't spend three years together to be off and on and constantly fighting because we're long distance now.

I love him and he loves me. Letting out an exaggerated exhale and pulling my dark brown hair up into a makeshift ponytail, I pretend I'm stopping right in front of his house just to catch my breath and cool down before I pull back the flimsy screen door and knock on the old worn door to the farmhouse.

We've been together all through high school, heck half of my memories are from that airplane hangar that doubles as a mechanic garage on the lower level. My first sip of beer... even though I'm only eighteen. Our first kiss... our first, everything.

My throat closes up tight as I tighten the ponytail and wipe the beads of sweat from my forehead.

I'm sure I look a mess, but that's exactly how I feel, so ... I suppose it'll have to do.

With one step, the gravel crunches under my feet, but then I halt.

The screaming from inside makes my already hammering heart go into high gear. Asher yells at his father in return. The two of them are going at it.

I take a hesitant step forward, unwilling to turnback and needing to know what the hell is going on. The two of them have had their issues butting heads, but the rage in their tones is something I've never heard before. He didn't tell me anything was going on.

I can't quite make out what they're saying, apart from the cuss words and his mother begging them to stop.

My body goes cold and begs me to stop as I near the wooden porch steps.

Swallowing thickly I pull my phone out from the back pocket of my shorts and check my messages.

He didn't respond to the series I sent him:

Hey I'm sorry. Can we talk?
I miss you.
You know I love you right?
Please talk to me.

Emotions swarm me as something is thrown from inside, glass shatters and I instinctively step back, my mouth parted in both shock and fear.

Are you okay? I'm here.
What's going on?

My fingers fly across the keys and just as I hit send, Asher storms out, nearly ripping the screen door off as it bangs against the house.

He gets three large strides out the door before he sees me. His tanned skin and rough around the edges decorum fits his blue collar ways to the T. His hair is a bit messy on top, his piercing eyes hitting me with all the intensity in the world. First the anger and hurt, then the recognition and with it a touch of shame. Like he didn't want me to hear that and he's very aware that I did.

Only I'm not sure what the fight was about.

He slows his pace, turning to look back once, and then focusing his gaze on the porch floor before looking back up at me. He licks his lower lip and all I see is a wounded man. Worn blue jeans and a graphic dark blue tee complete the image.

"You okay?" I whisper. Cause really that's all that matters.

His parents don't come after him. It's far too quiet for far too long. He doesn't answer me, but emotions filter through his expression and every second that passes it crushes me more and more.

"Want to get out of here?" I offer, feeling the heat at

my back and knowing right now the only thing I need in life is to get that look off his face.

I can't even try to count the number of times Asher has held me while I cried. Fights with my friends, with my parents, losing my grandparents and so many other things throughout the years.

I've never once seen him cry and I'm not sure he's going to now, but I think if I wasn't standing right here, right now, he'd have gone up to the apartment in the hangar and… and I don't know.

"I wanted to talk, but we don't have to, we can go anywhere you want," I offer him when he doesn't respond.

All I want to do right now, as the porch creaks with his shifting weight, is love on him.

However he needs and never leave his side again.

CHAPTER 2

ASHER

"You should come with me," she pleads with me.

My hands fist at my side, a cold sweat lines by back although everything inside of me is do damn hot. Anger forces adrenaline to surge through me.

None of it is for her. Not an ounce of this is for my Bri. I hate that look in her eyes. That hurt and even sympathy she has for me right now. My face flames with embarrassment.

My throat's tight as I swallow and attempt to calm down. With a tension ringing throughout my body, I attempt to answer her without any of that shit back there being shown to her.

"What all did you hear?" I question.

Her head shakes, that ponytail sways and her gorgeous green eyes widen as she tells me she couldn't make out what we were saying, but she heard us arguing.

I love this girl more than anything, but I don't want to share this with her. I can't. I can't let her know what happened.

Heaving in a breath, I take a look behind her and I don't see her father's car.

"Did you walk?"

"Yeah," she whispers at the same time that there's a commotion behind me. Probably my dad pushing the sofa out of the way. A heat flows over my body and I move before either of them can come out here.

She can't see this.

"Come on," I pull her by her elbow as I walk passed her. All I want is to get to to my car and get the hell out of here. Her flip flops catch in the gravel as she tries to keep up.

"Shit," she curses beneath her breath.

My sweet little Bri cursed. *Fuck*. I stop everything and turn to face her fully.

"You alright?" She's bent down, those little shorts creeping up as she grips her toe and hisses.

"Fine," she mutters, her expression scrunched and then she reaches up, grabbing my hand in hers. That right there. There's a shift, an immediate change.

It feels like breaking down though and I'm quick to turn back and head to the car. Focused on keeping my shit together.

I can't speak, I'm barely conscious of opening the car door for her. But I'm all too aware when I squeeze her hand and she squeezes back before letting go.

After I close the passenger door, I nearly stop before heading around to the driver's side. Just so I can deal with this shit before getting in. Just a moment.

I just need one fucking moment but it never comes.

Pushing through it all, I get into the driver's seat, turn the ignition of the Chevy and drive off. As the car is pulling away, I peek up into the rearview to see my father walking out onto the porch. Arms crossed and a beer bottle dangling from one hand.

I hate it here.

I hate him sometimes too.

"You okay?" Bri asks, her small hand landing on my thigh as I turn down the gravel road, my family home from view.

Words tumble at the back of my throat, all the thoughts that have been weighing me down compete to be heard. I don't know what to say. That's the God's honest truth. But I settle on one thing as I flick on the AC to high.

"I just want to leave sometimes." It's far too simple. But at least it's true.

"Where do you want to go?" The innocence and surprise isn't hiding in her question.

"I don't know." Truth is, I've never even let myself think of where. Because the moment I think of leaving, I know I can't. I barely passed high school. I put all my savings into the garage to start my own mechanic shop … and I can't leave my mom.

"I don't know, but right now I just need some space I think," I tell Bri honestly as I drive down the long road to get to town.

I could go to Robert's. I could stay there. He'd let me just like I've let him for years.

"Please don't say that," Bri whispers.

I have to take my eyes from the road to look at her. It's a quick glance but then I take another. I love Bri, I've always loved her, but she keeps at it with needing more from me that I can give her.

Hell, I have nothing. No way to come see her across the damn country and that's all she wants from me.

"I don't know what you want from me," I tell her. The last she text me, she gave me an ultimatum. Come up to see her or we're over. I almost tell her, as far as I knew we were done, but that vulnerable look keeps the thought locked in the back of my throat.

"I want you to come with me," she murmurs. Her hand shifts on my thigh and I think she's going to take it away, but she doesn't. She turns in her seat to face me, the leather of it groaning.

"Just come up north with me."

"And how am I supposed to do that? Really Bri? I don't even know if we're together anymore." I can't help it as my hand twists on the steering wheel. It just flies out of my mouth. "You change your mind every five fucking minutes."

"Don't cuss at me," she scolds and takes her hand back to cross her arms. Just like my father just did.

"Don't--" I start but bite my tongue. I'm frustrated and worked up. I know better.

"I'm sorry," I apologize and she doesn't react other than to soften slightly in her seat.

I glance up and see the sign for main street but I drive passed it. I don't even know where we're going.

"I'm sorry too," she tells me after a moment. And her hand comes back, I'm quick to grab it and steer with my left.

"I need you right now," I don't know where it came from, but I'm guessing something in me had to tell her that truth too.

"I'm here. I'm right here."

CHAPTER 3

BRIANNA

My parents went to the movies. I know they're doing a grocery run when they're done that. The back door to the patio slides open easily as Asher and I sneak in. The thought hits me for a moment that it's crazy of us to *'sneak in'* at all. We're nineteen and there's no reason at all to not go right up to the front door and waltz in... except that this town likes to gossip. They make a big deal out of everything.

Whether or not Asher and I are going to last is a topic of conversation in the hair salon according to my grandmother. With the floor creaking as the back door closes softly, all I can think is, it's none of their damn business.

Asher's hand, hardened from years of working in the garage with his father, slips into mine. The lock clicks up into place at the same time that I peer up at him.

We've been together for years and I've never seen him look at me like this. With a hurt that can't be covered up by an asymmetric grin or a halfhearted, dry humored joke. The dark circles under his hazel eyes tell the story of him not sleeping well. We're only just learning what life and being adults really is, and it's so very apparent that it's taken a toll on Asher and I have no idea why.

Turning fully to face him, I ask again, "Can you tell me what happened?"

Instantly his gaze is ripped from mine and he tries to pull his hand away, angling his body towards the kitchen.

"Let's go upstairs," I'm quick to push the words out and grip his hand tighter, adding my second hand as well and giving him a gentle pull. "We can just lay down and if you don't want to talk, that's fine."

"Just lay down," he repeats my words with a hint of humor and a smile that doesn't reach his eyes. "Since when do we just lay down?" he jokes.

It awards him a playful smack to his chest and in return I get a rough chuckle and he squeezes my hand back. There's a shift, something more natural and more 'us' that happens with the small moment.

I cling to it and to him as we climb the stairs. Taking them slowly. Every step he gets closer, to the point that when we're at my bedroom door, his arm wraps around my waist like it's supposed to. Leaning back, I fall into him slightly, until the door is opened and I make my way to the bedroom, kicking off my flip flops.

"Hasn't changed a bit," Asher comments. He's right. I've had the same off white furniture since high school. The poster of the boy bands I love are still hung up, the stacks of fantasy novels haven't budged except the top one, my comfort read, and the matching off white desk is still cluttered.

"Mom said they might paint it and if they do she's going to rearrange somethings for me," I tell him easily.

"Your parents love you," Asher slips his hands into his jeans and looks around as if he hasn't been in this very room a thousand times before.

"Come on," I urge him. The bed groans as I climb in and crawl to the side pressed against the wall. It's not a large room, my older sister got the biggest room apart from my parent's.

"I don't know that it's the best idea, Bri," Asher confesses with a shrug and a spike of fear races through me.

Sitting up, I stare him down. "Just come lay with me," I request and when he hesitates, shifting his weight, I add, "please. Please just come lay down."

I nearly add that we don't have to talk but he asks me, "Do you even want to be with me or do you just feel sorry for me right now?"

Emotions swell in my throat. "How could you think that?"

"Don't be mad… for all I know you were coming over to formerly break up with me."

"Firstly, I'm not mad and secondly—"

"You didn't answer me Bri."

Tears prick my eyes as my voice raises. "Answer what? Do I want to be with you?" I've never felt regret like I do now. "It's been hard not seeing you," my bottom lip wavers and I strengthen my voice, "but all I want every day is to see you. To be with you. To have you more in my life. Of course I love you and I want to be with you." Every sentence his expression softens. The resistance is all but gone when I'm finished. "Come here," I pat the bed and take in a deep steadying breath. "Please, just come here and lay down with me because I miss you and I love you and all I want is to make us right again."

"Can you stop giving me ultimatums?" he asks me and my head feels light and dizzy. "I know I don't come to see you like I promised I would but I need you to be with me if we're together. Really be with me and not sending texts at three am that if I don't do x y or z we're done."

"I'm sorry," both hands raise and all the reasons I've

been upset with him this last year races to the forefront of my mind but I push them away. Summer break is almost here and then I'll be home and we can figure those things out. "I won't," I promise him. Right now I just need him to be okay and for us to be okay … and then everything will be okay, won't it?

Asher swallows thickly and that hurt from downstairs comes back. "You sure you still love me?" he asks and for a moment it looks like his eyes glass over but then that emotion vanishes.

"I love you, I'm in love with you and every way you can say it." I confess and ball up the floral navy comforter in my hand. "You?"

"I might be a little bit in love with you," he answers with a smirk and a grin spreads across my face as I grab the closest pillow and chuck it at him.

That's how he told me he loved me for the first time behind the bleachers at gym. *I might be a little bit in love with you.* The pillow thuds as he catches it and a small genuine laugh is rough and masculine as he smiles back at me. Before I can press him for more of a reassurance he says, "I'll always love you Bri. Even when you're mad at me and overthinking everything, I love you."

CHAPTER 4

ASHER

First I pull the shirt over my shoulders and drop it to the floor, then I pull the covers back. I keep them up so Bri can get it inside me. I know every little movement she'll make as she slips in. How her shoulders do a shimmy when she nestles down beside me and the contented little sigh that slips from her sweet lips as she rests her head on my shoulder and I lay my arm over the covers and over the curve of her hip when she's settled.

We've done this a hundred times before, and I'd take this every day for the rest of my life if I could. I love the moment when she's right here and everything is safe and still. There's not a worry in the world. Just me and her.

"Are you trying to sleep?" she questions and my heavy eyes open as I tile my head to peer down at her. The comfort rustles as she lets the tips of her fingers skim over the rough stubble lining my jaw.

"I'm exhausted but no," I joke and tighten my grip on her. I worked all morning to finish the jobs that were due to be done by my father last night. "I only slept a few hours last night," I tell he and leave it at that. My father was screaming at me for taking over his job – I can't have peace in that house. Not if there's beer in it and my father's reddened face and clenched fist. There's never any peace anymore.

She's quiet a moment, before she says hesitantly, "Was it because of my text?"

My throat tightens, I don't even want to think about her texting me that I needed to be a better boyfriend. I can't. I'm barely hanging on as it is.

"I promise you I'll do the best I can, Bri. You know that right?"

"I know." Her head falls to my shoulder and I know there's something she wants to ask. It's from the way her lips stay parted and how she glances up at me before down to my chest where her fingers play in the bit of hair there. I almost tell her I bought a ring. I almost ask her to marry me right here and now, but I don't have it on me and I don't want to propose like this. All I want to do is give her the security she's begging me for and I may not be able to fly out to see her every weekend, but I show her she's mine. I can show her I'm serious.

"You smell like you just got out of the shower," she changes the subject and I let out a huff of a laugh. "I love the way you smell," she murmurs and then kisses me on my throat. My cock stirs slightly from how tender and soft her touch is.

"Bri baby, don't..." I warn her.

"I'm not doing anything," she teases under the covers.

"I know that hip roll"

"Which one?" her tone is tempting. "This one?" she mocks and a grin forms on my face before both of us laugh. She's just playing around and I pull her in closer, kissing her temple before she settles back down.

Everything about her is warmth and comfort. Before I can stop myself I tell her, "I missed you."

She doesn't hesitate and doesn't hide the agony of longing in her voice, "I miss you every day Asher. Every single day you're not with me, I miss you."

She's quick to kiss me again and this time it's on the lips. It's short and isn't meant to tease me but she does.

I kiss her back if for no other reason than to soothe that bit of pain. But one kiss turns into another. Testing and tempting, her soft body never leaving mine. I'm cock's hard in an instant and when she kisses me again, I deepen it. Slipping my tongue along the seam of her lips until she parts them for me. The moment my tongue strokes against hers, she moans into my mouth, her thigh slipping around mine until she's straddling me under the covers, her forearms resting on either side of my head.

When I break the kiss, I look up at my gorgeous girlfriend. Her sun kissed skin and the kindness in her green eyes. "I thought you said don't?" she questions teasingly.

With an asymmetric grin, I wrap my arm around her waist and flip her under me in a swift motion. A squeal leaves her as she grips onto my shoulders in surprise. The moment her back lands and she's under me, that smile hits her face.

The genuine one that I wish I could see every day. That thought forces me to take her lips back, mid laugh of hers and kiss her with everything I have. She moans again, this tortured sound of need that I fucking love.

Her legs are spread for me, her heels digging into my ass. As I rock myself against her, she writhes against me.

"Too many clothes," I scold her playfully as I pull back. The heat around us more than working us up. I work her shorts off first, letting my fingers glide down her skin as I do. A beautiful blush hits her cheeks when I move my hand between her thighs, the thin lace that'll go next separating my palm from her pussy.

"Already wet for me?"

Her gaze rips from mine as her cheeks redden even further. Leaning up, I nip her neck and her entire body tenses with a wanton gasp. "Answer me baby," I command.

"Yes." She whispers.

"Yes, what?" I look into her eyes and she stares back. There's a skip in my chest, one beat and then another that's harder and more needy. Like she can control the beat of my heart.

"I'm ready for you."

Knowing what this woman does to me makes me pause as I realize I can never lose her.

"Take your hair down," I tell her and she obeys. Then I help her with her own shirt and flick the snap of her bra undone. The moment her breasts are exposed, I tease her nipple, suckle it into my mouth. My tongue flicks against them as they peak and harden.

I take my time toying with her, but my girl is needy and so damn ready. She pushes against my jeans with her feet, as if they could be enough to rid me of them.

"Too many clothes," she mocks me with a lust filled gaze as her chest rises and falls more heavily than before.

It's tense between us, the pull not letting me take my eyes off hers as I kick off my pants. I stroke myself once, a bead of precum already at the head of my dick.

Slipping myself between her slick folds, I tease her clit as I kiss her.

The way she gasps with my lips right there is everything. It's all I want and need.

"Bri," I whisper her name as I line myself up.

Her questing look meets mine. "I love you."

With both of her hands splaying in my hair, she tells me she loves me and kisses me with every ounce of sincerity there is in this whole damn world.

Her lips press and mold to mine and I slam into her in one swift stroke, filling her and forcing her head to fall back from the sudden sensation.

She's tight as all hell. So I give her a moment to adjust. A mewl leaves her and I rock against her, not moving just yet and kissing down her neck. It doesn't take long for her body to remember mine and I pull out then thrust back inside of her in an easy rythym, then harder and faster.

A cold sweat lines my skin as her nails gently scrape along my back. As I fuck her deeper and her small cries of pleasure fill the room, she tightens and spasms on my cock. Coming undone so easily for me.

I ride through her pleasure, kissing along her jaw and she clings to me. It's only when my thumb finds her clit again, that her piercing eyes find mine and she moans my name.

"Asher," my name on her lips is wrapped in desperate need for love.

And fuck do I love her. We nearly say it at the same time and I take her again and again, not wanting this to end.

I've learned my lesson before, so before I go down the hall to get what I need to clean her up, I slip my jeans on. She's still as can be on her bed, trying to keep the evidence of what we've done from getting onto the sheets.

I can't help but smirk as I stare down at her with that just fucked look. Her hair is a messy halo and her chest is still flushed.

Once all is taken care of, I get back under the covers to cuddle with her again, and it's not long before reality sets in.

"When are your parents going to be home?"

"You thinking of going back to the hangar?" she answers me with a question of her own.

"I don't know," I answer honestly. I don't want to go back home at all "I know I don't want to be naked and in your bedroom when they do come home though."

"We could go downstairs and turn something on ... would that—"

"I'd love that," I cut her off. We have time to go from cuddling on the sofa to sitting up right when her parents come home. We've done it a thousand times before.

As I gather her clothes for her, I can't stop thinking about what's going to happen when I do go back home. They'll both probably pretend it didn't happen. They won't talk about it and if they do, it'll be a promise that it won't happen again.

My expression my show my thoughts, because Bri looks back at me with nothing but concern. I'm far too late to hide it from her.

"Asher?" she questions and I just kiss her. A quick peck as I hand her the bundle of clothes for her to put back on. That doesn't satisfy her though.

"Are we going to be okay?" She's the only thing in my life that is okay in this moment. I can't lose her. I love her too fucking much and I need her more than she could ever know.

"Of course we are. I love you and you love me. That's all that really matters."

"You promise?"

"I promise you, Bri; I'm going to love you forever."

ALL I WANT
IS A KISS

CHAPTER 1

OLIVIA

The butterflies in my stomach just won't quit it. I've searched the lobby with baited breath, but he's not here. Nick's all I could think about the entire flight. I was so convinced I'd step in through those double glass doors behind me and see him standing right in front of me, not this thin crowd of people I don't recognize.

The entire flight I pictured him at the end of the mahogany bar, seated on the leather stool with his gray tailored suit. He knows the one I like; it brings out his steely eyes. They're such a pale blue, I swear sometimes they're silver. At least they look that way under the dimmed bar lights late at night in this very hotel.

I imagined coming up beside him at the bar, and casually ordering a drink, pretending not to recognize him. As if I wouldn't know his cologne, his confident, dominating demeanor, that rough stubbled jaw in a heartbeat. I swear my body can recognize his in a crowd a mile away. I'm simply drawn to him. I even changed into this red dress that clings to my curves at the airport and touched up my makeup, just for that moment. Last time I saw him, he told me I look gorgeous in red. Pouty red lips. Check. Sultry red dress. Check check. Man I've been dreaming about for days? Nowhere in sight.

Sighing, I roll out my shoulder, letting my luggage bag fall to the crook of my arm for only a moment. It gives me enough time to take in the place without thoughts of *him* making me an anxious, excited mess. The gust of cold from behind me urges me forward, away from the front entrance and back to reality.

It's bitter cold in the Pennsylvania mountains and I happen to despise the cold. We aren't friends. No way, no how. But the fireplaces in the ski lodge resort this hotel is based in, made of large stones and surrounded by plush leather couches? We may as well be old lovers.

"There you are!" Over the din of chatter from the crowded bar across the lobby. I recognize Autumn's voice instantly.

"Hey, hey love," I greet her with a peppy voice and a tight hug when we meet halfway. Her embrace is only half assed, but she's got a good reason. Standing two inches shorter than me with big brown eyes and a brunette bob, Autumn has a wine glass in each of her hands. Red for her, and white for me. The red in her glass matches her soft chenille sweater perfectly too. As if she did it on purpose.

"I freaking love you," I say gratefully, tossing down the weekender duffle and graciously accepting the glass. If I can't have him, my heart flips in protest at the thought, at least I can have a little wine to take the edge off.

"I'm telling you," my friend of over a decade is always "telling me" something. She's also typically right. Maybe always right, I'm not sure, I don't have the mental energy to keep track. She's the creative one, I'm the workaholic. Together we kick ass. "It's so much better when you come a day early."

"I seriously wish I could, but--"

"Work," she finishes the sentence for me and rolls her eyes when she does. "I know," she comments before sipping her red wine. Her bottom lip is already slightly stained, but it only adds to her charm.

"You would think with the way you said 'work' that you don't know we're actually here for work." With my glass in my left hand and my luggage in my right, I make my way to the elevators.

"A conference is different and you know it." Autumn follows behind me, offering to take my glass. With a smirk I tell her she'll have to kill me to get it from me. It's chilled and delicious and exactly what I need after a long flight. I thought I would be here hours ago, but the flight was delayed, and here I am arriving at eleven at night with tired, dry eyes. A glass of wine is exactly what I need.

"Fine, give me your bag," she insists, downing the rest of her red. I want to ask her if she's seen Nick, but I don't. I keep my lips sealed tight, grateful that she's at least here to greet me. Besides, I know she knows I'm looking for him. I always am at these events. If she saw him, she'd tell me. The simper on my face wavers slightly, but only slightly.

A lobby attendant passes by and collects the now empty wine glass from her just as the door to the spacious elevator opens. "Thank you," she offers the uniformed gentleman. Maybe it's the uniform, or maybe I'm just really in need, but the guy is *hot*. Like he came out of a People's sexiest men alive list, *hot*. His smile is charming, a little too wide and Autumn actually blushes before pushing me into the elevator.

"You aren't kidding," I tell her as the doors close and I take another sip, "I really should have gotten in last night." The smile that creeps onto my face is fitting for the Cheshire cat.

Autumn only laughs. She's all sorts of good bundled into a beautiful little package. "Oh fuck off," she jokes back. "I wish I had the balls for a one-night stand."

There's a little blip in my chest, and heat rolls down my shoulders, yet it gives my arms chills at the thought. I was hoping for a one night stand with a man I've had plenty of those with. Disappointment lingers, he knows I'm here for the conference and every time I come to the East Coast, we meet up. Every single time. One to two times a month for nearly two years now. He's not my boyfriend; and I don't want him to be. We want different things in life and we live on opposite sides of the country. There's an unspoken commitment though. I'm the only one he sees, and he's the only one I see. It's casual and low maintenance. But why does it feel so crushing that I haven't heard from him yet?

I text him yesterday and he said he'd be here.

He's just not here yet. That's what it is. I try to convince myself and then resort to sticking my nose into Autumn's business to take my mind off of it.

"I mean...," I tease her, "we are staying for an entire weekend. And since you came a day early, it could be a four-day-stand."

I can tell she must be at least half a bottle in by how

loud she laughs and it only makes me want to catch up as we make our way to the room. I have an order to things though, before I can have more than this one glass. I don't just drop off my luggage in the room like Autumn does, I unpack everything. I put it in its place. I get bottles of water and my ear plugs and put them on the night stand too. I'm just a little OCD like that. It helps me feel settled.

"This one's for you," she hands over a keycard without acknowledging my comment, simply shaking her head in feigned dismay.

This is the same lodge as last year and it doesn't escape my knowledge when we get off the elevator that this is the same floor Nick was on last year. I spent an extra two days with him last time, lost in the sheets and taking off from work for the first time in months just to prolong saying goodbye.

I have to blow a stray piece of blonde out of my face and focus. This trip is not about him, no matter how much my libido may disagree.

Autumn's already plopped herself onto a bed. She knows the drill.

At first, when we started going to all of these events so frequently, she would stare at me like I was an alien with two heads whenever we bunked for a conference, but now, she lays back on her bed, kicks her feet up and gives me the itinerary while I do my thing. All the while, her bag lays on the floor, unzipped and spilling out everything she packed. Except her dresses, which are always hung up in the closet. She gets the right side, which she barely uses, and I get the left.

"I'm glad you're finally here. I was thinking I wasn't going to make it and by the time you got here I'd be dead asleep."

"I should have just gotten on the flight with you."

"Yes," she says pointedly as I unzip my bag. "Yes you should have." The way she says it makes me laugh. She is *always right* after all and her tone doesn't hide that fact.

"Hey," I finally get the courage to ask her although I turn my back to her, busying myself with my clothes, "did you happen to hear from Nick?"

"Mmm. Not yet." She answers and I let the frown stay in place as I put everything away. "Am I already boring you?" she asks with humor dripping on every word.

I turn to look over my shoulder, folding a pair of jeans to slip in the dresser drawer, "You know I love you."

We may be completely opposite in a lot of ways, but we're also a perfect match. Autumn and I started this marketing meet up company together and when we did I questioned if we really should. I didn't want to risk a decade long friendship over business. I'm so glad we took the risk though. Three years later and we're closer than ever and the business practically runs itself. We connect businesses with the firms they need to take their companies to the next level. I evaluate them, every nook and cranny and data point they have to offer to identify what they're lacking and how they can improve. Autumn does the socializing and connecting and most importantly, updating our clients and keeping them on track.

"So it kicks off tomorrow with a key note speech at noon, lunch served during. Then we have a workshop with the promotional team."

"You sound bored as all hell," I call out as I make my way to the bathroom to put my toiletries in their place. We've been through these conferences a dozen times this winter already. All the clients are new, but the talks are the same. So "bored" is a word that's rather accurate to describe how we'd feel if we had to sit in on the talks. This is the last one before the holidays then we have a decent break. I'm looking forward to PJs and downtime.

Autumn gets stuck attending the workshops this time around. Luckily, I'll be meeting with every client one on one, face to face, making sure we're on the same page and they're comfortable with the conclusion we've come to. Change can be unwanted, and even scary at times. But, like I tell each and every one of them, change is necessary. If you want to be at a level you've never been to before, you need to do something you've never done before.

"I don't come here for the lectures." Autumn stretches on the bed and adds with a yawn, "You don't either."

"Let me guess, is it for the lobby attendees and booze?"

She belts out a laugh and corrects me, "Again, I freaking wish." I'm still busy unpacking when she comments, "Speaking of getting some—"

"You're getting some?" Both of us have been single for nearly two years. My reason is easy; I'm only interested in what I have with Nick at the moment. I don't see a reason to stop or to want more. Although that's not something I shout from the rooftops.

Instead, I stick with something simple for an excuse as to why there's no ring on my finger: I'm a workaholic and my expectations are unreasonable. At least that's what my therapist said. And by therapist, I mean a bottle of Cabernet and a slurring best friend by the name of Autumn. Even though she's well aware of the truth, after all, Nick is her brother. She's known since day one, a few months into working together, and she doesn't judge. One more reason I love her.

She finally answers my question regarding whether or not she's getting laid. "Unfortunately no, not since the Rivera Maya."

My brow lifts at the memory of sunshine and mojitos on the white-sandy beaches. "That was a good trip."

Another trip I met up with Nick on. *Damn, I can't get him off my mind.*

"Mmm hmmm," Autumn hums and reaches into the mini bar, grabbing a bottle of water for herself before sitting cross legged on the end of the bed.

"I have no idea why you don't snag someone and settle down," I comment after plugging in my charger and then fishing out my phone from my bag to plug in while we're up here. I already have a dozen emails and four messages waiting for me. And wait they will continue to do. After the flight I had today, everything can wait until tomorrow morning. The conference doesn't start until noon and regardless of how late we stay out tonight; I'll be up at six. It's something about these events, maybe the excitement or the social interaction... whatever it is, I can never sleep. It doesn't matter how comfy the mattress is or how plush the pure white comforters are. Unless Nick happens to wear me out in bed. My thighs involuntarily clench at the thought. I check the messages just to be sure. None are from Nick and my heart drops a little.

Autumn holds up her finger, closing her eyes for a moment of silence so she can yawn again and oblige, and then dig into the bottom of my now nearly empty bag for the foldable steamer and set it on the floor of the closet, next to a set of sexy black heels, although they're simple the heels are so thin, they reek of sex appeal.

I make sure my heels are hot, my lingerie a class-A knockout and my dress, professional and nothing less. Simple and natural makeup, but a bold red lip. I love confidence and I wear it subtly, but to pack a punch. It may seem like an oxymoron, but it works for me. It keeps me lifted and motivated. So long as I have sexy panties and a pedicure, I'm convinced I can conquer the world.

It takes me a minute of digging at the bottom of my nearly empty bag for the extra charger for my laptop before I realize Autumn isn't talking anymore. Lifting my gaze, I see her fiddling on her phone.

"Hey, I thought you said something about 'getting some'?" I remind her.

She smiles brightly at me even though sleep is written all over her expression, holding up her phone and says simply, "Your star crossed lover is here."

CHAPTER 2

OLIVIA

The bar is slightly darker than everywhere else on the main level of the hotel. The lights are softer. So dim that the lit glass shelves lined with glass bottles behind the bar are really the main attraction. Although it's a Friday night, it's nearly midnight and most of the guests on this level are gathered around a stone fireplace, leaving the bar stools vacant and perfect for a private conversation. There's only a single couple seated at the bar and then there's me and my red dress.

My heart's been racing ever since I left Autumn in our hotel room to come down here. I don't remember being this eager before. I don't remember missing him as much as I am right now. "What'll it be?" the bartender asks me. Resting her palms on the bar, she leans forward to tell me when I purse my lips in indecision, "The cosmos here are pretty stellar." Her perfectly pluck brow raises as if to ask, *want one?*

"I'll have one of those then," I answer with a smile that's relatively genuine. All the nerves have me on edge. With a pat on the bar and a "coming right up," the bartender turns her back to me to make a pretty concoction of liquor in a tall skinny glass. I can't help it even though I'm irritated with my own impatience; I peek at the clock on the wall at the far end. It's only been ten minutes of waiting. It's still ten minutes too long for my taste.

With a tap on my phone, I bring up the text messages. *Meet you at the bar.* He texted it nearly fifteen minutes ago. Not even a half minute after Autumn telling me her brother was here, he texted me. And that's all he said: *Meet you at the bar.*

He gave the command and I obliged.

I don't remember being this needy ever before. But then again, I can't remember ever waiting on him. This time feels different. And I don't like it.

"Here you are," the bartender's voice is soft like the smile on her lips. Thanking her and then taking a sip, I pretend like I don't want to text him. I've never been *that* girl. Clingy, and left wanting. I've been busy all my life and for the last few years, Nicholas has been right there every step of the way, never making me feel like things weren't enough.

I just want him here. The second he's here, I know everything will be alright and this weird anxiousness will be gone.

"Did you wear red for me?" The seductive cadence and deep voice behind me eases everything in me in an instant. From my head to my toes, including those butterflies in the pit of my stomach. I don't have time to turn around, his strong arms wrap around my front, his shoulders cradling me as Nick kisses my neck. Right there, in that spot just beneath my ear that's so sensitive. His rough stubble tickles my neck as he leaves me. It leaves me hot and bothered, but so relaxed. So very at home. That's how it feels with him. He feels like home even though I never see him there. It's always hotels. Still, that doesn't change how I feel.

I reach up and behind me, my fingers trailing along his short hair until he brings his lips to meet mine. Pressing them lightly at first, until my lips mold to his. I part mine for him, and he nips slightly before deepening the kiss.

Even when he kisses me, the smile doesn't leave. It never falters. The electric tingle races through me, from head to toe. Until he breaks the kisses, leaving me breathless and trailing the tip of his nose against mine.

"So did you?" he asks, taking the seat next to me and I'm in such a haze, I don't remember why he's waiting for an answer. His handsome smirk widens into a grin when he sees the effect he has on me. "Wear the red dress for me?"

"Oh," the blush rises to my cheeks before I answer, "You know I did." I haven't an ounce of game in me. That's what Autumn says and she's right. I don't care to either. I'm not here for games.

"I love it," he comments and before I can let my smitten comeback get the better of me, the bartender's back.

"Hello, there. What'll it be?" she asks Nicholas and takes a glance at my glass, still nearly full as Nick looks at what's on tap.

He's going to get the lager. I know it. He knows it. But he takes his time, looking at each one before telling her, "A lager please."

"Short or..."

"Tall," he's quick to answer.

"Tough day?" I tease him as he slips off his jacket and gets comfortable, adjusting on the stool.

"Long," he answers and slips his hand over mine. The tips of his fingers toy with mine. "It's got a good ending though." He smirks, before lifting my hand to his lips, kissing my knuckles one at a time.

"Hasn't anyone told you, flattery will get you everywhere," I joke and he laughs. A deep rough sound that I love.

"Maybe once or twice," he answers and thanks the bartender as she places his beer in front of him.

He doesn't waste any time, taking a long swig although his left hand stays over mine. He doesn't look at me after and suddenly the air feels different again. That instinctive flip in my stomach goes off and I pull my hand away to readjust in my seat.

"You doing okay?" I ask him. My nerves get the better of me. I always trust my gut, I have all my life and it's never steered me wrong. If things feel off, it's because they are off.

He hesitates before letting out a small huff that's a humorless laugh and running his hand up the back of his neck.

"I might be moving soon," he tells me and wraps both of his hands around his beer.

Flip, skitter, halt. That's what my heart does.

"Oh yeah," I suck at keeping the nerves out of my voice. "Where to?" I ask him because it's the polite thing to do. It's the obvious question. Even though nerves dance along my heated skin.

"Out of state, the company is still nailing down the

details," he answers me and I watch the cords in his neck tighten as he swallows.

"Oh, when will you know?" Anticipation and slight relief are there, but still, this is a serious conversation. And we don't have those. Not about us. If ever one of us needs something, we're there for each other, but those moments are few and far between. I don't recall a single conversation we've ever had about "us." Although I'm completely aware, that's exactly what this is.

"This week."

"Really?" My brow shoots up my face and I can't stop it. It gets a huff of laughter from Nick, who nods his head and takes another gulp of his beer. "Really," he answers. "What do you think about that?"

"About you no longer being available for our get togethers on a whim?" I clarify, merely to take up time so I can find the right answer.

"Yeah," his voice is low, coaxing. "Will you miss me?"

There's a pitter patter in my chest that lights up every nerve ending in me. "Of course I will," I answer honestly.

"Yeah," he agrees, "I don't know for sure yet." The thick air around us dissipates into a casualness that's familiar.

"Company decision?" I question and he nods.

"Yeah, something like that," he teases and absently runs his thumb along the dew of his beer glass.

"It's weighing on you?" I question, noting how he seems lost in the conflict of whether or not to move.

"It's a big decision," he says but the way he says it sounds as if it's not so unordinary.

"So if you moved… we wouldn't be able to meet up in hotels anymore. And have our dirty little secret rendezvous."

"Is that what this is? I'm your dirty little secret?" he toys with me and I gently smack his arm and then return to nursing my drink.

"Seriously though, is that why this feels different?" I almost ask, why it feels like all of this is a long goodbye, but I don't.

"Things just… they might change a little and I wasn't sure what you'd think about it," he tells me and a nervousness settles in my gut. Change. Sometimes when I use that word, my clients get this wide-eyed, defensive look. I can feel it coming over me.

"We don't need to talk about it," I'm quick to shut it down. "All I want tonight is a kiss. Is that too much for a girl to ask?" I don't want to talk about this right now. There are too many unknowns and what ifs and I am not ready to say goodbye when he's just sat down. I know that's where this is headed and I'm not ready. I'm not willing to agree to goodbye. Or to going back to being friends. That's exactly what this feels like.

"Mmm," Nick hums and then leans close to me, kissing me and silencing my inward complaints. The kiss isn't deep, but it's soothing and when he breaks it, I keep my eyes closed for just a moment longer, wanting to make sure I remember it forever.

I whisper with my eyes still closed, "God, I missed you."

CHAPTER 3

NICHOLAS

Her long blonde hair is a messy halo from her running her fingers through her locks. It only adds to the sex kitten look she has going on. I love that she did it for me, even more that she's not ashamed to admit it out loud.

If only I wasn't afraid of losing this, these moments of inhibition with this captivating woman, I'd tell her right now what's happening. I'd tell her everything's changed and lay it out for her to accept or to walk away.

"Your room?" she asks, her eyes half lidded as she bites down into her bottom lip.

"Damn right," I answer her beneath my breath,

leaving cash on the bar and then helping her off her stool. Her small hand slips into mine and I lead her towards the elevators, listening to click of her heels and loving how she holds on to our clasped hands with her other, her shoulder brushing against mine as we walk, as if she needs to touch me, needs to have her body close to mine.

I get it. I more than get it. I love it. Which is why I'm not ready for change, but something had to give. I live for these moments with her, after tonight, it'll never be the same again.

"You smell like man," Olivia hums when the elevator dings and the doors slide open.

"Is that right?" I question, hitting the button for my floor and waiting for the doors to close as my cock hardens to an unbearable degree.

There's a hair of an opening, before they shut completely, and I lift her hands above her head, gripping her wrists and pushing her small body against the elevator wall with mine. It's quick, it's instinctual. A simmering want and desire rushes through me, when she gasps and I catch it, sealing my mouth over hers with a kiss.

"Nick," she moans in my mouth and I love it. She rocks her body against my length and my response is a deep groan of need that vibrates through my chest.

Nipping her bottom lip, I release her the second I

feel the elevator slow. I only have a moment to adjust my cock in my pants and stare down at her breathless, sagging against the wall.

"Two more minutes," I tell her, hoping to ease the ache so obvious on her face. With my hand out, she takes it, righting herself and the doors open. No one's here to watch us, no one in the hall, but still, we're professional. Her clients could be on this floor after all, and she prefers discretion, apart from a kiss here and there.

I can't count the number of times I've slipped a key card into the door with Olivia behind me, caressing my arm and waiting patiently for the soft beep and gentle click of the door being opened. It's a heady rush each and every time. The anticipation, the desire that flows freely between us. From the first time, a drunken night with a goodnight kiss turned into more, to two weeks ago, it only gets better with Olivia.

She leaves me wanting more.

Pushing the door open, I motion for her to enter first, and whether she's tipsy from the wine or drunk on lust, Olivia slides past me, making sure her curves brush against me as she does.

Her hips sway and the simmer in my blood only gets hotter.

The door closes with a resounding click and I don't have to command her, she turns at the foot of the bed, facing me as she unzips her dress and lets it fall from the curve of her shoulders down to a puddle of fine fabric at her feet. She makes a move to take her heels off next and I stop her.

"No," I order, "keep them on tonight." My voice is deep and I let her hear every ounce of need I have for her. Her lips part just slightly, her breasts rising with the quick inhale in the quiet room, and I swear my cock leaks precum at the sight of her, turned on by the simple fact that I'll fuck her tonight in those sex kitten heels.

I could imagine her lying on the bed behind her, her legs in the air as I pound into her, then the slim heels dragging down my back as she screams my name. I could, but I don't, because her hazel eyes entrance me, reflecting the same concoction of need and want in the moonlit room. The thick curtains are open, but the sheer ones are closed, giving a breathtaking view.

The mountain range behind her, the bright moon that filters into the room against the plush white comforter. And in front of it all, a beautiful woman who wants me as badly as I want her, slowly but surely, unstrapping her bra and letting it fall to the floor.

With her fingers moving to her hips, I motion for her to stop and finally move, closing the distance between us in three long strides. Every step closer, the collar around my neck feels tighter, suffocating me for still being dressed.

She tilts her head for me to kiss her, but I don't. Her eyes are closed and it takes a moment before she opens them, staring up at me as I tower over her naked form, all but heels and thin satin panties. "Hands at your sides," I tell her and she listens. She loves the submission as much as I love the domination. She knows it all now, every command, every wish I have. "Fucking perfect," I mutter beneath my breath, letting her see my gaze roam down her body.

Trailing my thumb down her bottom lip, I let it fall to her collarbone, then lower, teasing her breasts one at a time. It's the only touch I give her for now. Her soft moan fills the room and her eyes close as her head falls back, lost in pleasure.

I take my time, still fully clothed, dragging my touch down her body to rid her of the red thong. She only touches me when I bend down, her hand on my shoulder, to step out of the underwear.

Tossing it carelessly beside us, I keep my gaze on her, and plant a kiss just beneath her navel, then lower, dragging the tip of my nose down further until I'm right where I want to be, my lips at her clit. I suckle gently and her fingertips brush my shoulders, but she's quick to correct herself.

"Nick," my name is a mix of a pant and a moan on

her lips. I taste her, parting her lips and dipping two thick fingers inside her. She's already wet, already whimpering. I stroke her, curling my fingers to be sure to hit the sweet spot at her front wall.

"Please," she begs with true desperation as she sways, without anything to keep her steady but the heels she chose to wear tonight. Her arousal coats my fingers as I stroke more ruthlessly, pulling her pleasure from her. Her smell, her soft sounds and even the heat of her body being so close is addictive. She's a drug and I've been addicted for as long as I can remember.

I can barely take it, crouched down in front of her, hard with my own need and desperate to be inside her. Quickening my movements, I suck on her clit and the instant gasp is followed by her nails digging into my shoulders as she clenches around my fingers and screams out my name.

I withdraw in an instant, all too aware that she's already gone over the edge, finding her orgasm.

Smack! My hand lands hard on her ass in reprimand and she can't even jump, her balance is so disturbed from her pleasure that she falls into me. "Bad girl," I growl at her ear as I lift her by her ass, throwing her onto the bed behind her.

I don't waste the moment undressing. In an instant I'm between her legs, still clothed and nipping her neck.

My right hand travels up her body, my left unzips my pants and pulls out my cock. I stroke it once, before slamming into her.

She screams out, her neck arching, her mouth the perfect "o" and I stay just like that, buried to the hilt for only a moment. Just one to let her adjust. That's when I finally kiss her, my tongue delving into her hot mouth and silencing her strangled screams of pleasure as I ravage her.

Pistoning my hips, gripping her own to keep her where I want her. Her heels thud as they hit the floor, one by one, unable to stay on as I fuck her ruthlessly.

She's so tight, so hot and so close to coming again already. Her second release is what pushes me to have mine.

I groan her name in the crook of her neck, feeling the warm air of her moans on my cheek as she cums with me. Pulsing around me as the waves of my own release pulse through me.

Both of us breathless, both of us sated, I slip out slowly watching her wince as I do. She rolls on her side, breathing heavily with her eyes closed.

I pull the covers around her before heading to the bathroom, finally stripping down and gathering a warm washcloth to take care of her.

It's silent until I climb in bed with her, everything

taken care of so she can fall asleep. "Sleep well," I tell her, knowing she'll stay with me tonight

She doesn't though and I'm certain I can't either.

This could be our last time together. There's no way I could possibly sleep. Her fingers trail along the grooves in my chest, and when she brings them up higher I lean down to kiss her hand.

She hums in satisfaction, but she still doesn't sleep. I could bore her to sleep, talking about the merger that just went through and how the company is sky rocketing, the stocks booming. She'd listen to it all, with the same expression she gives me now, as if I'm her beloved Prince Charming.

"I don't want to sleep," she finally breaks the silence.

"What do you want for Christmas, Olivia?" I ask her, running my thumb down the curve of her neck and feeling the pull of my lips into a smirk when she shivers.

Naked and tired, Olivia stretches lazily and then sidles up closer to me under the sheets, "More of this," she answers and I have to keep my expression the same, unmoving, so she doesn't see the loss I feel deep inside. Her eyes are closed, but I don't want to risk her seeing.

"Nothing else?" I question, knowing she isn't going to get more of these meet ups. Not for a while at least with all of the changes coming.

Slowly peeking up at me, her hazel eyes a mix of

wildfire and calming ocean shores, "Fine, all I want is a kiss." Her voice is soft and her hand on my chest even softer. Leaning down to kiss her, I let the kiss linger, waiting for her to hum in approval. She does and I knew she would. I love that sound. I love how easily she kisses me.

"I hate that I have to leave you tomorrow," she says it so easily, so used to it. She's alright with what we have. She would be fine with this for as long as I let it happen.

"Hopefully I'll see you soon," I answer her and her eyes open, staring at my chest rather than meeting my gaze.

"Do you know when that will be?" she questions.

I hate that I have to answer her the way I do, "No," I tell her.

I bet she thinks she's gotten away with hiding her disappointment, but I see it. "That's alright," she tells me, even though I know she feels that same ache in her chest I do at the thought of not having another night like this planned. She can't say goodbye so easily.

Her pointer traces my collarbone when she whispers what we've told each other every time for years now, "It's never goodbye. Only until next time."

CHAPTER 4

OLIVIA

"Why do I choose the walk of shame?"

Nick's first response to my groggy morning question is a rough chuckle that jostles the bed. "I can go get your things," he offers, "Or Autumn can bring them?"

I shake my head, brushing my cheek against his firm chest before resting my head back against him, "It's okay, I'll walk it with pride," I answer with a simper and lightheartedness.

The early morning sun is peeking in and I check the clock to find it's nearly eight. Last night filters in as my eyes adjust to morning and the easy rest in Nick's bed changes into the reality that I need to leave it and I may never share one with him again.

"You're really leaving?" I question but I didn't mean to. The disbelief simply slipped out.

He breathes in deep and his chest moves with it, so I remove myself from the cozy spot and sit up, covering myself with the sheets. As I do, the ache between my thighs intensifies. I'll feel him for days.

"Yeah, just one night this time. I have to get somethings settled," Nick doesn't look at me as he talks, instead he reaches for the bottle of water on the nightstand and hands it to me.

"Thanks," I tell him and my smile is weak. I drink down as many gulps as I can, trying to pause the unwanted thoughts filtering through my mind.

"You okay?"

"Huh?" I look up into Nick's steely blues to find them riddled with concern. "Fine," I lie. "I just have to get going."

With the excuse spilled, I gather the sheets, pushing them out of the way and search for my dress and underwear.

"You don't have to go. We can order in breakfast," he offers but there's no hope in his voice.

I was already a drink down last night, but still. How did I go to bed with him one last time, knowing that he was leaving? How did I think I could do it? Stay here with him and say goodbye?

I struggle with my strap and Nick climbs out of bed, still naked and in all his glory to help me.

"Olivia," his voice is gentle. "You don't have to run off," he whispers at my neck and then pulls my back into his chest.

"I'm not running off," I lie. "I just need a shower and to prepare."

I turn around, conscious of the fact that I haven't brushed my teeth. I usually use his toothbrush, but I also typically stay. This morning isn't typical. I can feel that in my bones.

"Never goodbye. Only until next time." He smiles when he says it and that's why I can only nod, not trusting myself to speak. With a wave of my hand, I leave him there, and put on a brave face when I open the door to my shared room with Autumn. I don't want her to know how much I'm breaking right now. Nothing is certain. He may not move. It may not be over. That thought is the only thing that keeps me glued together. I wish next time was a given. For the first time since we started it, I'm all too aware that it's not a given. No matter how much I want to lie to myself.

The taxi ride is almost forty minutes long and it's excruciating. All I want is my pillow so I can bury my head in it and let all of these unwanted emotions out.

"I miss you already," the second the plane landed, I messaged Nick first. I haven't heard from him since we said goodbye at the resort and again, I find myself not used to the waiting. The lack of an answer from him. I check it again, and a good thirty minutes later, I have nothing. No answer from him.

I have loved every conference we've ever done, but not this one. This one is stained with loss. Undeniable and irrefutable loss. I glance at my phone again, to see no response from Nick. With tears pricking at the back of my eyes, I'm tempted to message Autumn. She's his sister and he's leaving me. Tension works its way into my gut and I shift on the leather backseats of the cab. They protest in response.

Is this really the end of it? It can't be. There's a sinking feeling in my chest and I need to talk to someone about it, but who? Autumn's the only one who knows, and what am I supposed to say to her? *Your brother is ignoring me?* We're grown adults and I knew what this was. I just wasn't prepared for this. We're never ready for goodbyes. At least I'm not. I thought I could avoid it with Nick, I thought I'd never have to say it. Checking my phone again and noting the lack of a message from him, I was apparently wrong. The conclusion I've come to is the worst of them all, because that's what my gut is telling me. *It's over.* He's moving on and that's all there is to it.

I keep thinking, it was too good to last. Wasn't it? It was so easy and natural. Everything always fell into place with Nick... I should have known better than to think it would last or become anything more. Fuck, it hurts. It's not supposed to hurt, when you keep yourself at a distance and make sure the relationship is casual. It's not supposed to hurt when it ends. But I'll be damned if that's not exactly what I'm feeling right now.

I check my phone and again, there's no response.

"Right up here," the taxi driver says absently and before I can answer, the words catch themselves at the back of my throat.

Oh my God, he's here.

My heart does that fluttering thing my stomach was doing only days ago. Sitting on the footsteps to my front porch, his large frame taking up the small threshold. I can't think straight, let alone breathe. He's right here. Waiting for me.

Nick must feel my eyes on him as the taxi slows in front of my townhouse because he looks right up at me. Those steely blues stealing my breath with their intensity.

My heart races, beating wildly at the sight of him.

"Mam?" the cab driver's voice alerts me that I need to pay and get on my way.

"Sorry, sorry," I answer breathlessly, frantically searching for cash so I can get out and go to the man I haven't been able to stop thinking about.

I don't have a chance to get my luggage, Nicholas gets it for me. Carrying it up to my porch steps and waiting there for me.

Anxiousness tingles its way through me and I barely hear the taxi drive off as I stand on the steps, looking up at him and whispering, "What are you doing here?" Praying and hoping he's here for more than a real goodbye.

CHAPTER 5

NICHOLAS

What am I doing here?

"Right now, I'm trying to gather up the strength to ask you something," I answer her. I can barely swallow, barely breathe. Even though it's winter and the cold is blistering, making the tip of Olivia's nose a rosy red already, I'm burning hot.

"I have to know, do you want me, Olivia? Do you want more?" Her bottom lip falls open and her hazel eyes widen with surprise. I can't bare for her to answer me without telling her everything, without giving this the best shot I can give it.

"Because I want you. I want all of you. I love our

stolen nights and I'll do everything I can to keep giving them to you, but I need more." A quick intake and a single step forward, closing the distance between us is all that pauses the confession I've been working over in my head all week. "I want to be with you, really be with you. Every day and always. Not just a secret rendezvous. I want it all. The picket fence, kids, I want it all… with you. And only you."

I don't know if I've said it all and I'm certain I've said most of it wrong. I'm nervous and I'm terrified. Terrified that she doesn't want this. It will destroy me if she says no. She's all I want and all I've wanted since I first laid eyes on her.

She still hasn't said anything, although she takes a hesitant step forward and I use that closeness to take her hands in mine, running soothing circles along her wrists with the rough pad of my thumb.

"Do you want me, Olivia? Because I'll move here, with you or get my own place, so we can be together like we should. If you don't, I understand, but I need to know."

The silence is awful. It rips at me from the inside as I wait for her to say something. Every deep breath she takes I prepare for her to tell me no.

"You asked me what I want for Christmas. At the hotel, you asked me and I lied to you," her voice is soft and riddled with emotion but I can't decipher it. I need an answer.

"I know. A kiss. You said all you wanted was a kiss." I can't bear it if she tells me that now. I'm not ready to say goodbye. I nearly backtrack, I nearly give in and tell her I'll go back to only hotel rooms and discreet rendezvous if that's what she wants.

"I lied. I lied to you," her voice cracks and it echoes the feeling in my heart. "I want so much more than a kiss. All I want for Christmas, is you."

Relief washes over me and it comes with a warmth I'm unfamiliar with. It's better than the heat between us when I first see her across the bar. It feels like home.

"I couldn't tell you because A, it's cheesy and B, I didn't think I could have you."

"Just say the word, and I'll move here. I'm ready to be with you, Olivia, I don't think I can fathom not being able to see you again."

"Same," she breathes the single word.

"That's a yes? You want this? You want me?"

"All of you." She nods, quickly and vigorously. Tears make her hazel eyes glassy. "I want all of you too."

Thank fuck.

I can't describe the relief, immediate and all consuming. With one arm scooping around the small of her back and the other spearing into her hair, I kiss her, the woman I love, with everything I have.

"I love you, Olivia," I tell her for the first time, solidifying what we have. What we've had all this time but neither of us was willing to risk bringing it to life.

"I love you too," she whispers against my lips, in the warm air between us. "You don't have to leave do you?"

"I took two weeks off to figure all this out. I want to figure it out with you. I told Autumn. She knows."

"She does?" her eyes are full of shock. It's comical really.

"You can't be mad; I swore her to secrecy." There's a smirk on my lips and before she can answer, I kiss her again. And again.

She nuzzles her nose against mine, before looking up through her thick lashes. "Two weeks to figure it all out?"

"Yeah, and if we need more time, I'll make it. I want us. More than anything, I know I need you."

"I figured it out. Move in with me and let's spend two weeks in bed." She says it so seriously, yet easily. As if it's so simple and I chuckle, planting a kiss on her forehead that makes her smile. She has the most beautiful smile.

"We can start with me helping take your luggage inside," I offer and she nods watching me while I gather her things and she opens the door. The moment it closes, she's on me, her arms wrapping around me with a fierceness. Dropping the bags to the floor, I hold her back.

"I thought... I thought we weren't going to get this," she whispers and before I can ask what she means, she kisses me, standing in my arms on her tip toes. "You make me happy and I don't want to be without you." She speaks so quietly, I barely hear her.

"Same," I tell her, brushing her hair back and waiting for her to finally look up at me.

"I've never been the girl for fairytales, but I want a happily ever after with you."

Resting my forehead against hers, all I can focus on is the warmth in my chest. Everything about this, about *her*, feels right.

"You can say it again," she tells me. "Tell me you love me again."

"I love you Olivia. I want to love you forever."

"I love you too."

Just A Little Crush

CHAPTER 1

AUBREE

Every Sunday night during football season, a game blares from the corner of the bar. The TV mounted on the wall was updated last year, the pool table is even newer and although the back room and one side of the bar is taken by men with gray beards who have come here for decades, this half of The Peanut Bar and Grill is ours.

It's been ours for three years now, ever since I moved to this small town. The only thing missing is our names carved into the tabletop at our regular booth.

Same crew every Sunday, and on Wednesdays too for half-price nachos. A smile grows on my lips as the bar cheers, someone shouts in protest and Dani, the bartender, breaks out in a laugh. She and I are alike; neither one of us really cares about football, but this is a part of home.

Nick and Michelle, high school sweethearts who have been married for five years now, are cuddled up in the corner of the booth. They'll leave early, just like they have since she found out she's pregnant.

It wasn't even on the menu until Michelle told the owner she was craving them during her first trimester. He's her neighbor and said it's the least he could do.

I take another sip of my pale ale just as the happy couple makes the rounds to say goodbye, root beer float in hand.

Jackson and Nate mock protest over them leaving although every single one of us knew it was going to happen. The other five of us will be here till close most likely.

Nate and his girlfriend, my close friend Anne. The rest of us are the single bunch: Jackson, Cheryl, and me.

"Have twice as much fun for me," Michelle says and sighs sweetly as she gives me a hug, her belly nudging against mine. Her flowy cream blouse peeks out from her jean jacket that wouldn't close around her if she tried. It's not maternity, but it's darn cute.

"Where's your sweater?" Nick questions, cutting me

off in a protective tone that's all too adorable just as she's snatching it from the seat with a smirk on her face. It's cute how he is with her, and just as cute how she toys with him.

His smirk matches hers once she gives him a peck on the lips.

I can't help but feel a pang of jealousy watching the two of them wave as they exit the bar. Hand in hand. Madly in love.

Another sip of my beer heats my cheeks as I peek at Jackson. Nick and Michelle had one side of the booth. Nate and Anne, the other. Then Cheryl and I took the outside seats while Jackson, Cheryl's older brother, sat at the barstool closest to the table.

That's been our setup for years.

Three years of sitting just feet away from a man I have a crush on, every single week. Ever since I moved to this small town.

"Another?" Dani calls out, catching my attention. Her dark eyes stare back at me and it's only then that I look down and realize my glass is nearly empty.

"Yeah," I answer and the tall brunette is already pouring me another. She works this side of the room. Her brother works the other. The Peanut Bar is a family place. Practically everything in this town is that way.

It's all close quarters and routines. Everyone knows

everyone and also their business.

Which is why my fingers fiddle with my drink a moment too long before I nudge Jackson, opting to hand him the empty glass, which he easily exchanges for the full one Dani's holding out to him to pass to me.

My heart does a little pitter-patter every time he looks my way. His sharp blue eyes and charming smile aren't what gets me, although they don't hurt. There's something else about him. And when his fingers brush against mine, in that small moment of contact, a heat blazes through me.

For three years it's been like this. And every day that passes without acknowledging what he does to me, only makes it harder the next.

The bar cheers again as the screen shows a playback of the game. Cheryl's busy chatting with Nate and Anne. The couple behind us, neighbors of Cheryl, leans over the back of their booth to join the conversation.

I stare up at the screen, pretending I don't want to glance back at Jackson, pretending I don't wish he was sitting next to me and the whole damn town knew we were a thing.

Jackson's my friend, tall, dark and handsome ... but *only* a friend.

The timing was simply never right for us to be anything more.

When I met him, the butterflies were there, the instant attraction undeniable ... but I tried to deny it, because I had a boyfriend. It was a long-distance situation—I'd graduated college and left that town to come here, but I was determined to make it work. Cheryl, my friend from college who convinced me to move here, introduced me to her brother and it was damn hard to keep my impression of him to myself.

Jackson greeted me with a charming smile and a laugh that made me feel things it shouldn't have. After three years of this charade, Cheryl is well aware I have a crush on her brother.

I wasn't the first of her friends to feel puppy love for him. Apart from some teasing here and there, she's kept that information to herself and we remain the closest of friends.

Thank God. I love her like family, and I don't know what I would do without her. Without any of them really. She became the sister I never had while we were in college. As far as I'm concerned, this town and these people adopted me.

Which is why I'll never cross that line with Jackson.

Back then, when she first introduced us, I thought: he's not into me like that, and he's not going to be hanging out with us all the time anyway. So I need to get the idea of the two of us out of my head.

Only he did keep coming around, and those feelings kept growing. I didn't realize just how tight knit this town is.

Over the following months, I realized I couldn't deny what I felt. So I did the right thing, I ended the three-month relationship I had so I could confess to Jackson how I felt. But when I went to the bar, in that spot across from me, right where Jackson is sitting now, there was a cute little redhead by the name of Mallory attached to his hip. And she made him smile, so I couldn't hate her.

Back and forth for years, one of us was always taken. I'd convinced myself it was meant to be that way because as time went on, he became my rock for so many things. Just like Cheryl.

"You want a root beer float?" a masculine voice murmurs close to the shell of my ear. My body heats with a flush that I'm sure is visible. And that baritone cadence elicits an ache of desire between my thighs.

He knows exactly what he's doing. The cocky grin on his handsome face tells me so as he stands back upright, a hand on the back of the booth. He towers over me in blue jeans and a simple plaid button-down.

"We could get one with beer and ice cream?" Jackson offers, lifting his glass in mock cheers before taking a sip. The bar erupts as our team scores, yet the noise seems to fade and blur behind him. Even with the scent of beer in the air, I know exactly how he smells. It's like amber and woods, mixed with a hint of freshness.

Instead of saying anything at all that's on my mind, I answer as I should, in a teasing, nonserious manner. "You want beer with ice cream?" I shake my head gently, a crease between my furrowed brow as I add, "What is wrong with you?"

He lets out a laugh and motions for me to slide down the booth so he can sit next to me.

The leather is still warm from where Michelle was sitting as I scoot back. It's quiet back here, slightly more private but not really.

"So you don't want to split ice cream with me?" he questions, a touch of his Southern drawl coming through, along with feigned vulnerability in his puppy dog eyes.

Yes. Jackson knows exactly what he's doing when he flirts with me.

And I know what I'm doing when I flirt back. "If by 'split' you mean I get a whole three bites before you devour it, then sure." I shrug and pull a leg up onto the seat so I can wrap my arm around it. My black leggings and baggy gray knit sweater keep my appearance casual. Although I did spend time on my makeup, keeping it relatively natural but with a hint of pink. Heavy mascara and a braid down my left shoulder were the finishing touches.

His hand runs down the side of his chiseled, stubbled jaw as he chuckles. "I asked you last time we split a dessert if you wanted more," he protests. Leaning closer he adds, "If I knew you were going to hold it against me, I wouldn't have touched your half." He's close enough now that I can feel his heat, I can smell him too and it's just like I knew it would be.

Before I can answer, a balled-up napkin hits Jackson square on his nose. "Get a room," a grinning Cheryl calls out from across the booth. Nate and Anne are laughing, and the couple behind them in the booth adjacent to ours is laughing too. Not at us, thankfully. They don't seem to notice and with a smile, Cheryl's already left the table. With a bit of a tipsy sway, she's headed to the bar before either Jackson or I can answer.

Thump, *thump*, my heart batters against my rib cage in protest, but this tension doesn't affect Jackson in the least. He's never bothered and I know it's because he doesn't feel what I feel.

He doesn't feel this pull between us like I do.

My throat's dry and I try to swallow down my nerves with a sip of the cool beer as Jackson leaves my side, the leather groaning as he goes.

CHAPTER 2

JACKSON

"You should just go for it, man," Nate comments, sidling up beside me at the bar as Dani puts in the order.

"And you should mind your own damn business," I joke back at him, pretending like Aubree doesn't get to me. Like I don't want to slide in next to her and press my lips against hers. I have to hold back a groan at the thought. I'm not a lightweight, but four lagers and apparently I'm feeling the effects.

"I think you two should just get together for a night. Just saying it might be good to finally clear that sexual tension."

My body reacts to the suggestion, but so does the last sober bit of me. "And ruin our friendship?"

Nate's smirk and lifted brow piss me off. "Don't act like it's not a possibility," I tell him lowly, leaning against the bar top, hoping he gets it. He's been joking about it for months since he caught me staring at her like some lovesick puppy dog. "If we did anything, you know damn well it would change everything between us."

Nate's dark eyes narrow as he seems to consider my dilemma. It's only ever been a joke. Nothing like the conversation we're having now and how I'm riddled with anxiousness.

"How would you feel if some guy came in and they started making out?" he asks and as he does, I set my glass down a little too hard on the bar top. It doesn't crack, but the sound is jarring enough that Dani turns from the tap, her brow raised.

I raise a hand in defense and say, "Didn't break it. Sorry."

"No harm, no foul," she answers with a grin.

"Come on, how would you feel," Nate presses, dropping his voice so no one can hear. Honestly, I'm not sure if they can or not in this crowd. I'm tipsy and the bar is loud, but in this small town everyone seems to hear everything even when it's whispered. "If some guy came in, hit on her and they hit it off." He gestures behind us. "If they were making out in that booth you were just sitting in beside her."

"She wouldn't do that." My head shakes and my entire body stiffens. I never knew jealousy until Aubree introduced me to her boyfriend years ago. I'm not a fan.

"If it happened, you wouldn't like that."

"I'd be happy that she's happy." I give him the lie and take refuge in my beer. It's crisp and cold still, even though it's the last of it.

"Bullshit," Nate says, not letting up.

Squaring my shoulders, I stare him down. "Let it go, man."

Every other reason gets caught in my throat:

If she was into me, I'd know by now.

If it was going to happen, it would have happened by now.

Nate shrugs, the jersey he's wearing pulling tighter on his shoulders. "Fine," he states casually, but then adds, "Don't come crying to me when some other guy is the one to get cozy with her 'cause you don't have the balls to kiss her first."

I'm paralyzed with a mix of emotions. I don't trust myself to answer. Nate seems to notice my lack of a response and glances over my way.

"Fuck, man, I'm sorry. Just ignore me. All right?"

Anger bristles along my shoulders as I turn to face the TV in the corner, although it also allows me to watch Aubree from the corner of my eye.

"I mean it, I'm sorry. I just … think you two would hit it off."

My tongue sweeps along my bottom lip as I watch Aubree finish her beer. Her cheeks are flushed, her hair's in a loose braid and a smile graces her face from whatever my sister just told her.

"I just can't risk changing some things, you know?" I say, finally answering Nate.

"They're going to change either way," he tells me in all seriousness and there's an ache in my chest. A familiar pull like the sense of loss. Loss of something I've never even had.

The moment Aubree scoots from the booth, her hand reaches out to me as she stabilizes herself, fixing her baggy sweater that swallows up her small frame. It's these little touches that get me.

How she knows she can rely on me. How she likes to even.

"You all good?" I ask her and she lets out a small laugh. That sound. It wriggles its way through me, warming me. Her hazel eyes slip to mine and she bites down slightly on her lower lip. "Just have to run to the ladies' room."

"You might want to walk, it's a bit crowded," I tease her. It's cheesy and the grin Nate has growing on his face tells me he heard it too.

Whatever, she still laughs.

Shaking her head, she brushes past me, and everything inside of me wants to wrap my arm around her waist, pull her in and ask her if she wants to come home with me.

It's a feeling I'm used to. And so is this chill that sweeps in the moment she walks away.

"Dani, she needs another," I call out to the bartender the moment Aubree's gone.

Dani's quick to place the beer down in front of me even though it's for Aubree.

"She didn't even ask who 'she' is," Nate comments.

Reaching over the tabletop, I snag an orange slice Dani forgot, and drop it into Aubree's glass. "Can't I be happy with this as it is?" I ask him genuinely.

Before he can answer, Aubree's right there, watching me place the beer at her seat.

"You looking out for me? Or just trying to get me drunk?" There's this small smile she gives me sometimes. It's there now as she lifts the beer to her lips and slips deeper into the booth to give me room to sit if I want to.

"Maybe a little of both," I joke, questioning if I should sit. If I should push it a little more tonight than I have before.

"Which one would you prefer?" I ask her, feeling this hot nervousness prick along every inch of my skin as she stares up at me.

She smirks back, all flirtatious and never breaking eye contact when she says, "Maybe a little of both?"

CHAPTER 3

AUBREE

Cheryl leans in close, a smirk clearly written on her face. "Just do it, Bree." She comes even closer to nudge me, her tipsiness making her sway as she adds, "You can't keep teasing him like this."

The grin on her face is as wide as it can be as her gaze lifts from me and moves to the topic of the conversation behind me.

My cheeks can't get any hotter.

"Your drink's empty." A deep yet flirtatious man's voice reaches us from down the bar. *Kill me now.* Cheryl and I grabbed barstools beside Nate and Jackson when the game went into overtime. Both of them have since moved. It's like musical chairs in this place.

It took a whole two minutes for the guys to my right to start chatting us up. They weren't paying attention to the game in the least.

"Let us buy you your next round. What are you ladies drinking?"

He raises his voice to speak over the sounds of the game on the bar's TVs. The crowd roars in the background. Whistles blow. I don't care much about the score, but the atmosphere is amped up. The end of the night is getting close.

Cheryl beams at me. "See? If you don't make your move, somebody else is going to step in. Those guys are hot."

"Those guys are hot because you're drunk," I joke, although I don't have much room to talk. I, too, am far from sober.

"No, they're genuinely hot." Cheryl sneaks a peek over her shoulder, her cheeks turning a bright pink as she takes them in.

The bar is emptying out. Quite a few people reached their limit by the fourth quarter and headed home, but Cheryl's having a good time. Nate and Anne made it through most of the fourth before they went home to make out with each other.

And Jackson ...

Jackson is still here.

I can feel him in the bar. Maybe it's just because I'm drunk as well, but I am acutely aware he's still here, even with my back turned. He's behind me now at the booth I was sitting at only an hour or so ago.

I wonder if he's watching. If those guys come closer, he's going to see. The Peanut Bar isn't that big, and there aren't many people left. Nerves eat at me as I wonder if he even cares. All I can think about while these guys are flirting with me, is whether or not Jackson can see. What the hell is wrong with me?

With a short sigh, I push my beer away and look back at my good friend. Her teeth are sunken into her bottom lip as she glances their way again.

Cheryl's right. I should make a move, one way or the other. Three years is a long time to shove my feelings down. Three years is a long time not to go home with a man because of a little crush that's never going to go anywhere. I should either get up and confess to Jackson that my heart skips a beat every time I see him here, or I should let those guys buy us drinks.

The moment I suck in a breath and peek at Jackson, I turn right back around.

It's silly to be afraid of rejection like this, but I am. If he outright turned me down, it would hurt like hell. And then I could never show my face again at this bar. Never ever. This place is like a second home to me.

"Pale ale," I call to the guys down the bar. The one closest to me nods and I shrug, offering a smile. "That's what I'm having, anyway." He's cute. Handsome even, although the jersey makes him seem a little young. He's definitely in college, and old enough to be in a bar so I'm thinking twenty-two maybe.

"I'm tempted to ask him if he's going to be a dentist because his teeth are freaking perfect," I comment to Cheryl and she pats my arm a little too hard.

"Hell yes," she says, a little too loud. "Now we're going to have some fun. Or at least you are." She gets up from her stool, the legs scraping against the wooden floor as if she's leaving me. The urge to grab her arm and cling to her has never been stronger.

"What?" The one word that spills out of my mouth sounds utterly pathetic and I don't even care. "You are not leaving me," I whisper in a hushed voice.

"I'm just going to the restroom. You get the first pick of the guys."

"Cheryl!" I reach for her sleeve, but she's already too far to pull her back.

The two guys don't miss a beat sliding down farther, like they're coming in for the kill.

"So, a pale ale?" the blond with the gorgeous smile questions and then motions for Dani. I don't miss how high her brow arches and that sly, comical smile she gives me.

"Mm-hm." I don't trust myself to speak, but I settle on some small talk.

"Hi, guys. Having a good night so far?"

"Depends," the blond one says. "Are you?"

My cheeks flare with heat. He's not subtle in the least but I play it casually. "I always have fun on Sunday nights."

The truth is, I'm always invested in being here on Sunday nights. Our crew has a good time together and it's my wind down time. My safe place. But I'd be lying if I said I wasn't here for Jackson too. My smile slips as I think of him yet again. I like being around him. I like having an excuse to look at him and listen to his jokes and just be in the same room. I've had to come to terms with making the most of it and enjoying my Sundays over the last three years. If it was truly painful to be here with him, that wouldn't be any fun.

The barstool scrapes as the blond hunk takes the stool next to mine, the one that used to be Cheryl's, and purses his lips. "You could have more fun, I bet." His tone is soothing, but I see through it all.

"Oh yeah? And how's that?" If I wasn't thinking of Jackson, I'd ask him if he wanted to cut to the chase.

As it is, even when I'm looking at this man who's obviously interested in me, all I see is the image of Jackson sitting here only hours ago.

My heart's beating faster, but I don't know if it's because I'm genuinely interested in this guy or because I'm nervous as hell about what's going to happen. If I click with some random man at the bar, what happens to my feelings about Jackson? Probably nothing. He doesn't have any for me, so we'd both move on with our lives like grown adults. All the while this guy talks, my thoughts scream in my head. I nod and comment when it seems appropriate. His friend hovers, more invested in the game now.

But damn if I don't want Jackson to be jealous. At least for him to notice that someone else has approached me. It sends a shiver down my spine to imagine his eyes on us, but I don't look to see if he's watching.

"What are you doing after this?" the blond hunk questions. My lips part but someone else speaks before I can.

"We're going to my place." Jackson's deep, masculine voice breaks into our conversation and heats my core.

My heart pounds and I let out a long breath. It's so damn hot in here. I hadn't noticed that before. I pull at my sweater, hoping to feel a little breeze.

Before I can say anything, shock and heat overwhelming me, Jackson's strong arm wraps around my lower waist. The thermostat must have fucking broken in this place.

Jackson's body curls around mine as he bends down and kisses the crook of my neck. Right there in that spot beneath my ear and I think I must have died. It's heaven, it's sinful. It's a fantasy come to life. "That's what she's doing after this." His chest is a deep rumble against my shoulder and I can barely look back at the man who just bought me a drink.

I don't even know how I'm sitting upright.

The brush of his lips fills me with butterflies. A fluttering mess of them. Gulping down the beer, I give myself a moment to steady. Jackson. Possessive of me in the bar just because a guy offered me a drink?

This might be my only shot to play along with him. I turn my face to his and kiss his cheek before I can overthink this. If he's going to cross this line for a joke or whatever Jackson's thinking … I'm going to cross it too.

My blond would-be hero throws his hands up with a smile when I glance back at him. "Didn't realize."

"Sorry, I should have said—" I'm not able to finish before Jackson cuts me off.

"No problem." His tone is familiar, yet harder, more dominating. He leaves no room for further conversation. And the other guys get the hint.

They back off, looking toward the hall leading to the restroom, leaving me staring up at him, his arm still wrapped around me. His hold is looser now, but it's still there.

"You drunk?" he questions, glancing down at me for only a moment.

Maybe more than a little tipsy. "Not so drunk that I don't know what I want." The words slip out before I can stop them and his brow raises in surprise.

I rip my gaze away and take another sip of beer, but it doesn't do anything to change the way I feel right now.

I've never been hornier in my life. I didn't come here with sex on my mind. I'm in leggings and a sweater. That should be enough of a clue that I didn't plan on doing anything but cuddling up with a hangover cure after this.

Jackson says something and I'm not quite sure what, but his hand leaves the bar and I'll be damned if I'm going to let him leave me like this.

"What was that?" I question, my voice sultry. I didn't mean for it to come out like that.

"Just cockblocking you," Jackson jokes. He picks up his drink from the bar behind me. That hammering in my chest intensifies. Is he ... is he toying with me? 'Cause that kiss is still burning my neck.

"Oh yeah? What would you call this?" I say, then lean forward, hook my arm around his neck, and kiss him full on the mouth. My lips press against his and at first they're hard, but they mold to mine instantly.

He kisses me back with an intensity I didn't expect. He tastes like beer and hunger. He tastes better than I ever imagined he would. I kiss him deeper, wanting to remember it after tonight.

That's when it hits me. We're in the freaking bar still. Everyone is here. His sister. Our friends. I pull away with a slight panic.

Jackson smirks down at me. A gorgeous, handsome, and somewhat cocky smirk. It's a look that keeps me calm while everything else blurs around us.

I almost ask him if he wants to get out of here, but the words fall short. My heart stops with the fear that he'll reject me. Tell me it was all in fun, and it's not like that. I'm just a friend of his sister. I just wanted those guys to back off. That's what he'll say.

In my short moment of fear, Jackson pushes a stray lock of my hair back and leans in again for a gentle, yet demanding kiss.

This time, he flicks his tongue against my lips until I part them for him. Inwardly I sigh with relief. It's been three years of waiting, and honestly, I thought it would be a lifetime. I never thought Jackson would kiss me at all and especially not like this. He's tasting me like I tasted him. I swear, he wants me too.

He lets out a groan against my mouth. "You want to get out of here?"

CHAPTER 4

JACKSON

There's no going back.

That's all I can think as my hands roam down her soft curves in the back of the car. Her lips haven't left mine and if I thought that this may not be the only chance I have with Aubree, I'd contain myself. I'd show a semblance of control, but as it stands, I have none.

There is nothing but desperation for her not to stop. To just let me kiss her.

Soft moans pour from her lips, subtle and just as desperate as my touch. The Uber slows to a stop and I barely look up, checking for a red light or a stop sign. Instead I see my front lawn.

I pull my lips from hers, but intertwine our fingers and keep her close. "Let's go," I tell her. Tomorrow is vaguely on my mind. The questions and concerns. Every time a thought pierces through the haze of lust, I shut it down by kissing her again.

As we climb out, Aubree kisses my neck in that tender spot above my shoulder and it only makes my dick harder. The simple act elicits a groan from me and the moment I close the car door, I lift Aubree into my arms.

With a gasp of surprise and delight, she wraps her legs around my hips. One of my arms supports her from under her ass, the other braces her back and keeps her close to me. Her lips find mine again and I swear to God I'm in heaven.

The scent of her hair around me, the feel of her warmth against me.

I want more. I need more.

It's dark inside when I unlock the door and kick it open. It's not as smooth of a transition as I'd like it to be, but I'm able to do it all while kissing her. Little nips of her bottom lip and the sweet heated gasps she gives me have me impossibly hard.

My front door bangs recklessly against the wall, and I don't give a fuck.

"Make sure it's locked," she whispers and I have to chuckle.

"Yes, ma'am," I comment as I set her down gently, for the first time letting her go. She flicks on the corner light of the living room. She's been here a thousand times before, but never just the two of us. With the click of the lock, I look over to see her standing in the middle of the living room, looking so out of place as she stares back at me. Her wide hazel eyes are filled with lust and desire.

As if knowing I've dreamed of this moment, she crosses her arms in front of her and slowly pulls the sweater over her head, letting it drop to the floor into a puddle of fabric beside her.

I can barely breathe, paralyzed by the sight of her stripping. The wooden floor creaks as I take a single step toward her. She sinks her teeth into her bottom lip, her cheeks flushed as she unhooks her bra, letting it fall to the floor. I take another step forward and another, so very aware of what's about to happen.

There's no going back.

Vulnerability shines in her hazel eyes as she looks back at me, but she doesn't stop. As her thumbs hook into the top of her leggings, I place my hands over hers and lower my lips to the shell of her ear to whisper, "Let me."

Her head falls back slightly as she murmurs her agreement. My lips travel down her body, leaving openmouthed kisses as I go. I take my time to pluck her hardened nipples and smile against her heated skin when she moans from the touch.

From what I do to her.

Groaning against her curves, I nip along her body as I lower myself to my knees. As I tug her leggings down, I pull her lace underwear along with it.

Her fingers spear through my hair the moment I peek up at her. She's bared to me and I lean forward, tasting her. Her eyes flutter as her head falls back and with that I take a languid lick and then another. Her arousal is sweet on my tongue.

Both of her hands brace against my shoulders as she struggles to stay upright when I suck her clit. I massage my tongue against her and my sweet Aubree digs her nails into my shoulders, sucks in a breath and then calls out my name.

My name.

My hands dig into her ass to keep her where I want her. Precum leaks from my cock as she writhes, the leggings still wrapped around her ankles, preventing her from moving much at all.

"Please," she begs me and I can't take it anymore.

In a swift motion I lift her up, stepping on the leggings to rip them from her and hustle to the sofa. I'm not as gentle as I'd like to be when I lay her down.

She gasps from the sudden change of pace.

My shirt comes over my head, and I kick my jeans

off as quickly as possible. All the while the sofa protests under us.

"Spread your legs for me," I murmur and she obeys, her wide eyes staying on mine. Without wasting a second, I slam into her.

Her wet, welcoming heat takes me like she's meant to. Her lips part in a gorgeous *O* and she holds her breath as I push myself deeper, rocking slightly so my groin massages her clit.

"You're so fucking tight," I groan and then lower myself down to her, bracing a forearm beside her so I can kiss her.

It's only then that I move. Pulling nearly all the way out before pushing all the way back in. The head of my cock presses against her back wall and I can barely take it.

"Jackson." She moans my name, her arms wrapping around my back. Her head thrashes from side to side as I push myself in deeper and fuck her harder with each thrust.

There's a moment when her hands brush against my chest, with her chest rising and falling with each heavy breath, that our eyes meet. My heart hammers, my blood heats and I swear she almost says what I'm thinking.

Instead she kisses me, pressing her lips to mine as if she would die without it.

I go slow for a moment, wanting it back. Wanting

that moment back and needing to know what she was going to say.

The three words are right there for me too, but I swallow them down and lower my chest to hers, holding her as I fuck her faster, but deeper still.

"Fuck!" she yelps and her pussy flutters around my cock. My thumb finds her clit and a cold sweat forms on my back as it all intensifies.

Her muffled cries of pleasure fill the room and I fucking love it. I've always wanted her, I've fantasized about it, but this? The sight of her getting off on my cock is better than I could have imagined.

"Jackson." She calls out my name again, this time with desperation as I hook my arm under her knee and pull it up so I can get even deeper.

"Don't worry," I say and kiss her neck. "You can take me." With that whispered, I piston my hips, fucking her deeply and roughly.

She comes again, screaming my name this time and I can't stop. I take her savagely. Without holding back a damn thing and I don't come until she reaches her third climax.

CHAPTER 5

AUBREE

It's all slow and fuzzy when I first wake up, which isn't uncommon for the morning after a Sunday night out. It all depends on how the game goes. If it's a close one, with lots of tension and shouting, I can still feel it in my muscles the day after. But something is off. I know it even before I'm aware I'm unfortunately hungover.

It's not the lingering effects of too many shots that's making me feel heavy and sated, though.

Since when did my blankets have this much weight to them?

It only takes one weak stretch to feel another person under the sheets. With wide eyes and a quick glance around Jackson's living room, all of last night tumbles into my memory.

Oh, no, no, no, no, no, no, no.

It comes back all at once, and the shock feels like a shot glass slamming down on the bar. Jackson. *I came home with Jackson last night.*

It's futile to pull the sheet up against my bare chest as I stare down at his naked form. How the hell did we both sleep on his couch?

I did more than *sleep* on this sofa.

The cushion groans slightly and I slow my movements as I attempt to slip out, still very much naked and groggy.

Every little moment flashes back and the conflicting emotions intensify. He kissed the side of my neck in front of the entire bar. He upped the ante in the game we played for years. Was he jealous of the guys who were hitting on me? Or ... I don't know. All I know is that it became something else when I kissed him back.

I barely remember anything about the ride home. All I remember is his mouth on mine, the deep murmurs and lust-filled groans. And how warm his body felt against mine.

Last night was better than I ever imagined it would be. The morning after, though? Well, there's a reason I've never dreamed of this moment.

Bottom line: we crossed a big red line last night in

front of everyone. That truth is a flashing bright light in my face as I tiptoe across the living room in search of my underwear.

Sex with your best friend's brother is a no-no. I can already see the look of shock on Cheryl's face. I can already imagine how awkward our group outings with friends will be.

Blood drains from my face and the regret slips in.

I never meant to take it this far.

My heart pounds as I stand paralyzed, clinging to Jackson's navy blue comforter which is pressed against my chest. His living room is neat and masculine in the pale early morning sun filtering through the blinds. Apart from our clothes from last night strewn across the carpeted floor.

Eventually, I take in Jackson's sleeping form. His firm—and bare—ass is fully on display, his arm hanging over the edge of the sofa. He's dead to the world and guiltily I lay the comforter across him. His face is turned toward the back of the sofa, and his other arm is tucked under his pillow in a way that shows off his muscular frame. Broad shoulders rise and fall with every deep breath. Just as I feel a touch of ease, he mumbles something I can barely hear and I freeze. A beat passes and then another.

All the while, the slight chill in the room skims across

my nakedness.

Clothes. For the love of all things holy. Where are my clothes?

It doesn't take long to spot them, but each quiet moment comes with a hint of regret.

Why does Cheryl have to have the hottest brother in the history of the world? It's not fair. That's what I've told myself for so long now. It's not fair, because I can never be with him.

Except I have been with him. We were together last night. He wanted me to come home with him, and I said yes, and now ...

Now I have to get out of here.

Part of me wants to touch his shoulder, wake him up, and give him a repeat performance. To fake it until we make it, so to speak.

A big part of me, actually. Most of me. I want to feel his body against mine again. He was powerful and confident over me in a way that no other man has been. At the same time, he was familiar. Safe. Jackson knows me really well, and for good reason. We've been friends for years.

Oh, Aubree, what have you done?

The reality, though, is that I have morning breath, bed head, a hangover and regrets a mile long, as well as a growing list of insecurities and uncertainties. So the only faking I'll be doing is faking that everything is okay until I am safely home and clinging to my own pillow.

I silently gather each garment like I've been trained by the CIA in extraction methods.

My purse dangles from one corner of the coffee table. The garments scattered around the room tell a definite story about what happened last night. Two people couldn't get enough of each other, and they couldn't even aim for the furniture when they took their clothes off.

Not that I need the clothes to tell me anything. I remember how amazing it felt to be in Jackson's arms. I remember how much I wanted him. Kissing him woke something up in me. Something that's been bubbling under the surface for way too long.

I step into my clothes quickly and quietly, then snatch my phone up from the ground. There's a text from Cheryl. It's from last night, about half an hour after I left the bar with Jackson.

Cheryl: *You did it!! Good for you!! Which of the guys did you go home with?*

I text her back with trembling hands. My pulse races as I press send.

Aubree: *Don't hate me. Jackson. I'm at Jackson's house. I spent the night here. I'm never going to be able to look him in the eye again.*

Never mind that I'll have to look Cheryl in the eye.

She'll know I slept with her brother. She did egg me on, but it was a joke. It was all supposed to be harmless fun. My stomach does a nervous flip. I won't be able to stand it if he walks out here all hot and handsome and plays it off like a joke.

Like it didn't mean anything. With both hands running down my face, I wish I could just get in my car and drive away. My fingers fly across my phone ordering my escape car.

My heart pounds as I glance over my shoulder back at Jackson. I don't think I'd be able to play it cool if he sauntered out and pretended it meant nothing.

I can see things going both ways. Next Sunday could be stiff, with us walking on eggshells and all our friends wondering what's going on. Or it could be normal, with both of us pretending to be comfortable. Like it was just a part of the flirtatious game we play.

Or maybe …

Maybe we could be holding hands at the bar. Maybe Jackson could be there as my real boyfriend and not just a decoy for the men who wanted to buy me a drink.

The phone buzzes in my hand and I clutch it to my chest, listening hard for any sign he's waking up. One beat passes and then another of me staring at him like a weirdo.

Without any sign he's woken up, I check my phone.

Cheryl: *It was just one night. No big deal. You guys got it out of your system ;)*

Out of my system. I swallow thickly.

Reality crashes down around me. Not a soul knows about the crush. The genuine feelings I have for him. No one is going to understand and nothing is going to be all right.

What was I thinking? This isn't the start of a new relationship. This was a one-night stand. In fact, it was a mistake.

My throat tightens. That's exactly what Jackson will say. It was a mistake for the two of us to jump into bed together. Our friendship is too important to screw it up with emotions.

What a mess.

The only way to begin cleaning it up is to leave before he gets out of bed. As if on cue, my phone informs me the getaway car is approaching. It's a little cowardly, I know, to run away after a one-night stand. But if that's all it is, then it won't be anything new. That's what you do when things aren't serious. You go back to your life before they get serious.

I hesitate at the door, my stomach sinking. He might worry about me when he wakes up.

Maybe I should leave a note. I half turn back to the kitchen, but stop myself.

What would the note say?

I had a nice time last night—see you at football!!

Or …

We should talk about this soon so it's not awkward.

Or …

No hard feelings, whatever happens.

Each idea I have is worse than the last. *Shit.* It's better if I don't say anything. It's best if I don't look back. It's better if I chalk it up to a tipsy mistake and leave it in the past where it belongs.

The future with Jackson has to do with friendship. Because we're friends. Really good friends. And that's all we're going to be.

CHAPTER 6

JACKSON

The thud of the front door is far too soft to be what woke me up. If I had to guess, I'd say it's the pounding in my head from a vicious hangover that did it.

With a foggy mind and a heavy body, I lift myself up before realizing what happened.

Aubree. Holy shit, did that really happen last night?

It only takes a moment of listening to the silence in this empty place before I hear a car door shut out front. *Fuck!*

I'm sober in seconds, jolting from the sofa and running toward the door although I don't get far. My foot bashes the coffee table and I seethe, sucking in a deep breath and wincing from the pain.

"Aubree!" I call out as if she could possibly hear me. By the time I get to the door, I realize I'm completely nude and can't open the door more than a few inches.

The bright morning light blinds me for a moment as I watch the four-door sedan head down the suburban street. Taking Aubree with it and leaving a sense of dread to creep in.

Shit, shit, shit. Running a hand through my hair, I search for a note or for anything at all.

Last night comes back in waves. The drinks, the kissing, fucking Nate texting his friends to flirt with Aubree. I know it was him, trying to prove a point and yeah, he was right.

Seeing her with them ... I lean against the wall with my bare ass pressed against the cold surface and regret swarms me.

Last night, I crossed a line, but she crossed it with me. That's the only hope I have, so I hold on to it. Even though she snuck out. Even though there's no note.

I'm quick to find my boxers, putting them on and then searching for my phone in the pocket of the jeans I wore last night.

It's dead ... great. Of course it is.

Letting out a sigh, I resign myself to coffee, an Advil and giving myself a moment while the charger brings it back to life.

As the coffee maker sputters and hisses, I remember how she kissed me. The passion and the desperation. A groan leaves me and my head falls back as my dick remembers last night too.

You can't fake that. She wants me. Or at least she did last night. And it was fucking incredible.

An asymmetric smile pulls my lips up as I add sugar and creamer to my cup and then stir it, the spoon tinking against the ceramic.

Suddenly, the hangover isn't so bad. My pinky toe that's stubbed? Not a big deal. The smile lingers until I check my phone, when it promptly vanishes.

Three texts wait for me, and not a single one from Aubree. My heart sinks further down with each.

Nick: *I heard you left the bar with Aubree ... what's going on there?*

Nate: *So you guys do it?*

It's the last one that leaves me wishing Aubree hadn't run off this morning. It's from my sister: *FYI she's freaking out a little. You might want to let her know your friendship is still intact.*

The phone clatters to the counter as I run my hand down the back of my head, cursing myself for taking her home last night. I should have kissed her and told her I wanted to see her. I should have said one damn thought

I've had for years about her rather than keeping it to myself.

My phone pings again and although I know it's not her, I wish it were. It's only my sister, asking if I even remember last night because the town is now being informed one text at a time.

Fuck, fuck, everyone knows and I have no idea what it means for us. Panic is something I'm not used to. Not at all when it comes to Aubree. But it's all that takes over until I shove it down.

I've wanted Aubree for so long and now I'm afraid I'm going to lose her ... but I'll be damned if I let that happen.

CHAPTER 7

AUBREE

At least I don't have to go to an office building. That's one small consolation as I stare at my phone wishing a message would pop up. None do, but I count my blessings on the Uber ride back to my apartment, which is on the second floor of a neat brick building with a hair salon on the ground floor and a couple more units up above. I don't mind the muffled sounds of the dryers and music coming through the floor. It's still quiet when I shut the door and lock it behind me with an exacerbated sigh. Not early enough for the first clients of the day.

Thank God I don't have a set schedule, because I

desperately need a shower. There's no way I can sit at my desk and go to work while I'm wearing clothes that smell like Jackson.

Maybe it's pathetic, but I can admit it makes me a bit somber to take them off and drop them in the hamper.

I go through all the motions. Shampoo and soap and conditioner. I dry my hair and put on makeup.

Unsurprisingly, it doesn't help. With a hot cup of tea at my side, I take my seat at my computer with a long to-do list and a mind that's full of Jackson. And what we did last night. And how I left him sleeping on the sofa. And how I wish I were still with him. I should have pretended to be sleeping for as long as it took.

In my defense, I'm not good with hangovers.

Graphic design has nothing to do with the man I slept with last night. For fifteen whole minutes, I concentrate on my projects. A new logo for a company based in the city. A banner for an artist's website. The background for a set of wedding invitations.

None of them are exactly presentable … but I try.

All of it takes way longer than it should, because I can't focus.

The only thing that draws my attention is my phone. Every two minutes, I stare at it, willing it to ping and let me know Jackson texted me to tell me how much he wants a repeat of last night.

After about an hour, I find the tea cold and my thoughts turning on me.

I don't know what's worse. If Jackson texts or if he doesn't. If he ignores what happened last night, then I guess that's something to go on. If he texts and wants to talk …

Butterflies flutter deep in my stomach. It's hard to tell if they're the nervous kind or the excited kind.

Of course, there's always the third option, which is that he texts and says we should pretend it didn't happen and was a mistake.

I fly out of my seat so fast the office chair nearly hits the wall as it rolls backward and I put my phone on the kitchen counter, plugging it in to charge. After that, I buckle down for a solid hour of work. There's not a chance in hell I'm going to miss a deadline and get laid off because I let my crush tear up my heart.

It doesn't take long, though, for it to buzz from all the way across the apartment and I'm out of my seat before I can think twice. It's silly to run across my little apartment just for a notification that could be a text from anyone, but I do.

Jackson: *You ran off this morning. I should have at least made you breakfast.*

Not even one emoji.

How am I supposed to answer this? How am I

supposed to respond? I guess I'll have to play it off like I'm fine and absolutely not obsessed with the outcome of sleeping with my best friend's brother.

Aubree: *Sorry—I just didn't want to be late for work!*

I sent the exclamation mark before I can think twice. Damn it, I should have changed that to a period.

The typing indicator dots appear on my screen and hover there for what seems like forever. He could say anything right now.

Option A: Let's forget about it. See you Sunday.

Option B: We shouldn't say anything about this. Keep it between us.

No, I correct my thinking, it's too late for that. Cheryl saw. She knows we left together. Everyone who was still at the bar knows. And even if they didn't, there's no way we're pretending it didn't happen.

Jackson: *Let me buy you dinner tonight?*

My heart's racing slows up slightly, hope in sight. I send a message back without thinking.

Aubree: *You don't owe me food just because we had sex :)*

I mean it as a joke, but no new dots come up on the screen.

Jackson doesn't say anything.

Not right away. And not in the next hour. Or the hour after that.

The afternoon crawls by. It's the slowest day I've

ever lived through. I leave my phone in the kitchen and force myself to work on my projects. This is not a good productivity hack, but it does mean my list gets smaller and smaller as the minutes pass. I answer emails I should have responded to a month ago and put in a couple bids for new projects.

I even cold email a handful of companies I think would like my work that have been on my to-do list forever. Sending cold emails is basically a new record for me. I put it off as long as possible because I hate writing those emails—they seem salesy and weird. I know putting myself out there is a big part of my job, but I still don't like it. I'm supposed to bring in a certain number of clients so I have to. But cold emailing ahead of the deadline … I am … desperate for a distraction.

All this to avoid deciding what to do about Jackson's text.

Do I say something? Ask for clarification?

Send him a message talking up last night as a joke?

That probably wouldn't play very well. Or—I don't know, maybe it would. He's always been laid back and funny. We've never had this much pressure between us.

In the afternoon, I give up trying to work and check his socials. He hasn't unfriended me. Hasn't posted anything there, either.

"Oh, God, Aubree." I bury my face in my hands.

He's probably working. It's Monday. Jackson works in finance and it's always busy, even when it's not the craziest part of tax season. He's busy, that's all it is. This isn't a disaster.

We've avoided disaster lots of times. When I first moved back to town, I had a boyfriend. We were going to do the whole long-distance thing and stick it out together. It didn't last longer than three months. My feelings for him cooled once we weren't in the same town. And ... my feelings for someone else were heating up.

Jackson.

I felt myself falling for him every Sunday at the football games. I waited for his calls and blushed when I got texts. When Cheryl and I would hang out with him, I tried to be the best, shiniest version of myself, all while I told myself I was being casual. The real me. At some point, those two people got mixed together. I got more comfortable with Jackson.

Too comfortable, to the point that I broke up with my boyfriend, intending to tell Jackson how I felt.

I was too late. He was already seeing someone else.

What's a girl to do? I told myself it was a crush. You don't bring up a crush to your best friend's brother when he's dating someone else. It was a reasonable crush too. Jackson had treated me well. He'd been kind to me instead of brushing me off as one of his sister's friends, and it would be hard for anyone not to feel something.

And he was sweet. And funny. And he liked flirting with me. But it wasn't … real.

Defeated, I sit back farther in my chair, pulling my legs up and letting the swivel rock me back and forth.

I still feel him all over me from last night. It doesn't matter that I've showered. Doesn't matter that I have fresh clothes and a day of work behind me. The imprints of his kisses are still on my skin. The places where our bodies met are still buzzing from the contact.

When I glance at the clock next, it's five fifteen.

I take my teacup to the sink and wash it. It's probably the most thorough bath the teacup has ever gotten in its life. Work's over. There are no new messages from Jackson on my phone. Nothing laughing off the text I sent him, or asking for a reply.

If he hasn't messaged by six, I'll text him and put myself out of my misery. I can't let this hang over my head all night. Or for the rest of my life. I can't go to the game next weekend feeling all twisted up inside, like I've ruined something.

I haven't, really. The way to think about this is as a nice, onetime thing. We both enjoyed each other, and that's enough. It's a choice to make it awkward with him. I can choose to make it normal instead.

Right?

Although that doesn't explain why I feel this sense of loss inside my chest. This ache for something more.

A knock at the door makes me jump.

I can't deny that it causes a flood of feelings. Embarrassment, because I've been waiting for this knock. Fear, because what if it's not him? And hope—hope that it's Jackson standing on the other side. Who the hell else could it possibly be, though?

I place the teacup in the drying rack as gently as my nerves will allow me and head to the door with even strides so it doesn't sound like I'm running. *It might not be him, anyway.*

I get up on tiptoe to look through the peephole. My heart beats fast and feels skittish. I've never had a crush as strong as this one. Not even when I was a teenager and all my hormones were out of control. The guys in my high school had nothing on Jackson.

Jackson's in the hall outside my apartment, waiting patiently, a bag of Chinese food raised in his hand. "Hey," he calls out. "You hungry?"

CHAPTER 8

JACKSON

I'm not hungry in the least. Even with the scent of Chinese food wafting from the coffee table. The TV plays some sitcom in the background but none of it means a thing.

Not when Aubree doesn't move for the food either. Not when she keeps stealing glances at me and blushing every time our eyes meet.

My nerves work their way through me as I stare at Aubree, needing to tell her exactly how I feel. It's now or never.

I told myself if there was even a hint that she didn't regret last night, that she wanted to be something more,

I was going to do it.

And now's my chance.

It's so quiet, my dry swallow is audible. My cheeks burn with the heat of embarrassment when she stares down at her plate, speechless.

"I loved last night. I've had feelings for you for years." I can't stop now. She has to know. I leave my hand on the coffee table, palm up and she notices. Her gaze moves to it and then back up to mine.

"I didn't know I was that good in bed," she jokes and I laugh, a genuine chuckle to match hers. But I don't back down.

My anxiousness scatters. The relief of knowing she's not running at the thought is all I needed.

Before I can say anything, she scoots closer on the sofa, her warmth immediately evident. "You were pretty good in bed too, if I might add," she teases me, her long lashes fluttering.

My thumb rubs a soothing circle over her knuckles as I debate on the next step.

"Just tell me what to say." I practically beg her like the desperate man I am.

"What?"

"I will say whatever I need to ... to get you to say you'll be mine right now," I tell her in all honesty. The subtle shock, the awe that follows, lets me know that she hears me. And that she knows I'm serious.

"I want to be with you. More than friends. I can't go back to being just friends."

"Jackson ..." Her hand leaves mine and she tucks it into her lap.

That slight panic of losing her comes back.

"I'll be damned if I lose you, Aubree," I confess, not hiding my desperation. "This isn't some one-night fling. I don't want that."

She whispers the one fear I've had for years that kept me from kissing her, "What if it doesn't work?"

"What if it does?" My answer is immediate and her gaze falls to my lips, then darts back up to me. "I want you. If you want me too, just say yes."

A beat passes. And then another. Too many seconds go by, filling me with an anxiousness until she whispers, "Yes."

That's all I needed for relief to take over and to lean down and capture her lips with mine. I don't even realize what I'm doing until this gentle kiss is over and a soft moan of satisfaction falls from her lips. With her eyes still closed, I take her in and this moment between us.

"I mean it, Aubree," I tell her, then clear my throat and wait for her to peer back at me. My heart hammers but I don't hold back anymore. "I could see you walking down the aisle ... I can see all of what I want in the future, happening with you."

Her chest rises with a slow, yet deep inhale at my admission.

"Jackson," she says, merely whispering my name, her longing gaze never leaving mine. With her small hand she fists the fabric of my shirt, taking what's hers as she pulls me down, devouring my lips with hers and letting her hunger take over.

Her soft body presses against mine and she climbs into my lap and all of last night comes back with a force. My cock is hard in an instant and I smile against her kiss as she pushes my shoulders back, easing me onto my back on her sofa.

As she sits up, straddling me and pulling her shirt over her head, I chuckle. "You are so damn good with your words, you know that?"

That sweet feminine laugh I know so well brightens up her face as she reaches behind her, unhooking her bra. It falls easily from her, revealing her supple breasts and rose petal nipples. I can't help the tortured groan that escapes me.

"Was that a word, Jackson?" she says, teasing me as she leans down, her palm resting beside my head. Her hair falls in front of her, obstructing my view. "I'm not sure I–"

In a swift motion, I grip her hips and flip her smart ass over so she's beneath me and I'm on top. Her gasp of surprise is accompanied by her legs wrapping around my hips.

I lean forward, pressing myself into her and rocking my hips.

"You teasing me, Aubree?" I murmur, letting the hint of a threat hang between us. "I think I could find a way to tease you back."

Her lips part with the sexiest fucking inhale I've ever heard in my life.

"Oh yeah," she says in a breathy voice. "I think I'd like that."

"Like?" I cock a brow.

"I think I'd love it if you teased me for the rest of my life, Jackson."

An asymmetric grin pulls at my lips. "Now that's the challenge I've been waiting for."

EPILOGUE

AUBREE

ONE YEAR LATER

The cheers erupt from every soul in here, including Michelle, who's got the baby in a carrier. The little one wears the cutest pair of baby earmuffs you've ever seen, which is a must for game nights at the bar. Technically she's too young to be allowed in, but this is a small town and even if she's not yet one, she can't miss this make-or-break game to see who's headed to the playoffs.

Just like old times, we're all here in our booth at The Peanut Bar. Nick and Michelle and baby. Nate and Anne. Cheryl and me.

The only one missing is Jackson.

Not *missing* missing. Just late. Late for the game

that takes place at the same time every Sunday. My foot taps erratically wondering where the heck he is.

"He's going to miss the second quarter," I fret to Cheryl. I'm not exactly worried for him. He's a grown man and The Peanut Bar is in the same place as always. We even planned to come here separately, me with Cheryl and him with …

Well, nobody. Since we're together. A smile creeps up to my lips as I check my phone again. *Together*, together.

We've been together since the night with the Chinese food. The awkward Sunday football game never happened, because it was never awkward. We simply showed up and announced we were a thing and ordered everyone a shot to celebrate. I'll never forget Cheryl's scream and Anne's hug of unadulterated joy. *About time* was said a lot that night.

"The first quarter's not over yet." Cheryl pats my arm with a gleam in her eye. "Relax. Want another drink?"

"I've barely had any of this one." The IPA sloshes in my glass as I tilt it.

Because I don't want to have fun without him. Jackson's easygoing, but I take my time with him seriously. If I'm going to get buzzed at the bar, I want it to be with him standing next to me and ready to take me home.

Fine. I want everything to happen with him

standing next to me. It's a huge victory to be with him, in my mind. He represents growing into myself as a woman and taking control of my own life. For once, I didn't shove down my feelings and pretend they were worthless. I acted on them, and now I have the best man I could imagine.

Our team kicks off the ball, and the players rush around the field, arranging and rearranging themselves for the next series. I like when we play defense. Cheryl thinks offense is more exciting, but I like standing up for what you've earned. Plus, there's a chance we catch an interception, which is the most thrilling thing that can happen in football.

The opposing team's quarterback lines up, catches the snap, and throws the ball.

One of our guys jumps into the air, his hands up high. Almost—almost—

He misses.

"Oh, man, that was close."

Nobody else in the bar reacts. I turn to Cheryl to see why not, but she's not looking at me.

She's looking at the man who just walked in through the front door of the bar.

Jackson.

He's not dressed for a football game. No well-worn jeans, no sweatshirt or jersey.

He's in a trim-cut suit that hugs his shoulders just right. A suit I've never seen him in. One that looks expensive as hell.

My mouth waters although my head is wondering if I've slipped and fallen. I could be dreaming right now and I wouldn't want a soul to wake me up. This is more than what he wears to the office. He's taken more care with his appearance, and everybody notices. How could you not? He's all dark hair and blue eyes and wearing a jacket that fits him like he was meant to be on the cover of a magazine.

"Hey, Dani," he calls out although his sharp gaze is pinned on me. "Can you turn the volume down a second?"

I barely glance to the left. The bartender smiles. The volume lowers on the TVs. To my shock, nobody protests. My heart flutters in my chest. *What's happening?*

Jackson strides over to me, eating up the distance too quickly for me to process that this is even real. He gives a wave to all our friends at the bar and everybody else who's come to watch the game. "I want all of you to hear this, okay?"

"What are you doing?" I whisper beneath my breath although he takes my hands in his.

With a nervous smile, he gets down on one knee.

Oh my God.

"Aubree, I've had a crush on you since the first day

we met."

My mouth drops open. He did not. I had the crush on him.

Jackson laughs. "I know. I never told you, because I didn't want to scare you off. But now the whole town can hear, and I don't care. I want them all to know how much I love you. I want you to know how much I love you. I want to spend every Sunday with you for the rest of our lives. Will you marry me?"

"Yes," I squeak. I take his face in my hands. "Yes, of course I do."

"Do you want to see the ring first, maybe?"

Laughter fills the bar, and it's so warm and welcoming. That's the sound of my friends being happy for us. Our friends. We didn't have to give any of them up.

I can barely get out the words as I tell him, "I'd marry you without a ring."

Jackson shakes his head and pulls a ring box out of his pocket. He opens it with a flourish. From behind him, Cheryl gasps. "That's way bigger than you said it was!"

"What?" he answers, sheepish and proud and before he can respond, I pull him to his feet and kiss him. Fisting his shirt and desperate to seal the deal. A cheer goes up from all around us. This is what it means to have a good life. This is what it means to be happy. As soon as I'm done kissing Jackson, he slides the ring on my finger and steps out of the way.

"What are you—"

Cheryl throws herself at me, wrapping her arms around my neck. "Do you have any idea how hard that was to keep a secret?" She laughs. "Let me see, let me see." Cheryl takes my hand and looks down at the diamond sparkling on my finger. "It's perfect." Then she tugs her brother back into place at my side. "You're both perfect together. I'm going to give the best maid of honor speech."

"Who said you were going to be—" Jackson begins.

"Oh, stop," I say, cutting him off. Dani turns the game back up on the TVs. "She's going to be my maid of honor. And you're going to be my husband."

He gives me that charming smile that makes everything around us fade to nothing.

"I love you, Aubree."

"I love you too."

PRETEND
YOU
LOVE ME

PROLOGUE

The front door creaks open ever so slowly and softly. The faint sound is immediately drowned out by the loud music, the laughter and the clink of chips falling onto the poker table in the back room. The space is filled with cigar smoke and brutal men whose faces hold genuine smiles as they gamble with stolen money. A half dozen of them are tucked away in the back of the modern home.

Seven men filter in through the front, dressed all in black, with leather gloves but no masks.

In that very front room there's a crib and next to it a lullaby sound machine on the fireplace mantel, meant to lull the infant into a sweet dream. Chubby little hands wrap around a rattle as wide eyes watch but can't see that far as the men take careful steps through the hall.

The floor groans in protest, but just like the front door, it's unheard. Not a single one of them expected anything more than drinking and betting during their monthly poker game.

The song's soothing refrain is punctuated by the staccato bang of guns cutting through the night. Feminine steps race down the stairs at the front of the home, rushing with the silent terror of a mother. Her screams are joined by shouting. Chaos only lasts a moment, one blur, one execution carried out seamlessly and planned for years.

The lullaby never stops as one of the assailants grabs the woman by her waist. The baby can't see how she struggles in the unknown man's arms to reach her child. She pleads and prays but can't do anything other than thrash in the arms of someone more prepared, and far stronger than she.

The sweet melody is at such odds with the silence that follows a bullet pinging on the tiled floor. Bodies lie around the poker table, blood seeping into the sides of tailored suits and what were once crisp white button-downs.

It's quiet, all but the cadence of a lullaby the infant

has heard since before he was born. Footsteps aren't so careful anymore as the music suddenly halts and the men filter out. The woman is carried away, all the while fighting for her child.

One man approaches the crib, and two rough, callused hands wrap around the top railing. A bundled baby, wrapped tightly yet those little arms somehow escaped, looks up at dark eyes.

A gruff voice whispers something to the man who stares down at the child, and he only gives a nod in response. He's murdered more men than he's shaken hands with.

The man carefully picks up the child, bringing the one-month-old to his chest. "Hush now, little one."

Madelyn

My breathing hardly comes in as another scream tears through my throat. Tears prick my eyes, burning them as I slam my fists against the trunk.

I've been taken, I'm trapped and nothing is in my control anymore. A terror that threatens to consume me takes over.

"My baby!" I cry out again, pleading with men who ignore me. "Please!" I beg them.

They won't listen, though. Even as panic tenses all my body, and adrenaline pounds through my veins, I'm all too aware they won't listen to me.

I know what he wants. My racing heart slows.

A chill settles through me as I hear a knock on the steel roof above me. "You be quiet now, you don't want to wake the baby," a man says, his voice carrying through the metal enclosure of the trunk.

"Please," I whisper so lowly, I'm not certain a soul could hear.

The command comes out final yet tinged with sympathy, although I may be wrong. Perhaps I only imagine a semblance of mercy. "You listen to me, and everything will be all right."

CONNOR
TWO DAYS AGO

My brother's footsteps crunch in the snow. Fletcher's silent, but I'm more than certain I know what he plans to say. A bitter wind whips by, my black tie waving in the breeze as I stare down at the carved stones in the ground. Two people who should have never been laid to rest will lie here for all eternity.

"What is it?" I barely manage to ask after I swallow the hard lump in my throat. It's all for them, for my wife and son I lost years ago, yet it feels like I've betrayed them.

"Is there anything I can do?" my brother questions behind me and it's so softly spoken, the harsh wind nearly drowns out the words.

Turning to face him, his hands are splayed across the front of his charcoal suit. Remorse wears itself on his face whenever we find ourselves here.

"It's been six years," I say, telling him a truth he already knows.

He only nods and then clears his throat as he takes the necessary steps to close the distance between us. He swallows so hard it's audible before he says, "Friday night, it's set."

With my brother in front of me and my past behind me, I'm all too aware that what I'm going to do next is cruel and unforgivable. He took my wife and child ... this is a fair trade.

"Are you sure about this?" he asks.

I don't answer him; all I know is that I need this to happen. More than I need to live.

CHAPTER 1

MADELYN

The trembling is constant and I couldn't stop it if I tried. Another shudder runs through me as the chill of the cell slips across my barely covered skin. My shoulders shake involuntarily as I bring my knees into my chest and stare at the vent where soft promises filter through of what awaits me. I can hear all the men, everything they're saying and how they're to leave me alone.

He said no one touches her.

Leave her there until he's ready.

They don't ask questions but they know I'm here, tucked away in the basement, huddled in a corner of my cell.

There's a soft drip from the spout in the cinder block wall behind me that's a relative constant and occasionally the heat kicks on, a loud click signaling its start but the warmth isn't for the cell, it's for upstairs.

The cotton nightgown I was wearing when I was taken is torn and thin, leaving me freezing, alone and waiting for the same person as the men upstairs: Connor Walsh.

Just thinking his name does horrid things to my heart. It skips and halts in place. The rough stubble of his jaw, the hard lines of his cheekbones and the depths of his dark copper gaze only add to the dominating air that surrounds him.

He's a damaged man with nothing left to lose. Men like him are dangerous. That's what my husband used to say. He knew that all too well and now he's dead.

Leaving my fate in the hands of a man hell-bent on revenge.

The unmistakable sound of a key turning in the lock from up the stairwell sends a pulse of shock and a new wave of terror through me. The first step on the narrow wooden stairs seems hesitant, as if whoever owns the movement is unsure of it. With my palms scraping against the grit littering the floor I attempt to scoot backward, as far away as I can get, but the stone wall at my back is unyielding.

Step by step, he takes his time.

His black jeans come into view first, followed by his black button-down with the sleeves rolled up to his forearms. The shirt is tight on his broad shoulders, and then those eyes ... they pin me where I am.

Connor is a hardened man; I've known him nearly all my life. Or at least I've known the whispers of him. In this small run-down town with corruption on every corner, two feuding families ran things for decades. There was my husband's family, the mob formed by his father, and there were the Walshes.

Now there's only Connor Walsh.

His heavy footsteps stop outside the barred door of the cell. The room I'm confined to feels so much like a prison, for a moment I think of Connor as my warden.

The tension is thick between us and even though he's feet away, I'm enveloped by his heat.

The cords in his neck tighten as he swallows, his gaze roaming down my body, appraising every inch as it travels lower.

Too much time passes in near silence and fear takes over, begging me to plead with him. "My baby—"

"You'll do what I say." His tone is low and his words spoken with a cadence that's calm and eerie. It's one I've never heard from him. One that paralyzes me. "Did you hear me?" he questions and tilts his head, as if willing me to defy him.

Something I have no intention of doing.

"Anything. I'll do anything you tell me to," I say, the words leaving me in a rush.

"Good."

"My baby?" I'm barely able to get the words out. He's only a month old. My little one.

"He's fine." He has the decency to pull his eyes away from me as he speaks. "He's taken care of, and you'll be with him soon."

Hope rises along with an eagerness to get to my baby.

"Come here," Connor commands and I don't hesitate. Unsure of whether I should stand or crawl, I crawl, lifting the torn nightgown and balling the fabric in my fists. The floor isn't gentle on my knuckles but I don't care.

It's not until I get to the bars that he tells me, "You could have walked."

Embarrassment colors my cheeks and just as I look up at him to tell him I don't know what he wants, he reaches through the bars, and his strong fingers wrap around my throat.

Instinctively my hands reach up to his, and I instantly regret it.

He isn't tight with his grip, just firm, not so much

that I feel the need to fight. Slowly, reluctantly, I lower my hands. All the while his amber gaze blazes and keeps me still.

"Stand," he tells me and I do as he wishes.

A chill filters through and my nipples harden; the thin gown does nothing to hide that fact. Staring down at the veins in his arms, I attempt to hide the shame of what comes over me.

"You know what I want from you, don't you?" he questions, his breath low and not hiding his desire.

I attempt to nod without looking up at him, but his grip tightens and my eyes flash to his.

"Yes," I answer in a whisper.

My heart pounds as heat floods through me with the way he looks at me. It's the same way he looked at me years ago, before the war, before the bloodshed, before he became the man he is today. Years ago when we were reckless and life hadn't taught us how harsh it could be.

His hand loosens just enough for his thumb to brush along my bottom lip, prompting me to open my mouth.

"Suck," he murmurs this time and I do as I'm told. The roughness of his skin begs me to scrape my teeth along it and I do. I suck the taste of him, I press my tongue against him and give him exactly what I know he wants.

It's only when my eyes close that he pulls away,

leaving me standing there with the bars between us and a power imbalance that puts me at his mercy.

He reaches into his pocket for the key, and plays with it between his thumb and pointer, as if debating.

My pulse rampages but before I can beg for anything from this man, he tells me, "Your child needs you. Get him back to sleep, then you'll come to me. Understand?"

CHAPTER 2

CONNOR

Voices come through the back door as I move through the house. My brother and three of our men are outside, having a smoke. Their cigarettes are orange flares in the dark. The wood beneath my feet doesn't creak to announce my presence. They don't hear me getting closer to the door.

I pause to listen. At times their voices are muffled by the sound of the vengeful wind. In general, they're not paying attention. The men talk freely among themselves, not bothering to give the surrounding woods more than a cursory glance. It's not the woods they should be worried about. It's me.

After years of working for me, and knowing how close to the edge I've been, they should be more than aware of that fact.

Their lack of attention will play into my hands, but it frustrates me just the same. I haven't had the luxury of letting my guard down.

Most people have no guard at all, even the men who are supposed to. They can't keep their mouths shut. A man who can listen is always better off. That's what it takes to survive in the world today. You have to keep track of what's going on around you, even with people you claim to trust.

I don't trust anyone. Least of all the men outside. My brother is the only one who deserves my trust, and he's the only one who will get it. Everyone else is expendable. Everyone else can be replaced in a heartbeat. The vast majority of the world simply takes up space until someone has a better use for it.

I wouldn't have thought that when I was younger. I had softer ideas about the value of human life. Now, I don't give a fuck.

Except when it comes to my new captive and prize. *Madelyn.*

Everything in me screams to go back to her. It's unsettling. I shut off my emotions six years ago. It was like flipping the switch to a circuit breaker. Every feeling apart from rage died out in an instant, and I haven't let any of the others come back. It would be impossible to focus with my mind occupied by sentiments and morals.

"What do you make of it?" Fletcher asks the men. They feel secure, out in the backyard. It's a mistake. The cover of darkness isn't a cover at all. Just because they've carried out the mission successfully doesn't mean it's any safer. Loyalty has been questioned recently. I deliberately chose the three newest men, fledgling additions.

If loyalty isn't given freely, I won't demand it. I'll simply cut their throats.

"She'll run the first chance she gets," answers the first one. I recognize the voice as belonging to Matthew. After a long drag of his cigarette he adds, "Had that look in her eyes. She's ready to bolt."

"Not if she cares for her child," my brother points out. I swallow thickly at the reminder of the little boy. Those emotions I thought long dead shove themselves to the surface and I clench my fist in response.

"You think he'll really keep her?" asks the second, Nathaniel. He lights a new cigarette and it casts orange light across his face. "Like he really wants to keep her as his ... what? Sex slave?"

"It's sick," Matthew practically spits out. "More than a little."

"Is that the first hint you ever got that my brother's

sick?" my brother asks in a light, joking manner, but there's a razor blade at the heart of his tone. I don't have to see him to know there's a smirk on his face. Right now he's seemingly charming and at ease, but it conceals a lethal side of him.

"You think I'm sick?" I say as I stride out into the backyard. They've been in the business too long to look truly surprised, but the first one frowns. He didn't want me to overhear him call me sick. It's a lapse. The third man has been silent and he remains still, his arms crossed as he leans against the brick of the house.

The other two exchange self-conscious glances, like they've been caught with their dicks out.

"She's in a cell, isn't she?" The question is followed by another drag from the first man's cigarette. "After all that screaming."

I'd rather stay cold, but emotions run hot. "She's doing what I told her to do."

He smirks. "How? Doesn't seem like she'll be very cooperative."

"That depends on who handles her. So it's a good thing you assholes won't be touching her."

He huffs a humorless laugh with his hands up. "I'm not the one who wants to. You spent too long in there. People are going to think you want her, and she's not like that."

"Not like what?"

The first man darts a glance at his buddy. This is risky territory, and he knows it. The mood is lightening but my face isn't.

"Worth it," he says. "What happens if she gets to you? What happens if she makes you even sicker than you already are?"

"I'll let you know if I feel ill when I'm done with her." I let a smile spread over my face. That's what he's watching. He doesn't see the quick reach for the gun at my belt. He's too busy laughing.

The safety's been off since we took her. I've been waiting for this moment. Waiting for one of them to step out of line.

Damn it, I wasn't supposed to care. None of the comments were going to get to me. I wasn't going to feel anything for her. Not at the house. Not in the cell. Nowhere.

Not until it was time.

The situation is already getting out of control, but my gun isn't.

I pull the trigger, sending a bullet through his head. Anger surges through my veins. There are things no one can ever know about Madelyn. There are things I'll have to keep buried deep until this is over.

A spatter of blood lands on my cheek as his body

drops with a dull thud. I've been at this long enough to recognize the sound of a dead man hitting the ground.

I wait a beat.

Watch him.

No sign of movement comes from the body, except for the blood seeping out of the wound.

I swipe at the blood on my cheek with the back of my hand.

The other men are silent. Cigarettes burn at the tips of their fingers. Not a soul makes a move. The second guy was standing close enough that he has to be bloodied. Impossible to tell for sure with our dark clothes and the dark night. His face is frozen.

"Mind cleaning this up for me, brother?"

Fletcher doesn't appear disturbed in the least by the death of one of the members of our team. His mouth quirks. Not quite a smile. Not quite a frown. More like acceptance. Like he expected this. All of them should have expected this from me. I've been this person for six years now. I'm not going to change because Madelyn is in a cell.

"Not at all, boss."

I adjust my sleeves as my brother steps over to the body. He bends down and feels for a pulse. It's not necessary. The man's dead.

"Did anyone else have any comments about my

future wife before I leave?"

I didn't intend to react to what they were saying, but my pounding heart didn't get the memo. *Sick*. I'll be damned. It was a simple bullshit comment that didn't mean anything. I felt it like a bullet through flesh.

The anger I've kept buried for the last six years is alive and well. It doesn't matter that I flipped the switch. It's all come back in an instant.

None of them has a damn thing to say. The only thing that surrounds us is silence and the threat of imminent death if they dare to say another word.

The third man taps the ash off his cigarette. He backs up half a step from the body, leaving room for my brother to roll the dead man onto his back.

"Get the wheelbarrow," my brother orders.

Everyone snaps into motion. They'll need to dig a hole at the edge of the woods, tip the body into it, and cover him back up. Not a single word is spoken in protest. Now that I've made my point, we shouldn't have any further conflict.

I've been patient. I've been meticulous. I've been planning.

Now that I have her, I'm going to use her to my advantage and use her for my pleasure.

If that makes me sick, so be it. It's time to enjoy the spoils of revenge.

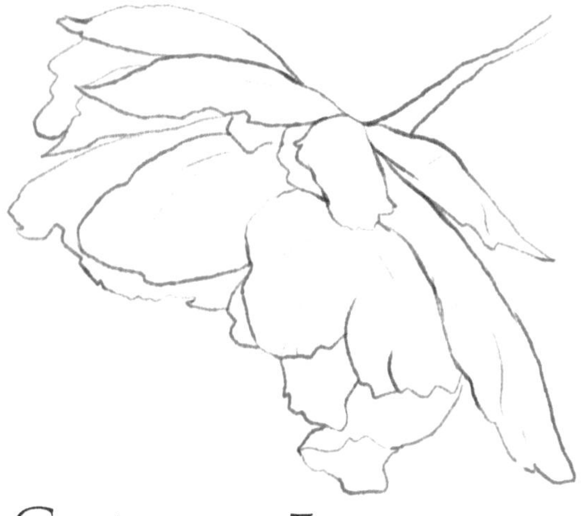

CHAPTER 3

MADELYN

With his hand on my shoulder and his rough heated skin against mine, he opens the bedroom door.

The baby is sleeping. Soundly and at a distance where I'll hear if he wakes.

This is the price I'll pay for the life I lead and the desires I've had for as long as I've known what it means to exist in this world.

A fire is already lit, surrounded by a stone mantel that reaches to the ceiling. The simplicity and masculinity of the room are undeniable. A gray textured wallpaper lines the back wall, while woodsy tones paired with blacks and grays add to the dominating atmosphere. The massive bed is a king and at the end of it is a tufted warm brown leather ottoman.

I've always seen Connor as a rugged man. Ruthless and foreboding. I never could have imagined his private room to have such warmth and elegance. The harsh lines and darkness certainly fit his persona, though.

With a heavy breath, I peek down at myself and my arms instinctively cover my chest. The torn cotton gown appears cheap and out of place in a space like this. My knees are dirty and although the room itself is warm and expensive, all I feel is cold and trapped.

"This needs to come off," Connor whispers behind me, his warm breath just beneath the shell of my ear. His light touch on my bare shoulders as he brushes down the straps of my nightgown causes me to shiver involuntarily. A line of goosebumps travels down my curves as the nightgown falls. It doesn't do so elegantly, as silk would have. As it catches at my wide hips, Connor uses both hands to push the garment down and his thumbs hook my underwear, tugging it along with the fabric.

Completely bared, my nipples pebble and I struggle to inhale as I stare straight ahead at the roaring fire. The flames lick and hiss while Connor takes his time, barely touching me, but exposing me exactly how he wishes.

My body isn't what it used to be and as his hand splays against my stomach, my eyes close with worry, but his hum of satisfaction spreads a new sensation through me. He nips the lobe of my ear and a gasp is forced from me.

As my breathing picks up, his hand lowers and his chest hits my back.

His fingers slip down to my sensitive clit. He takes his time, toying with me until my body buckles forward. His forearm braces me against him and he tsks.

"You'll stay still as I play with you," he tells me, his tone holding a note of warning. His hardened length presses into my backside through his jeans. His hard body demands that I take it.

My hand, though, acts on its own accordingly, grabbing his wrist as his hand moves lower still to my slit.

His body stills and the air changes. I can barely breathe knowing what I've done. I've stopped him, I've deliberately disobeyed.

"I haven't—" I start to say but can barely speak. "Since the baby," I add, pushing out the excuse. I haven't touched myself or been touched.

My chest rises and falls chaotically, uncertain how he'll react.

All at once, he leaves me, and I only turn when the sound of the sheets and comforter being lifted is louder than my pulse racing in my ears.

In the near silent room, all I can think about is my now dead husband's cruelty. Random flashes greet me of every time my needs were denied. Memories drift into my mind of my brother and how he died needlessly. Every dark moment passes in the flick of a second. My throat closes and the strength I thought I had fades to nothing but a facade.

I watch the dark shadows play along Connor's body as he pulls his shirt over his head, dropping it to the floor to form a puddle of clothing. His hands move to his belt and it comes off nearly violently to the point where I'm tempted to take a step back. He drops it, though, and it lands with a heavy thud. His jeans are next, and in one swift motion his cock juts out.

In only a moment, the damaged man is completely bared to me and waiting.

"Get on the bed," Connor commands and my body moves immediately, instantly obeying. Everything in me is at war; every want, every need, every thought and memory.

The bed groans softly as I climb onto the center and lie down on the luxurious sheets. My head sinks into the pillow and my gaze finds the spinning fan.

He's deliberate as he crawls up the bed, but his touch still startles me and brings me back to the present when he asks, "Is there something on your mind?"

My answer is immediate and submissive. "What would you like to be on my mind?"

Sliding between my legs, he spreads my thighs and his hard body covers me. His warm skin presses against my chest and he caresses my curves. His mouth greets me, his lips molding to mine instantly as his tongue parts my seam.

It's been so long since I've been kissed like *this*. Heavily and wantonly. Since I've been moaned into by the mouth of a man. His tongue strokes against mine as his fingers press into the flesh of my hips and he keeps me pinned. It feels as if he's everywhere all at once.

Consuming me and demanding attention equally as much as desire.

When he breaks the kiss, I breathlessly stare back at him, transfixed by his copper gaze.

"You will think of nothing but this. Of how much you need me to take you."

The light of the fire displays the harshness of his collarbone and corded muscles as I part my lips to answer. I can't, though, because he's far too concerned with silencing me with another kiss.

It's demanding and brutal, but the gentle motion of his hand slipping between my thighs is very much at odds. He's focused on my clit until I writhe under him, unable to stay still as he told me I should.

Every nerve ending lights on fire, a bundle explodes in the pit of my stomach and I cry out my pleasure as an orgasm rocks through my body. It happens so quickly and so unexpectedly, smothering every thought and doubt along with it.

He's off of me the moment I've come, and it doesn't take me long to figure out why. From his nightstand he gathers a bottle, and I watch him stroke himself with lubrication before pouring more in his hands.

It's only then that his fingers slip lower once again, spreading the lube at my entrance.

On his knees between my thighs, he slips the head of his cock between my folds, toying with me before pressing in slightly. My breath hitches and my hand splays against his chest as if that could stop him. With his dark gaze focused on mine, he tells me in a murmur, "I will ruin you for everyone else, but I intend for you to enjoy every moment."

With that he presses in deeper, stretching me and making my lips form an O. The sensation stings for a moment until he's fully inside of me, pressing against my walls. Connor stills, allowing me time to adjust.

My blunt nails dig into his shoulders as I wrap my arms around him, the heels of my feet digging into his muscular ass, as if I could hold on. As if doing so will save me from the far too intense sensation.

As I stare above me wide eyed and attempting to breathe, he kisses and nips my neck, relaxing me slowly as he pulls out gently and presses back in.

His lips find mine again and I'm able to kiss him, to cling to him, grateful and relieved. My body heats with every small movement. Every rock of his hips causes him to brush against my clit and it isn't long before I tilt my hips, wanting him deeper.

The moment my body instinctively welcomes him, he smiles against my lips. "You're my good little whore, aren't you?"

At his question my eyes meet his and he slams inside of me, brutally.

My head falls back and a strangled moan leaves me.

"Your cunt was made for me to fuck," he tells me as his hips piston.

His body pins me and his left hand finds my neck. Fingers wrap tight around my throat as he pounds into me, relentlessly and bringing about an intense sensation I've never felt before.

The bed bows with every hard thrust.

"Come on my cock like you want to," he groans into the crook of my neck. My pebbled nipples brush against his chest and it's all too much. "Come for me, my good little whore."

I do it. Unashamedly, I come undone for him.

The moan of satisfaction only extends my pleasure.

The orgasm is still raging through me as he kisses me again, riding through my release and fucking me deeper and harder. "That's my good girl. You're so fucking perfect."

He doesn't finish like that. He turns me over onto my stomach, grabbing the base of my hair and tugging as he fucks me from behind, dragging out every orgasm and pausing before he reaches his own climax so he can take more time with me.

"I'm going to enjoy every inch of you. I'm going to make you completely mine."

CHAPTER 4

CONNOR

She's terrified with the men watching.

At least that's how it looks from my perspective. Her previously timid glances have turned to wide-eyed stares. Her chest rises and falls rapidly. Are these real nerves or is she pretending? Or is she just feeling the effects of what we did together?

Fuck knows I am. She's perfect. I already knew she would be. But last night was fucking perfect.

When she's cleaned up, presentable as she can be given the circumstances, I bring her out to the kitchen. She barely slept. All she wears is my T-shirt and an oversized pair of pajama pants rolled up at her hips.

Her hair is combed through but her fragility and delicate features are entirely exposed. For a split second I question my pride given her fear. But she's fucking perfect and she's mine. All mine. Forever.

She is the only good to come from chaos and war. How could I not be obsessed with her?

With hesitant steps, I have to press against the small of her back to bring her to the kitchen. It's modern, much like the entire estate, with clean lines and granite and stone that touch nearly every surface. I imagine she'll change it. As far as I'm concerned, it's hers to do as she wishes and needs.

Her delicate hand forms a fist, balling up the fabric of my shirt as we enter the room. Her bare feet pad softly, almost silently, on the cold tiled floor.

The men have arranged themselves there around the table. None of them appear to have slept last night. There's always the risk of retribution. No one will be safe or secure for weeks, months, maybe even longer. Not until the last enemy is snuffed out.

My brother watches Madelyn and I get closer without so much as a glimmer of recognition in his eyes. Best for everyone that way. He's the only one who knows her. He's the only one who knows the whole story. And it'll stay that way.

"Madelyn, this is my brother." I bring her over to

him first. She's shaking like a leaf as he holds his hand out for her to shake.

"Hello, Madelyn," he says easily with the charming air he's known for. Although he's kind, she's still hesitant and looks to me first before she takes his hand.

"Hi," she says. I can hardly hear the words as they make small talk.

Madelyn lets me introduce her to all the men. She's a good actress. She's known who these men are for years. Knows their faces.

And they know her. They know far too much.

I don't care for the way they look at her, gazing too long and appraising. My hand itches to clench a fist, to express my rage for their indecency. I don't. I have to pretend I don't feel the anger surging inside every time one of them looks down at her body instead of her face. I have to pretend that there's nothing behind this but revenge.

That she's my captive, that this was planned in the way they're aware. That we haven't used them and there weren't ulterior motives.

The sound of the baby crying drifts into the kitchen. It's soft. He has the calmest cry.

Madelyn reacts instantly, her body tensing up as she looks over her shoulder, toward the hallway to her child. She bites at her lip but doesn't take a step toward the sound.

"Go," I tell her.

She hesitates, those wide eyes peeking up at me.

"Are you going to make me repeat myself?" I question lowly with a hint of playfulness, although she doesn't let on that she registers it.

Her eyes meet mine, and I swear I can see real fear there. *Of them? Of me?* I have to admit I like the look of it in her eyes. If that makes me sick, then so be it.

I take her jaw between my thumb and forefinger and tug her lips toward mine. I have to pretend I don't enjoy it. That it's part of the job. But it feels damn good to have my fingers on her skin. Her pulse is right at the surface. Her heart is beating hard, and something else flashes into her eyes. Desire. She can't hide it from me, no matter how well she pretends with the other men.

It's a good thing I have practice in following the plan. I want to drag her back to my bedroom, but this little performance is important for what happens next. The men need to see us together. They need to see me controlling her and her submission. There can be no question about what's happening between me and Madelyn.

Revenge. Ownership.

Nothing else. There is only one truth now: she is mine.

"What did I tell you?"

Madelyn parts her lips. "That I'll do what you say."

I want to say that she needs to do more. That she needs to kiss me, right here, right now. Make me believe it. But that would end my ability to speak, and I have more to say. The baby cries out again. He sounds more desperate now. Hungry or lonely, it's hard to tell. I don't let on that I'm responding to the noise too. A man like me shouldn't ever want to comfort a crying child. Certainly not one that everyone believes is another man's child.

"What else?" I ask her. "What else did I tell you? There are only two things that matter. You will do what I say … and what else?"

"That I'm yours." *I'm yours* sounds sweet on her tongue. It doesn't matter that we're in a room full of killers. It doesn't matter that I'm the most dangerous one of all.

"Do you think what's mine hesitates in my own home?"

Madelyn shakes her head, pressing her face more firmly into my hand.

It's going to be hell to let go of her. I keep thinking I can make this easy. I've endured many difficult things over the years. Staying in control is my entire life. I even planned this operation from start to finish. Everything about it was my doing. This should have been the simple part—pretending she's just a captive who will marry me against her will.

"You're a mother. And you're my fuck toy. You'll

marry me and love me in every way I crave." I say these words in a cruel, mocking tone that's meant to hurt her, but they're true. They're the only real thing about this situation. Madelyn will marry me. She'll stay my fuck toy. And she is a mother.

The baby cries again, and my fingers tighten in spite of all my control. It's a sound designed to attract attention, but I can't give in. I can't be the one to scoop the child from the crib and give it whatever comfort it needs. Not with the eyes of my men on me.

"Don't you love me?" I say in a taunting tone.

Madelyn flinches, and once again, I'm flooded with confusion. Is she flinching because she doesn't believe me or because she's afraid of reality? Now is not the time for that conversation, but damn, I wish it were.

"I love you," she says, her voice soft.

I pull her in for a brutal kiss.

This—this is the thing I can't stop. I meant for it to be quick, but once her mouth is against mine, I'm consumed with how sweet she is. She doesn't pull away from the harsh bite. Instead, she gives into it. She's obedient that way, but it only makes me want to keep her here with me.

It's a dangerous line we're walking.

Until we follow this situation to the end, everything will be as uncertain as it is now. Anything could happen.

That's one thing this life has taught me. It's not over just because you want something to be done. It's over when the last threat is finally defeated.

We're not there yet. Not even close.

I pull away from her, and Madelyn stumbles. It takes all my willpower not to pull her into my arms and steady her. She catches herself before I have to and straightens slowly, her breath coming fast.

"Now go," I order.

The baby wails now, sustained cries. I can see the physical pull he has on her. Maybe it's similar to the pull she has on me.

Once Madelyn has her balance, she leaves quickly, not glancing back at any of us.

Not surprising. She doesn't want the other men to look at her. It was hard enough for her to be in the kitchen with all of them. Still, I would have felt some satisfaction if she'd looked back for me.

It doesn't matter. I'm the one who ordered her to go. That doesn't include hesitating to see if I'm watching. I made that clear enough when I spoke to her. I can still feel her warm flesh pressing against my fingers when she shook her head. It's unreal, how this woman gets under my skin. I almost wipe my palm against my pants just to get the sensation to go away. I can't let it influence me.

I can't bring myself to do it. The tingling where our

bodies touched lingers on my hand.

I want to follow her more than anything. Instead, I imagine her entering the baby's room, her body relaxing as she sees her child again. She's a good mother, and she would soften. Murmur something to him as she came in so he'd know she was there.

I was right. The cries taper off. She must have him in her arms now, holding him close.

If we were different people, I'd be in there with her. I feel more regret about that than I should. Having feelings like this is almost overwhelming, given how hard I've worked to keep them suppressed over the years.

It doesn't matter. I won't let them interfere. Madelyn and I will get to the end of this, whether it goes as planned or blows up in our faces.

I turn back to the men gathered at the table. If they noticed anything different about the way I treated her, they don't give any sign of it. That's a relief.

"Time to move on," I tell them. "Any movement or word? Has anyone heard anything?"

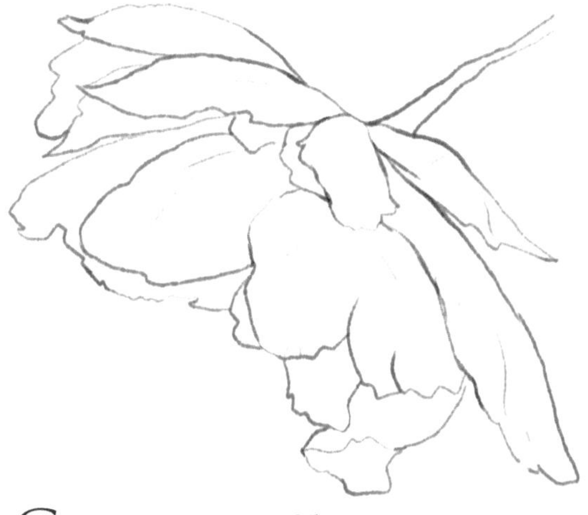

CHAPTER 5

MADELYN

He fills me with every thrust. Each motion is forceful and brutal, yet it all brings nothing but pleasure. With a pillow under my hips, he fucks me deep and rough. A cold sweat breaks out along my skin. I'm sore, deliciously used and my entire being is exhausted and sated.

As he buries himself fully inside of me, his hand roughly plucks my nipples and his pubic hair grinds against my clit. He's an expert at playing me, at depriving me of pleasure until he's ready.

It's been that way for years now, and the memory of our first time against the brick wall of an alley flashes before my eyes as he tells me to come like the good little whore I am.

Just like he did then.

And I obey, dutifully coming undone for a man I've loved in secret for years.

As he loses himself to pleasure, the rhythmic pulses of his cock press against my walls and I swear I could come again just from the sensation.

He holds me, kisses me for a moment and then climbs off, leaving me waiting for a damp cloth to clean up. He's gentle as he does it. I've always been in awe of how this man can be so cruel and so hell-bent on murder and vengeance, yet in the dark of night, alone with me, he has a side to him no one else sees.

Although I suppose it's the same for me. I'm a duplicitous woman who married a man only to get back at him for my brother's murder.

The bed groans as he wipes between my thighs and the cuffs attached to the bedpost clink.

"Do you want to use these?" I ask, only because they've been there since I arrived and he hasn't once mentioned them.

"No, it's for if they come in," he states simply, even though dread consumes me.

No one can know I was a rat. No one can know we planned this for years. So much is in the hands of deceit. "You'll say I put them on you at night," he tells me, tossing the cloth into the laundry bin and then climbing back into bed, pulling the sheets and comforter over us.

I can only nod as words evade me. I don't know what all his men think or what they're telling one another. I don't know if I'm playing the part well enough.

My whispered words are laced with fear when I ask, "Do you think they'll find out?"

"My brother knows and no one else. No one can ever suspect you were a rat, even if I told you exactly what to do. They would never trust you."

"I know, but have they said anything?" I ask him as I turn onto my side, staring into the eyes of a man I fell in love with before I was even on his radar. Years ago, before my brother died and I vanished. Before he met a woman who gave him his first son.

Before tragedy. Before this life requested we pay our dues.

Back when all I wanted was him and I thought that would be easy.

"You're giving me that look again." Connor breaks up my thoughts with a gentle murmur, his fingers tipping my chin up and forcing me to look at him.

My handsome brutal protector peers down at me.

"I know I used you. I know you fell for me before I

fell for you."

"I loved you so much, I was willing to marry the enemy." My heart aches knowing what I've done.

"You wanted vengeance too," he reminds me and I nod in agreement. I wanted to kill him, but Connor convinced me to destroy them all. Every last one of them from the inside out.

"When did you want me?"

"Always." His answer is easy and confident, without hesitation. "When did I fall in love with you, though? When did I ... feel this possessiveness over you?"

"Was it when I got pregnant?" I ask him the question I've wondered for the last nearly year. Everything changed when I told Connor I was pregnant.

"Before that." He admits, "I couldn't stand the idea of him touching you." I remember the argument we had. Connor didn't want me to go back. But we were so close to having our plans realized, and I wanted vengeance more than I cared to protect myself.

"He could have found out the baby wasn't his."

"We were careful ..." I start and all the thoughts and worries race through my mind. "If Nolan wasn't yours—"

"He's mine." His answer is final. "That is all that matters. No one will ever hurt him."

My throat closes, wanting nothing else than for my son to be safe. With the feud between families ended by bloodshed, he should be safe.

"I will do anything to keep him safe."

"What if they find out?" It is my only worry. The only thing that keeps me from sleeping peacefully now.

"Fletcher and I would kill them all before we let anything happen to you or our son."

The anxiousness doesn't leave me. "I just want it all to be over," I whisper, my gaze falling to his chest.

His hand wraps around mine and he brings my knuckles to his lips, planting a kiss there before telling me, "I asked too much of you." The remorse and regret are evident in his tone.

"What's done is done."

That's what we've said for years as we fell deeper into each other's arms and more and more consumed with plotting an execution to right the sins of the past.

I'm only grateful I'll no longer be sleeping with the enemy.

"You did everything I told you to. You are my good girl." He kisses my forehead and the pride and comfort that come with his praise nearly lull me to sleep.

"I love you. Not only for what you do for me, but because I know you. I know all of you."

His hand slips down my curves when he tells me he loves me too.

"You didn't answer my question, though ... When did

you fall for me?" I don't know why I need to know so badly. But I do.

"Around the time I told you we were pregnant?" I guess.

"I loved you before that … you know that."

"I know, I just—" I have to steady my breathing before I can get out this pain that radiates inside of me. "But when you … when you wanted to stop it all … when you wanted me to run away from him and be with you because I was pregnant … I was afraid to tell you because I knew you didn't feel for me what I felt for you but something seemed different that day."

He smiles weakly and stares at the spinning fan as he says, "I'll never forget that day."

Before I can press him again, wanting to know when, he tells me, "I fell for you when you came to me with a proposition. It was slow, not all at once. When you told me you knew how I felt." His words are choked and I remember that moment. When I met him at his wife and child's gravestones. My dead husband took from us a love that will always be missed. But Connor and I found each other and he won't take that away now.

He pulls me in close. "I fell in love with you when my soul realized I needed you to exist. I don't know how else to describe it. Without you, I didn't want to live."

Silence surrounds us as I realize the depth of our connection.

"It's our secret, though," he reminds me.

"I know."

His voice is reassuring when he tells me, "You'll do well playing the part, you have before."

"I'll pretend as long as you want, whatever you want. So long as you love me."

His grip on me tightens and he pulls me in as close as I could possibly be. He's my savior, though everyone else thinks he's my enemy. I can only hope I'm the same to him.

"Tell me you love me again," I whisper against his lips.

"I love you."

"I love you too."

A
Kiss
To Keep

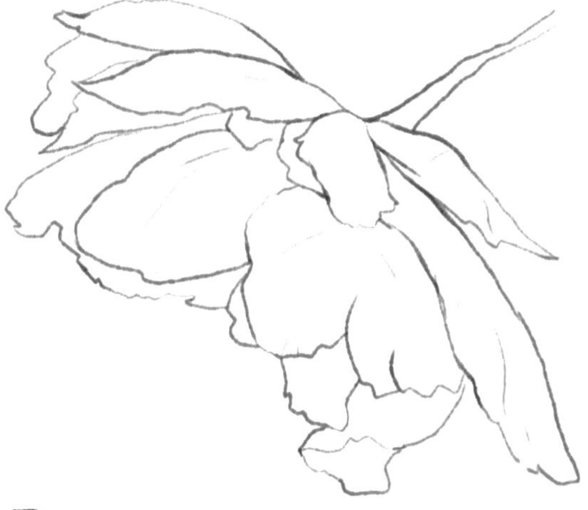

Prologue

Chloe

I remember the hum of the engine. It's funny how that's what stayed with me all this time. We took off in the shadows of the night, with what little bit we had that was worth taking with us and we drove away as fast as we could.

We didn't stop running, not for a long time, and I didn't have to ask him why.

No one leaves that place and gets away with it.

Crescent Hills is nothing but sin and misfortune. It's designed to keep every soul trapped there in a fog of devastation. I grew up surrounded by violence and agony. Living in fear and in anger. The constant turmoil kept me fighting, but I knew I would never be anything more than a name on its list of victims. That's the truly unfortunate part. I never wanted to call it home, but back then, I knew I'd never have another.

Until Sebastian.

He was always the only one for me, because he stained my lips with his and scarred my skin with his burning touch before I ever considered letting a boy touch me. Well, any boy other than him. No one else could have compared.

It all started with a kiss.

He followed me behind our high school. I didn't know it and I never would have guessed he felt even a fraction of what I'd felt for him. He had to have though, because that unfortunate day, I turned around after crying so hard and there he was. I was embarrassed to be inside with the other kids, so I hid outside, trying to suppress the shameful tears. The second I heard him, the second I turned around to see who'd followed me, Sebastian pushed my back against the brick wall and crushed his lips against mine.

Stunning me. Stealing my breath from me. Forcing me to think of him. Which was worlds better than being consumed with the tragedy that plagued me. That moment changed everything.

Because he kissed me, and I never forgot that kiss.

Because I took his hand and he led me away.

A sad smile plays at my lips as I rest my cheek against the cold glass. It was freezing cold when we ran away over a decade ago. We were barely more than kids then. Time's changed us so much. But it can't change everything.

It's fitting that it's bitter cold now that we're returning.

Now that we're going back into the nightmare.

"I never thought we'd go back," I whisper into the silent cabin of the car. The stereo works just fine, but I can't stomach the idea of music right now. I don't want to ruin any songs with this ominous day, knowing they'll be forever associated with this memory.

Bastian lays his hand on my thigh, and I merely glance at his touch, ignoring his warmth when he tells me, "I didn't either."

I think he just says what he thinks I want to hear.

I think he knew one day, he'd be drawn back to this life.

"I love you," he tells me in a rough voice, one that's been silent for hours. My sad smile lifts just slightly, and I lay my hand on top of his although I don't want to.

I love him, but I hate this place.

He says we're coming home.

But this was never my home.

I don't say "I love you" back. And Bastian doesn't react when I don't. That's what hurts the most. He knew what this would do to us.

And he did it anyway.

CHAPTER 1

CHLOE

We've been driving for days now. The snow's barely slowed us down. The prolonged silence, however, makes every minute seem longer than it is.

The closer we get, the faster the snow falls though. And we're close now. I know we are. I recognize these streets, even the backroads that have no names.

The air has changed, and it makes my stomach churn harder every time I breathe in.

"So you had a good time then?" I ask Bastian, picking at some barely perceptible fuzz on my sweater. My heart ticks faintly in my chest, almost like it's afraid to really beat and pump life through me. Instead it's this timid movement, leaving me counting the seconds until things are right again.

Clearing his throat, he shrugs. The motion draws up his jacket, pulling it tighter around his shoulders as he turns the wheel and the car takes a left down a back alley.

It takes real effort not to close my eyes as we pass the bar. A bar I know so well and wish I didn't.

Everything is different, yet it's all painfully familiar.

The sign looks worn and old, but even when I was a child, it looked just the same. Ragged and decrepit. Time's aged it, but not enough to really change it.

"It was a good week," he finally answers me, and his answer pulls my gaze from the gutters full of dirty snow to his steely blue eyes. "I'm sorry I had to go so quick and for so long. I missed you though," he adds with a warmth in his voice that travels straight to my veins.

He's my drug. A living, breathing drug. He's been gone a little over a week, leaving me all the way across the country to come back here. Now, I'm joining him, which is a nightmare come true for me.

"I missed you too," I admit although the words come out strangled still and I have to rip my eyes away to stare back out the window.

As if beat-up houses and barren streets were something I'd ever want to look at.

This particular road has stayed with me all my life. As the disquiet forces me to readjust in my seat, I ask Sebastian again, "Are you sure we should be here?"

Tick, tick, goes my heart, then a pause. My heart refuses to do anything at all, leaving a chill to travel down my arms as we pass Dixon Street, and Sebastian gives me a pointed look. We grew up on the same street, this street, but we've never lived in the same world.

I don't know how I fooled myself into thinking running away from here would change that.

"I know this is sudden…" He trails off and reaches his hand for mine, but I'm already crossing my arms so I pretend not to see it.

I swallow my response along with the regret from saying anything at all.

He can comfort me, but he's ignoring the flashing red light warning that this is exactly what we shouldn't be doing. I don't want comfort in that. He can keep it for himself.

"Never mind," I whisper and my warm breath fogs the window.

As the car moves over a speed bump and then a pothole in the old road, I jostle with it, passively letting the movement take me how it wants.

"How are you feeling?" Bastian's voice is low and apologetic, yet strong. He's always strong. Never faltering, never needing to lean on me.

It should be a blessing, but it feels like a curse.

"Second trimester is worlds better," I tell him and breathe in deep, feeling my shoulders stretch and rise before settling back down against the heated seat. "And I love this car," I comment.

"Smooth ride, huh?" he says just as we go over another pothole and I have to let out a small laugh at his dry humor and irony.

The second of ease between us is spoiled when we drive past our old high school, filled with haunted memories.

Mostly. The only two days I want to hold on to are the first day he kissed me and the day when we drove away years later. Every other day I spent here can rot in hell.

"It took me years to get over this place," I tell him, feeling the raw admission scratch up my throat with every word. Like I had to drag them out of me.

A second passes as the car slows to a stop under a red light.

"I know," Bastian says and this time when he lays his hand down for me to take, his eyes stare at me. His eyes pierce into me, begging me to feel what he feels. "I have to do this, Chlo."

I can't resist pulling down the seatbelt to lean over the center console so I can kiss his cheek. His rough stubble is short and it nearly scratches my lips as he tries to capture my own with his. But I avoid the kiss, settling on giving him a peck on the cheek.

Sebastian leans closer to me, ready to take one regardless, I know it.

With the groan of the leather seat protesting the movement of his broad shoulders, I prepare to give him a cheek and nothing more. I just can't kiss him; I can't give him that bit of me, not when he's hurting me the way he is.

He won't tell me why he *has* to be here. Why now? Why are we back?

Without a straight answer, things can't go back to being right between us. I won't allow it. He needs to know that. And all I know is that it has something to do with Carter Cross.

The red light turns to green as he sits up, and with it the car behind us beeps. Bastian's focus doesn't budge, not until I grip his hand. I thread my fingers between his and pull his hand to my lips, kissing the back of his hand as the car behind us beeps again.

Sebastian's frustration shows with his sharp, narrowed gaze aimed in the rearview mirror at the person behind us.

Always with a temper. What did I expect marrying the man everyone used to fear? He earned his reputation, and some bad habits die hard. The very thought makes me close my eyes with contempt. How could I think they'd died at all?

"Let's just go." I push out the rushed words as Bastian sits there, staring in his rearview and ready to pick a fight. "I want to lie down," I say, giving him the excuse and he buys it. His expression softens, but only slightly.

He doesn't ask and I don't tell.

I ask and he doesn't tell the whole truth.

We can't live like this, but we can suffer in silence until it kills us.

Well, mostly silence. The quiet hum of the engine keeps us company for a moment until he speaks.

"You can't hold back from me forever."

His words are heard, but not answered. Not for another two blocks.

"And you can't keep lying to me and keeping secrets," I finally counter, although my voice isn't as strong. It never comes out as strong as his, but it doesn't need to. My words are just as right as his are, and we both know it.

He's reticent again until we drive out of Crescent Hills, away from where our past lies restlessly. I don't understand why we didn't stop or where we're going.

He said we were going home. And Crescent Hills is the only home I've ever known, but we've driven out of it.

It's not until we pull into a long gravel driveway,

nearly fifteen minutes away from the world I once knew, that I give him a questioning gaze laced with worry.

"I thought here would be better," he tells me and with his words, massive iron gates part, creating a large opening for us to enter.

They're beautiful and behind the gates is a grand estate, but it's far too much and there's no way in hell I want to live like that. In a massive house with more rooms than I would ever fill.

"We could never afford something like this." Anxiety consumes me, wondering what the hell he did, who he stole from, or if he sold his soul to the devil until he speaks.

"Not this one," he tells me when he catches my gaze. "That one's not ours." The relief is only slight.

"None of these are ours," I remind him. "Our apartment is on the other side of the country. I said I'd come for a week, but none of these are ours unless we decide together." I stress the last word, *together*, waiting for him to look me in the eyes. I can hear the gravel lift up under the tires just as easily as I can hear the pounding of my chest. Even if it still feels like a faint tick. That damn tick is loud.

"I know," he finally agrees with me, rounding the large white stone home and driving past it, down into a tree line for a slow minute and then another. The trees are a mix of burnt auburn and evergreen. And the evening light casts shadows and sprays of light on the gravel road and barren dirt path.

We have to drive deep into the winter forest before I see a much smaller house. I almost want to call it a cottage, but it's too contemporary. I have to lean forward in my seat to get a better look as he parks the car, although he keeps it running.

The word "motherfucker" nearly leaves me under my breath. If I could pick a dream house, it would be this one. It's set back deep under a canopy of mature trees, but with an opening for sunshine. There's a wraparound porch and so many windows with pale blue shutters.

"This isn't going to be like the last time, is it?" I ask him and he doesn't answer immediately. "You're not going to buy this house and wait for me to cave, are you?" I push him. Suddenly, that tick is becoming more of a slam with his ever-passing silence.

"Do you like it?" he asks me and I close my eyes, refusing to believe he did it again.

"You didn't," I whisper, praying he really didn't.

"I bought it," he tells me, letting the words slip out as if they don't matter. Just like the last time he decided to have a house built here.

"Motherfucker," I mutter, finally speaking the profanity aloud.

"I'll sell it if you don't love it, Chlo. We can up and

leave and sell it no problem," he's quick to tell me, but that's not the point.

"You can't keep doing this shit!"

"Keep? It's only here, only about finding a place to stay," he argues back, letting his voice rise.

"Yes! Only here, the place I told you I never wanted to see again," I retort, and my voice cracks with outrage. "Do I have to remind you what happened to the last place? Good things don't happen here, and you should have taken that as an omen!"

The sky darkens at my words, the sun setting further into the trees, and I don't like it.

"This isn't okay," I tell him in the calmest voice I can manage. I focus on taking one deep breath and then another.

"Don't get worked up. I didn't mean to upset you."

"How could you have thought this wouldn't upset me?" I bite back. And then snidely add, "Oh, that's right, because you don't listen to me. Because I say words that don't mean anything."

"Don't do that." Sebastian's voice is low as he stares at me. His gaze is heated and so penetrating I can barely look at him, but I do. "Don't make it out like I don't care, Chloe. All I care about is you."

"Then why are we here?" I can't control the emotion in my voice.

The quiet forest seems to get darker with every minute we sit here arguing in the car.

"Because Carter needs me," he answers me in a tight voice.

Carter. His best friend. The one he left behind in order to run away with me.

I could never relate to that friendship. A friendship he calls family. Because I had no one to leave behind. Friend, family, or otherwise. I only ever had Sebastian.

"And that's his place?" I surmise. "The big one when we entered?" *Big one* doesn't quite do it justice.

"This is all his property, but the place we're going is deeper in the land. Private but safe and close. He lives there with his brothers," Bastian answers, all the tension leaving him. He knows I have a soft spot for Carter. What he doesn't know is how guilty I feel about everything that happened. But how could he, when he doesn't even know I'm very aware of what actually happened all those years ago?

"And what did he need you for?" I ask him, meeting his gaze. I can already see that he's going to lie. His tell is the way he narrows just his left eye, ever so slightly.

"You never tell me anything," I say before he can disrespect me with another lie.

"What you need to know is that you're safe here, and that I love you and I would do anything for you."

My first instinct is to correct him and tell him it's not about what I need to know, it's about telling me everything because I'm his partner. And those are the words sitting there on the tip of my tongue until I look in his eyes and see a hint of worry, and I let his statement digest.

Safe here. Are we in danger? My hand moves to my belly and the fear of loss is all too real. The last time we left this place, death remained behind. The lingering memory of the nightmares and the fears creep into my mind. But I know what happened back then, and it can't be that. I pray it's not that.

I don't know if it's just being back here that causes chills to trail up my arms and down my spine, or if it's something else. I swallow my question, knowing Sebastian won't answer me anyway.

"Just come with me," Bastian asks, holding out his strong hand for me to take.

It doesn't mean I forgive him when I place my hand in his. And it doesn't mean we're okay when I follow him up the paved walkway to the gorgeous red walnut French doors.

All it means is that it's getting late, I'm tired, and I don't want to fight right now.

I fought all my life just to get by. I thought I was done fighting.

I thought wrong.

CHAPTER 2

SEBASTIAN

"Is he going to be a problem?"

I ask Carter the only question that's been eating away at me as we drove down here. The hate, the anger... the fear, it's all mixed into a deadly concoction that's been destroying my sanity for days. Ever since I left Chloe, all I could think is that this prick would go after her. That Romano would take her away from me.

Even though I knew she was safe, I couldn't sleep not having her right here by my side where she belongs. I don't know how we lived so long thinking we'd get away from it forever, but we can't. I'm not running away; I'm not going anywhere. "I'm going to fucking kill him."

"Romano's a dead man and he knows it," Carter answers, the early morning light filtering in from the large window behind his desk.

"While he's still breathing, he's a fucking problem," I respond and run my thumb along my jaw. "I thought about how we could do it on the way over to pick up Chloe and then that cop had to show up."

"Officer Walsh is a menace. He thinks he can question everyone and wait in parking lots for shit to go down and that he'll somehow be the hero? He doesn't know shit. Not about how things work around here, or about how deep these cuts go. All he's doing is delaying the inevitable."

"He has damn fine timing." I blow out the statement, sitting back farther in my seat and hating that this new cop had to come down here and force us all to wait for what's rightfully ours. Even though he's former FBI from New York, all we have to do is wait until he turns his back, just like they all do. He'll learn what it's like down here and how far a piece of paper and a badge will get him.

"Romano's not going to make a move or leave that gaudy piece of shit he calls home. Not unless he has a death wish."

Fuck, just hearing his name causes adrenaline to rush through my veins and I have to sit up straighter, gripping the arms of the leather chair as I struggle to stay still. "I hate doing nothing."

"You and me both," Carter answers.

"You didn't screw him over, though. He didn't send out a hit order on you," I tell him. Chloe is everything to me and I would do anything for her. Leaving the mafia behind and being marked was a risk I was willing to take for her. But I'm back now, and I'm not going anywhere. Not when so much is at risk. The fucker has to die. No one is coming after me or my family.

"I heard about his guys going to Chloe's when I didn't show up and he realized I'd left that morning after we got the hell out of here when we were kids," I say. The sickness burns up my throat and I have to swallow it down, along with the hate and the rage. "Romano didn't try to kill someone you love."

I take my words back when I remember what Jase, Carter's brother, told me last week. The little bit of information that changed the reluctant relationship the Cross brothers had with Romano. "I'm sorry. I heard about your brother." I'm not the only one Romano went after. I'm the only one to get away though.

Carter reacts more strongly than I thought he would. He's younger than me by only a few years. In a lot of ways, he was the younger brother that I never had. But back when we were just kids, he never liked to talk about his emotions. Never. He'd always preferred to just be alone.

"Romano will pay for what he did—to you, and to the rest of my family." His statement is strained. I don't miss that he says "the rest," which means he still sees me as his family too. Even though I haven't been at his side through all of this bullshit.

Some blood you're born with. Some blood you choose.

He leans back slightly and a grimace mars his face as he touches his chest. He's still healing.

"You all right?" I ask him and he nods, still taking a moment to process the pain. To process all of it.

"I miss him," Carter confesses after a minute and his eyes get glossy. He coughs it away, pretending to be nothing but cold on the outside. But with no one to fight in this cold war, you can only look inward.

"Aria's changed you," I comment, knowing it has to be her who's brought out this new side of him.

Carter grins at me, not denying it. He knows it's true.

"I'm sure Chloe's changed you too."

Chloe. Just hearing her name does something to me. My Chloe Rose. "You could say that."

Carter chuckles, a knowing grin growing on his face. "What'd she say about coming back?" he asks, the smile never wavering even though every trace of humor vanishes from me instantly.

I have to look away, feeling a hint of shame that she didn't want to come back. She fought me on coming back. "She doesn't know what it feels like being away and missing it, you know?" I finally settle on that truth. "She hates this place."

Carter's smile dims, but the corners of his lips kick up at the last comment. "Don't we all."

"She doesn't have anyone left here."

"You think she'll come around?"

"I fucking hope so." The temperature of my blood drops and I tap my foot restlessly against the leg of the chair as I watch the early morning sky turn darker with the gray clouds moving in. I stayed away for as long as I could. I needed to so I could keep her. The only worry that keeps me up now that I know she's safe is whether or not she'll stay with me. She was always meant to leave me, she's too damn good for me and for this life. But I'll be damned if I let anything happen to her, whether she stays with me or not, she'll be staying here, where it's safe and she's protected. We had to come back; I have to end Romano.

"Does she know? Does she know about what you did before you left?"

I hold his gaze, letting the memories of the life I used to live, the one I'm walking back into, play before us. The violence, the murders. It was an exchange I had to make, one I don't regret because it means Chloe's by my side.

"No." I answer him in a single word, spoken so firmly that it practically ricochets off the walls of the room. "She can't know."

Carter gives me a single nod of acknowledgment.

"And what about Marcus?" I ask Carter, quick to change the subject so I can get rid of this revolting churning in the pit of my gut. I know where I stand with Romano. One of us will kill the other, but he has everyone foaming at the mouth to end his life. I don't know where I stand with Marcus, though. No one ever knows where they stand with him until it's too late. "Is Marcus going to be a problem?"

Carter's eyes are assessing as he stands from his desk, turning around to look out of his window as the snow starts to fall. I know somewhere beyond those trees Chloe is in bed still, sleeping, safe and sound.

"Marcus is always a problem."

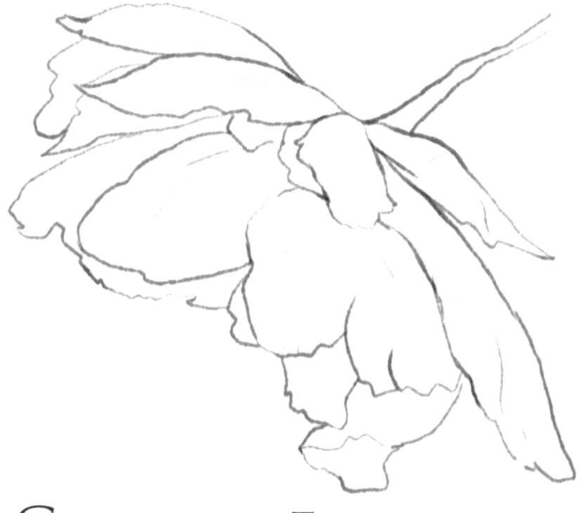

CHAPTER 3

CHLOE

"You hungry?" Bastian's voice startles me and I jump back from the opened suitcase of clothes I set on the sofa.

His rough chuckle at my expense makes me want to smack him, but his strong arms wrapping around me send a warmth through me, calming all those nervous feelings that wormed their way in. "Didn't mean to scare you," he says low and deep, pulling my back into his chest.

As I reach up behind me to wrap my arms around his neck, he kisses the crook of my neck right in the small gap my baggy sleepshirt allows him.

With my eyes closed and breathing in his woodsy scent, I remind him, "I'm still mad at you."

Last night we slept together, my legs tangled with his and my entire being happy to be by his side again. We avoided the argument for the time being ... and then I woke up alone. It wasn't until I found his note on the nightstand that the hollowness in my chest went away. He was only going to see Carter while I slept.

I don't like this insecure feeling. The nerves are a permanent stitch in our relationship. Like one day I'll lose him. I'll wake up alone, and that's how it will be for the rest of my life.

I don't want another man to take his place. I only want Sebastian. His lies and hidden truths are what give me that feeling that it's all going to unravel though. Lies he's carried for years. Secrets he needs to let go of.

He rocks me gently, and that's how he gets me every time. He didn't use to give me this so easily, so freely. The touches, the kisses, the obvious need for me to feel loved.

And I didn't use to feel like I needed it. But I do. I need him. I need this. Just like I need the air to breathe.

"So food? Yes?" he asks again and I stand up a little straighter, nudging him away because he doesn't acknowledge the fact that there's this gaping hole between us. How can we fix what he refuses to admit is broken?

"I'm going to unpack this stuff first." My knee prods the suitcase and the insides of it jostle slightly as I get back to the unpacking I've been tending to. It's mostly clothes and bathroom essentials. "I assume you're having everything back home packed up and moved here without my knowledge?" I ask him, peeking over my shoulder just in time to see him cross his arms and lean against the wall.

My gaze drifts to the corded muscles that line his arms and I know he's doing that shit on purpose.

It's quiet and I hate that I think he's not going to answer me, when suddenly he does.

"It can wait until you tell me you want to stay." He readjusts and adds, "I know you like the apartment, I wouldn't do that to you."

"Are you thinking we could keep it? And have both places?" I ask him, noting his every moment as I fold a sweater I'd pulled out of the suitcase before he came in here.

"We have options," he answers and I huff out a sarcastic laugh.

Options. I have to stare at the plush cream sweater as I toss it onto the sofa and then retrieve the next piece of clothing from the suitcase. It's an old shirt of mine, but one of my favorites that reads *Carpe Diem.* I have never felt so much betrayal from a shirt before. Even this garment has taken Sebastian's side.

"With you writing, we can go anywhere, do anything. Remember how you told me that?" he reminds me.

"I didn't mean you could drag me along to wherever you wanted to go against my will," I answer him flatly.

"You said you'd go wherever I wanted to take you. Change your mind?" he says, and the tone of his voice changes. The way the words float in the air longer, needing more attention and wanting to be heard so much more than any other words... the way he says them makes me pause.

Tick. My heart's counting the seconds. That's what it's been doing. Savoring each one and recognizing that they matter.

"I came here, didn't I?" I ask him, leaving out the emotional damage threatening to spill into each syllable. I remember the way I felt when we were first together. Counting each day and waiting for the one where we inevitably said goodbye.

I don't want that. Ever.

It's quiet, too quiet. The kind of quiet that turns to nights filled with loneliness and heartache.

I focus on the room and change the subject as I ask, "You had someone decorate this place?" It's a bitch move to cower away from the argument because I'm afraid to lose him. I hate myself for it.

This is the exact reason he thinks he can keep secrets from me. He knows I don't want to fight. Not with him.

He stares at me hard for a moment, reading into every detail of my expression the way he always does. I wish he wouldn't.

"Yeah," he answers and his single word tests the tension between us.

It's still there, smoldering, but I don't add fuel to it. I don't want to fight with him, ever. Not when he's the only hero I've ever had. The only knight in shining armor I've ever wanted. Even if he's all dinged up and damaged but pretending he's not.

I can pretend too.

"I like it," I tell him as I toss the shirt onto the pile, folded nice and neat even though I'm debating on finally donating it now that it's taunted me. Taking in a slow breath and releasing it, I say, "I really like the whitewash on the furniture with the light woods. And the cream walls, it's very calm and relaxing." All the while I talk, I fold another sweater and toss it down, making my pile lean a little. "It needs some pops of color I think, but I really like it."

It looks like I could have plucked this house straight from the pages of a *Good Housekeeping* magazine. I attempted something like this at the apartment, but it wasn't quite right. It was just items I bought and put in the rooms, but they didn't fit the way I thought they would. "I think I may even love it."

"Is that right?" he asks me easily, and even his lips tick up into an asymmetric grin. My heart recognizes something powerful between us: I love to make him happy and make him smile ... in turn, he wants that for me too.

It's still just ticking along though.

I don't know how long my smile will last here.

"Yes, that's right," I answer, avoiding the unknown and focusing on the here and now. On the fact that if I'm not ready to fight, I want to love him. It's only one or the other, with no happy medium. Because either way, we're together.

Knock, knock, knock. The three timid knocks save me from a strained breath.

Bastian makes a move to get the door and turns to walk out of the room, letting me return back to this new reality.

It is my reality and it's already better than I anticipated, but I can't shake the nervousness. "I'd like it better if you'd tell me the truth," I whisper lowly under my breath, knowing that's exactly why the ticks are being counted.

"Chlo," Bastian calls my name from the foyer, a gorgeous foyer with whitewashed floors and an iron lantern chandelier. I wasn't being complimentary for the sake of a truce; whoever decorated this place knew what they were doing.

My bare feet pad on the floor as I make my way to the front entrance, following the sound of a feminine laugh.

"I hope so," the woman says as I enter. That ticking turns to something else when I see her. Something like a war drum being beat with the handle of a machete.

I'm in shapeless pajamas and feeling the heaviness of the bags under my eyes and she's... put together and chic and beautiful. And a woman I don't know.

"I know she'll love it," Bastian tells her and then they both spot me in the threshold.

"Hi," the petite brunette says with a shy wave. She rocks on her heels as I look between her and Bastian, who's holding a tray of something covered in tinfoil.

"Chloe, this is Aria," Sebastian tells me and I look between the two of them again as I say hi. I have no clue who she is. The name Aria means nothing to me.

"I wanted to give you guys a housewarming gift. Food for Sebastian... because ... well, because he's a man and I don't know what men like... and this for you," she says clearly, politely, matter-of-factly as she hands me a brown kraft gift bag with a white lace design and white tissue paper. Something tells me she's already been here, given that the bag matches the décor.

"It smells delicious," Bastian comments and then looks at me pointedly to inform me, "Lasagna."

"The guys all love it when I make pasta, so ... I hope you like carbs," she says with another one of those laughs I heard before I walked in. A nervous kind of laugh which has me wondering what she has to be nervous about.

"The guys?" I prod.

"Carter and his brothers," she clarifies as I absently open the gift and mentally try to place her from back when we lived here, but I don't remember an Aria. A single sheet of tissue paper's already out before I realize she's intently watching me open the gift bag as she chews the inside of her cheek.

I don't have to pull out the rest of the tissue paper to see it's a frame I can easily remove from the bag.

With the empty bag cradled in my right, and the frame in my left hand, I turn it over to see a beautiful drawing of Sebastian and me. It's a sketch of a photo I remember from years ago when we first got together.

It's all done in a deep blue charcoal, but so finely sketched and on a thick cream canvas. The multiple shades of blue add dimension and capture the details perfectly. I'm awestruck for a moment at how thoughtful the gift is. And how breathtakingly beautiful it is.

We were only two kids really, barely out of high school and trying to find our way through the shit life we were born into.

Sebastian's holding me on his sofa, and I'm nestled in his lap with my knees pulled into my chest, looking at the camera while he's looking at me. I remember when Carter took this picture, only days before we ran away. Bastian asked him to. I remember it like it was yesterday.

"Do you like it?" she asks nervously, and her voice brings me back to the present.

"It's beautiful." I have to clear my throat as I set it down on the round beechwood table in the center of the room. "I love it," I admit honestly. "Thank you."

"Let me see," Bastian asks and even though I move to hand it to him, he stands behind me, both of his hands on my hips as he peers at it over my shoulder.

Watching his reaction, I see how his expression softens. I can tell he remembers too. Some memories here weren't the worst. Some of them are the best.

"Carter showed me the picture a couple of days ago when he was telling me about how him and Sebastian were so close growing up." Aria's voice grabs my attention. "He told me all about how you stole Sebastian's heart. It was such a sweet story," she says, and her voice is nearly singsongy.

I wonder which version of the tale she got, because I don't remember it being "sweet" exactly.

"You drew it?" Bastian asks, and my mouth drops

open when she nods.

"You're so talented," I comment.

"I'm so happy you love it," she says cheerily, more at ease than she was a moment ago. "Carter thought you'd like it but ... you know, he's a guy and I think he likes to make me feel like I'm good at drawing, so he'd say just about anything to make me smile."

"Is Carter your...?" I don't finish, not sure if Carter's married or dating. The least Sebastian could have done is told me that much.

"Oh," her eyes widen and her gaze moves from me to Sebastian, then back to me. "I'm with Carter. I'm his ... fiancée," she tells me and when she says the last word, she smiles, a kind of sweet, innocent smile and then looks down at her hand. Her ring finger is barren. "No ring yet, it's been a little crazy recently."

"Let me take this to the kitchen. I've got to make a quick call and I'll be right back," Bastian says and without waiting for a response, he leaves the two of us. The kitchen is in the back of the house and I listen carefully as his footsteps disappear.

"Crazy, huh?" I prod, not wasting a moment to get details on what happened this past week while Sebastian was here and I wasn't.

"We found out we're expecting," she says and lifting her voice a little higher, immediately tells me,

"Congratulations, by the way." She shakes her head and rolls her eyes. "I meant to say that first thing, but I swear my head isn't on right."

"First, thank you. And second, you can blame that on the baby now and for probably the next eighteen years or so I've heard."

My comment makes her laugh again, and any bit of jealousy I had vanishes knowing she's with Carter.

"Congratulations to you too," I tell her and prod again, my left hand resting on the table, "I haven't seen Carter in … gosh," I blow a strand of hair from my face, remembering him as a sixteen-year-old kid, "in years."

"Really?" she asks, seeming surprised. "Well, he has a lot of respect for you and for Sebastian. He speaks really highly of you two. And he seems really happy to have you two back."

Guilt is what makes my smile slip the way it does. I feel it falter and I can't stop it.

I know why we left, even though Sebastian doesn't know that I know.

I know what happened when we took off too. What happened to Carter specifically.

"He's a good guy," I tell her and try to ignore the regret. If I'd known everything he'd go through at only sixteen and have to face alone because his best friend left, I would have made Sebastian come back. It's ironic that I can admit that, yet coming back now, the thought never occurred to me.

"So, how far along are you?" I ask her, trying to hide everything I'm feeling, but she sees it just like Sebastian does, if her wary expression is anything to go by.

"Not far at all," she tells me and offers a small smile as she touches her lower stomach. "We only just found out."

With a nod, I acknowledge what she said, but new words fail me.

"You okay?" she asks with hesitancy.

"I just wish Sebastian would tell me why we're here," I blurt out the truth. "Why now?" I don't bother keeping my voice low as I spill the truth to a perfect stranger.

"It's funny how they keep things from us," she says a bit lower, a bit more serious than she's been, "as if we aren't going to find out." The small eye roll and shake of the head are meant to add humor, but I can see how she really feels in her eyes, in the way her smile struggles to stay where it is.

"Carter too, then?" I ask her, feeling the race in my pulse.

"He tried; I think he knows better now." The moment the words leave her, she bites down on her lower lip and peeks over her shoulder at the door, as if he could come in any second. For a moment I think she's worried he'd come here, worried he'd see her talking to me about him.

But then she mutters, "He better know better now," in a tone not meant to be negotiated.

"He's an asshole sometimes," she tells me, playing with the nonexistent ring missing from her finger. "He's rough around the edges and difficult at times. But he loves me, and I told him I want to know what's going on. Even if he thinks I shouldn't know, not knowing makes it harder on me, you know? Which makes it harder on us."

She's saying every single thing that I could say right back to her.

"I told him, I'd let him know if I didn't want to hear." Again she looks over her shoulder, this time as if summoning him, but the man doesn't show himself. "And if I want to know something, he answers. And I do the same for him."

"Right." I nod in agreement.

Her last sentence is spoken with finality. "Being raw and open is scary as fuck, especially in this life, but it's the only way I know how to survive."

Those words, each and every one, settle into the very marrow of my bones. "I don't think I can stay here if Sebastian doesn't tell me what's going on," I confess to her. Bastian isn't anywhere to be seen or heard; I have no idea what he's doing, but he needs to hear those words. "I'm afraid he's going to choose this place over me, to be honest." There's the truth. The heart of the matter.

He's wanted to come back since the day we left, and now he's done it, without my permission. If I say I don't want this, I am certain he's not going to choose me.

"Why would you say that? You're all he talks about."

"Because he's been waiting for me to leave him for years. He'd let me walk away if he thought it was the right thing to do by me."

"Do you want to walk away?" she asks.

"No," I say, and the answer is easy. "I don't even mind this place. It's not what I was thinking when I told him I'd never come back. This isn't Crescent Hills and I could be happy here. The only thing I really care about is that he's not telling me what's going on. And with the history of what happened before, I want to know. I don't want to go crazy worrying."

"I know that feeling," she mutters beneath her breath. "What did he tell you?" she asks me, and I shake my head along with giving her a shrug.

Swallowing and feeling my dry throat tighten, I answer, "He said he wanted to come home. He said Carter needed him." Every word feels drier and drier in the back of my throat. Like it's suffocating me to tell this woman and admit how little he tells me. "I know something's wrong," I confess to her.

She only nods her head in response, her eyes darting behind me, but when I look she finally speaks. "He's not there, I was just checking."

Feeling an oncoming chill from the draft of the front door, my right hand absently rubs my opposite forearm.

"Do you know why he came back now?" I ask her and again, she nods and answers, "Yes."

"Is it bad?" I question.

"The bad just passed, now it's just waiting for things to settle, I think. There are some loose ends, but they'll be tied up shortly."

A beat passes, and the ticking in my chest speeds up, feeling each second slip by me faster and faster.

"I'm sorry, I'm a little guilty. Carter asked Sebastian to come back because of things with me, I would think. Things were the worst..." She trails off as her bottom lip wobbles, but she catches it between her teeth and swallows her words.

"Are you okay?" I ask her, feeling for the first time that she's more like me than I could have ever known.

"I am. I am now," she adds.

"Do you want to talk about it?"

"Maybe one day, but I don't think today is a good time. I'm grateful Bastian came back. I'll tell you that much. And if you're worried, I wouldn't be. But I really think you two should talk." Her gaze again moves behind me, and this time I know he's there. She lets her gaze linger and the floor softly creaks behind me.

"We should," I answer and hear the floors protest once again, but still far behind me, maybe in the doorway. As if he's stopped there and doesn't dare to move any closer.

"Sorry to intrude... I just wanted to say 'hi.'" She gives me a small smile and an odd wave before tucking her hair behind her ear and turning to leave.

"Thank you so much for the gifts." My response is nothing but polite, even though inwardly I'm prepared for confrontation with the man standing behind me.

"If you ever want to hang out or just talk, I'm right there or happy to come over even."

"I'm going to take you up on that," I answer her and then watch her leave.

Chapter 4

Sebastian

"What did you two talk about?" I ask her before Aria's even through the doorway. Anxiety spreads along my skin. I thought the two of them would hit it off. But the atmosphere in the foyer reminds me of a funeral home.

"About what's going on."

My pulse picks up. "And what is going on?" I ask her, swallowing thickly and refusing to believe Aria told her anything specific. Chloe's pregnant, for fuck's sake. She doesn't need the stress or the fear. The last thing she needs to do is worry. I've got her.

"I don't want to not address these things anymore.

We need to talk about it." Her words echo off the walls of the foyer as the door closes and the biting chill of the bitter weather joins us.

"What things do we need to talk about?" I ask her, as if I don't know. There's so much shit she doesn't know. And if she learns the truth, how could I ever keep her?

The thought sends a prick down my neck that doesn't stop until it reaches the base of my spine.

The uneasy feeling stays where it is when she turns around, staring into my eyes and swallowing thickly. "I want to know everything."

The hell with that. "No."

Her baby blues widen, the shock apparent. Even I'm surprised by the way the single word sounded so harsh. "You don't need to know this shit." I give her the simple explanation, and a light sparks in her eyes.

"It's not about need, Bastian. It's about want," she grits out. "I love you and I'll never stop loving you, but I hate how you think I'm so delicate and easily broken." Her tone is severe and unrefined. "I deserve to know the truth."

"The truth about what?" I ask again, knowing the one truth I will never tell her. Never.

"Everything," she demands.

I was her savior. That's how she looked at me. Like I was one of the good guys, and it did something to me.

It made me a better man. I will never let her take that back, because I don't know what will happen to me if she does.

My lips part, ready to give her a partial truth, enough to keep her at a distance. Something to satisfy her curiosity, but her bottom lip quivers and her arms cross, showing me her swollen stomach. She's only just started to show.

"Tell me why you needed to come back right now," she asks when I hesitate.

I question if Aria told her something I'll have a hard time explaining, or if she told her anything. Fuck, what was I thinking leaving the two of them alone? "Carter was in trouble," I start and she cuts me off.

"What kind of trouble?"

"The kind that wound up with a lot of people going to funerals this week," I answer her sharply and wait for her reaction. I get none. Nothing. The blunt answer doesn't faze her in the least.

"Why now?" she asks and when I feel a deep crease settling in my forehead, she elaborates. "Why didn't you come back before? It's obvious..." she hesitates, but doesn't hold back when she continues, "It's obvious he's been putting people in the ground for a while now... yes?"

I nod, and my heart hammers. The skin across my knuckles draws tight as I flex my hands into fists and then relax them, thinking about all the shit that's happened since we've been gone.

"He didn't need me, but this time, it was important to him that he did everything he could…" I almost tell her how it was the first time he was fighting for something that mattered, but I don't have to.

"Because of Aria?" she questions and again I nod.

It's silent for a moment and I watch as the tension in her shoulders lessens. The hope that she's been given just enough to drop it toys with me until she asks, "Did he need you to do what you used to do?"

I can barely nod in confirmation. Every muscle in my body is tight, waiting for her to run, to cower, to be afraid or angry or disgusted. I never liked the man I was without her, but it doesn't change the fact that's who I am. I can run away for years, but I'll always be a murderer. I don't want her to look at me that way. I don't even know if she knows the extent of what I've done, both years ago and just last week. And what I'm willing to continue to do.

"Did you want to hurt them?" she asks quietly.

I answer her with questions of my own. "Why would I want to do this? Why would I want to hurt people?"

Another question is all I get. "Why wouldn't you? That's what you did before, and living out there, away from all this… nothing made you happy. You moved from job to job and you hated them all."

"I was happy with you and bored with work... that's life."

"No," she responds sharply, "you lost your passion."

"I lost my family," I correct her, raising my voice and stressing the statement. I feel the harsh words linger between us. The room feels colder than it ever has before. Anger simmers, although not for her; anger at my past, anger at this shit life I was dealt.

"You are my family, we are family. But Carter was too."

She starts to speak, but her words turn to ghosts of thoughts as she stares back at me and starts to cry. "I wish we'd never left him behind," she croaks and I swallow my confession that I wish we'd never left at all.

"Come here," I say and hold her close, forcing her body to mold with mine. "I love you and I don't want to see you like this."

A shudder runs along her shoulders as she tries to calm herself down. Can't she see this is the exact reason I don't want to tell her these things? I don't want her to live with the pain. I can bear it for the both of us.

As if reading my mind and finding fault in my conviction, she whispers against my chest, "I don't want you to lie to me." Her hot breath sends goosebumps down my skin in a wave.

"I don't lie to you. I've never lied. I just keep some of

this shit from you, so you don't have to deal with it." It's a half truth. It's always only a half truth.

"You don't think I know? Or that I wouldn't find out?" she questions as she lifts her gaze to me. Staring back at me are worry, sadness, and desperation even. And it stuns me.

"I know more than you think," she says in my silence.

"I would never bring you into danger," is all I can say, because it's the only truth that matters to me anymore.

"Is that why you came up here before me? Because it was too dangerous?"

I almost lie, I almost hide it from her so she doesn't have to know, but I can't. "Yes."

"Why not tell me?" she asks as if it's that simple. As if I could risk her knowing who I am at my core and leaving me.

"I don't want you to know. I want you to be happy and to trust that I'll take care of it. All of it."

"That's not fair. I don't want it to all lie on your shoulders. I want to help you. I want to be there for you."

He sounds desperate when he tells me, "You do help me, and you are there for me."

"How can I, when I don't know what you're going through?"

"I just want you to love me."

"You already know I do."

"Show me. Kiss me. Kiss me like you love me." I miss her kisses the most. When she's angry and she's holding back, I know she keeps them from me. And all I can think is that she must not need them like I do. She must not feel the same thing as I do when she lets me kiss her.

I can keep secrets so easily. But I can't keep her touch as easily. I need to feel it every day. She makes me feel like it's all worth fighting for.

"Kissing doesn't make it better," she says softly, but her gaze lingers on my lips and the fight in her cadence is weak at best.

"Fighting won't either," I answer her and that's when her eyes lift to mine.

"Are you sure about that?" The seductive tone doesn't go unnoticed, and neither does the challenge.

One large step is all it takes to dwarf her small frame under mine. She doesn't back away, she doesn't reach out to me, but her breathing quickens and her baby blues spark with a heat I've longed for.

"Kiss me, Chlo. Even if it doesn't make it better, it'll feel better, and that counts for something, doesn't it? Life is what we feel. That's what keeps us alive."

Leaning forward, she places one hand on my chest, barely touching me, hesitant and careful. She stands on her tiptoes next, taking her time to plant the smallest of kisses against my lips. Her soft, feminine touch may feel like nothing to her as she brushes her lips against mine, but to me it's everything, even if it's only miniscule to her.

I can feel the faint wetness she leaves behind as she pulls away, her eyes still open. I can even hear her heart running wild so close to mine, no matter if she's so restrained in front of me.

"There," she whispers and tries to move back, but I wrap my arm around her waist and pull her in closer to me, forcing her breasts against my chest, her hips pressed to my thigh, and a small yelp of surprise slips from her.

"Again," I command her, barely breathing. Moving my other hand to the small of her back, I keep her pinned to me. "Kiss me again." Although my voice is strong and the words are a demand, both of us can hear my desperation, so why hide it? "I'm fucking begging you, Chlo," I whisper the strangled truth.

It's only a single beat, a single moment before she crashes her lips against mine, hungrily, greedily, searching for the same thing I need.

The feeling of being loved. Of knowing it and wanting nothing more than it. I could tell her a million times and she could do the same for me, but it's only when we kiss like this, raw and with everything we have, that we can feel it burning in our blood.

Her nails dig into the back of my neck as she parts

her lips and my tongue dives into her mouth, massaging hers with swift, powerful strokes.

Lifting her ass up with one hand, she wraps her legs around my waist and I don't waste a single moment bringing her back to the sofa, knocking off the suitcase and placing my wife down in its place. She heaves in a breath when I finally pull away from her.

"Bastian," she breathes my name, rather than the oxygen she needs. I barely get a glimpse of her as I rip my shirt off and I hate it. I hate that anything gets in the way of what we both need.

I'm savage as I rip her clothes from her, tearing down the front of her shirt and pulling her pants and panties down as if they're scorching her skin and she'd be scarred if I didn't remove them this instant.

Her panting, her soft moans, the way she lifts her hips to help me and then tears at the button on my jeans, it all fuels me to move faster, to eliminate everything that keeps us apart.

She stares up at me, watching as I kick off my jeans and then grip the top of the sofa as I move between her legs. "I love the way you kiss me." That's all she says.

Cupping her bare pussy, I find her wet and hot and wanting. Her lips form a perfect O, and her eyes go half lidded as I finger fuck her, bringing her closer to the edge but not letting her get off.

Her little whimper of protest makes me smile. Her pout, the way she wraps her leg around mine and then digs her heel into my ass... Fuck, everything about her makes me hard.

I wait for her eyes to find mine and hold her stare before telling her, "Don't stop kissing me."

She isn't given the chance to answer, because I thrust myself inside her to the hilt, making her scream out in pleasure before slamming my lips against hers.

Our lips crash and our moans mingle in each other's mouths as I thrust into her over and over again. Moving out slowly, ever so slowly to tease her and then pushing myself into her in one swift stroke. Each time her head begs to fall back, but she keeps her lips on mine, struggling to breathe, to move away from the intensity, to get closer and have more.

A cold sweat breaks out along every inch of my skin as I pick up my pace, ruthlessly fucking her and claiming her again and again until her tight cunt spasms around my length and I groan as I lose myself deep inside of her.

Even then, she doesn't stop kissing me. Her body trembles under me and her nails scratch down my back, but her lips stay on mine. The two of us never parting, my Chloe Rose never leaving me. And we unravel together.

She's still panting, still feeling the waves of aftershock when I pull out of her slowly and move quickly to get beneath her, laying her limp body on my chest to nestle beside her.

"I love you." She doesn't moan the words or whisper them, but they get lost in the air just the same.

I kiss her hair, her cheek, her shoulder until she brings her lips to mine and kisses me gently, but with undenied passion. And it's only when she breaks the kiss that I tell her, I love her too.

I always have and I always will.

I don't know that she'll ever know just how much. She is my everything. My only. My hand moves to her belly, to the life we made together. I would do anything for my family. I will do anything and everything to make sure they will never have to be afraid. Our child won't experience the same life we had.

I won't allow it.

"What do you want to know?" I ask her, feeling her bare skin pressed against mine. Her hair slips through my fingers and I wait for her to ask any question and I'll answer it. "I don't want to lose you or lose this ever again, Chlo. If you need to know something, ask me. I'll tell you. I'll tell you anything." I breathe in deep before confessing, "But you may not love me anymore when you hear the truth."

"Sebastian, you're crazier than I am if you think I could ever not love you. Right now I want to know where and when you're working. I don't like waking up alone."

While kissing her hair and running my fingers down her back, I answer her, "I can show you one place I may be a lot." She readjusts on the sofa, moving her small body so more of her is on top of me. I fucking love it. I love how she wants me and how she shows me that she does.

When she lifts her head, her brunette hair tumbles down her shoulder, exposing more of her and I lean forward to kiss that crook in her neck. "You love it when I kiss you here," I whisper against her skin and she gives me a small, feminine moan of feigned protest.

With her hand splayed on my chest, she straightens and I'm forced to pull back. "I want two things," she says, staring in my eyes.

"What two things?"

"Show me this one place. And tell me something you've done that you think will change things between us. Tell me the worst thing, Sebastian."

I can't; I won't. I won't willingly lose her like that.

Her baby blues are bathed in desperation when she tells me, "I want to show you what I think of that side of you. The side you like to pretend I can't see."

CHAPTER 5

CHLOE

"A club?" I say, and the humor of the word rests in its cadence. "Thought you were tired of clubs?" My brow arches as I look up at Bastian when he opens the doors to The Red Room for me. The second he does, the vibrations of the music hit me, and somehow the dim lighting feels even darker than the night behind us.

"It's different when I'm not working in it," he comments and I have to clarify, "So you're not working here?" There's a small sputter in my chest, afraid that he's holding back. Afraid that he's not going to hold up his end of the bargain. It doesn't matter if he does or doesn't; I'm ready to tell him what I know. And that I love him for it. I love my dark knight. He's always been my hero.

His lips quirk up as he splays his hand on my lower back and leads me to the long L-shaped bar in the far right of the room. "Not exactly." Although he's casual, there's a tightness in every small feature of his stance and the way he walks.

His answer is one he would have given me a week ago. Hell, even two days ago. He would have left it there, and I wouldn't have had the balls to push for more. I would have let the unsettling feeling push us farther apart.

Not tonight though, not as we brush by the crowded room, past high tables and men and women whose outfits range from both custom suits and short dresses, to tattered jeans and thin white tank tops. "I'm working with the Cross brothers, and Jase owns this place, so if he needs me here, I may be here, but I won't be the bouncer or bartender."

His eyes hold a brightness, even though they're dark and in them I see the reflection of the bottles that line the bar, and more, so much more.

Passion, desire, a challenge, and ... purpose.

It's disconcerting in some ways as I take a seat at the bar, sitting down on the leather stool. I could never give him this. I don't want him to fight, but that's what dark knights are meant to do.

"You want anything to eat?" he asks me and I shake my head, telling him I just want a cranberry juice. He signals for the bartender easily, but I can tell he's on edge like I am. On edge that the wall of mistruths and hidden secrets is breaking down between us.

"Bastian," the bartender greets him and then turns to me. "You must be Chloe," he says without missing a beat. With his sleeves rolled up and his tattoos showing on his forearms, the man looks deadly, even if he's smiling at me. Italian. Dominating. And sexy as hell.

"Sebastian's told me all about you and the little addition," he says, and his eyes drift lower as he searches for the baby bump. "Congratulations," he tells me.

"Thank you," I respond but I don't even know his name, and I could cringe at that. I know so little. I don't know anyone here, but that's going to change. Sebastian's only been here a week longer than me, but it's obvious that he belongs here. That he's welcome here.

There's a small piece of me that wants to be welcome here too. For once in my life.

"Chloe, this is Seth," Bastian tells me and Seth smiles broad and wide.

"It's nice to finally meet you," he tells me and then someone calls for his attention, taking him away but not before Bastian orders his beer and my drink.

"He works with Jase."

"Well obviously, since this is his bar."

"No, I mean…" Sebastian trails off and runs his hand along the back of his head. "Seth likes being behind the bar when he's not working. But he works really close with Jase," he tells me and then pauses. Even the music pauses a beat, as if to let the words sink in.

"What does he do?" I ask, and Bastian reaches for his beer. I turn around to thank Seth, seeing my drink right next to my hand for the first time. I hadn't realized he set it there, but he's already moved on to someone else.

"He does a lot of things. Whatever needs to be done. Fixes situations that get out of hand."

"You like him?" I ask, letting my finger sit on the rim of the glass. It slides along the edge and I wonder if it makes a sound given that the edge is wet, but it doesn't matter. The club is so loud, the soft sound would drown in it. Bastian nods, not showing me any emotion on his face, but steadfastly observing my reaction.

"Is that what you do too?" I ask him, not sure if I really want to know, but I damn well know that I want him to know I'll still love him regardless.

"No." Bastian takes a drink and then tells me, "I'll be staying with Carter, going places with him to make sure things go down the way they're supposed to."

"Situations?" I ask and before he can even say "yeah" again, I ask, "Like what you used to do?" His tax returns said he was a butcher for Romano, but the scars on his knuckles say otherwise.

This time he only nods, his lips pressed in a tight line. "If it needs to be handled. Yes. I handle it."

"So you're the muscle," I comment and take a sip of the bittersweet drink. I appreciate having to be sober for this. It's surprising how it doesn't bother me. How it even excites me. That's what surprises me the most.

"I know it's not what you thought I'd be doing when we settled down." He starts to talk, and I don't bother to let his mind wander down that path.

"I never thought I could tame you, Sebastian Black. I never wanted to either."

"Tame?" he says and huffs a humorless laugh. He swallows thickly, staring at the ring of bubbles on the edge of his glass as he adds, "I just want you to know ... who I am."

"I've always known who you are."

Shaking his head slightly, he stares blankly ahead. "I've hurt a lot of people," he tells me in a voice so cold and low, as if I still don't get it.

"You killed them. You didn't just hurt them; you killed them."

The club life seems to get louder, but it bleeds together when he looks at me with that intense icy gaze.

"I know what you did," I choke out, needing to finally

tell him the truth. "When we left, I know what you had to do before we could leave. I heard you talking about it on the phone."

"What?" Disbelief lays in the breathy syllable. His stern gaze hardens; the depths of the man he is showing. And I love it. I love this side of him. Dare I say, I may even love this side of him more. Not because I love what he does, or the actions. But because he's willing to risk everything to fight for what he believes in. I don't know what Carter's gotten himself into, but back when we were only kids, Sebastian did something I know I never could. He made an injustice just.

"We hadn't been gone long, maybe a few weeks?" The words race from me, so willing and eager to finally be heard. "Something happened with Carter and you wanted to go back. I thought we were coming back here, but we didn't. They told you not to. You were talking to someone about the people who were murdered, about the list ... about Marcus."

"Chlo." Bastian says my name like he's daring me to tell him it's a lie, but the words keep running from me, running away like we did all those years ago.

"And when you came back to the bedroom, I waited for you to tell me what had happened. I wanted to know if Carter was all right. And you didn't say a word." Tears blur my vision, but I don't cry. "You never told me anything, even though I knew you were hurting."

"All I needed was you and you didn't need to know," he tells me in a single breath, the impact of my confession hitting him and turning his jaw hard.

"Did you think I wouldn't love you anymore for it, Bastian? Did you think I would leave you?"

"Chloe," he says, my name strained like it hurts him to say it.

"You would have never told me, and I get why. I get it."

I don't wait for him to respond before I continue on.

"And what you did after. When someone came for us." I barely get the words out, because I know that night changed him. It was right after he got the call about Carter, so we'd been gone maybe three weeks, constantly moving from place to place, not stopping anywhere. "The night after you got that call, there was a knock on the door."

"Chloe, don't." Bastian's words are only a breath of a wish. A wish to not just keep me safe, but to make it so I don't even know about the danger. It's an impossible task and he needs to know that, even if that means he thinks he failed me.

"I was awake when you grabbed the gun. And I hate that I pretended to be asleep. I know that's what you wanted, you didn't want me to know."

"It was Romano. I knew he'd send someone."

"And I heard everything." I whisper the confession that tears down the wall of pretenses between us. "I heard you nearly beat him to death, I heard the message you told that prick to give to Romano…" I swallow my words about how I heard him in the bathroom, cleaning up the mess and trying to hold back his own emotions. There's more than anger and rage inside of him. The fear that he couldn't protect me was almost palpable. "I was there behind the door with your other gun, Bastian. I was ready to fight with you, but you've never wanted that."

"No, Chloe-"

I cut him off before he gets carried away, before he can focus on something other than the problem that's keeping a wedge between us. "I don't want to be in this world, Sebastian. I belong here nonetheless, and I don't want to fight. But I won't be left in the dark, and I don't want you to think that I shouldn't know the truth or that when the time comes, I wouldn't be able to be at your side. I know it's my fault to let you think I don't know what you do… but you need to talk to me. I need to know what's going on."

His head falls back and the air leaves him as I grip his hand and beg him to listen to me. "It's one thing to let my mind run wild and think these things. It's another for me to know it. But Sebastian, I know. I know *you*." He turns to look at me as my last word cracks. I whisper,

"How could I not?"

"You were never supposed to find out," he finally speaks, looking away from me and staring straight ahead, failure clearly written in his gaze.

I have to stop and take a drink, calming myself down. I thought letting the words out would feel freeing, but that's not at all what this feels like. Instead it feels like the unraveling I've been terrified of all this time.

"Did you keep it a secret because you wanted to protect me? Or because you wanted me to think you wouldn't do something like that?"

"Both," he answers me sincerely, looking me in the eyes.

"Well you protected me, and I love you regardless."

My chest rises and falls quicker, and I can't shake this nervousness, not until he asks me with a rawness in his throat, "You know that I love you more than anything. That I would be anyone you need me to be?"

"You don't need to change who you are, but you need to tell me if that's why we're back."

"It doesn't have to do with that. Romano's still here, but not for long."

"Then why?" I ask him, even though I think I already know. "There was a note?" My assumption brings his icy blue stare to mine.

"From Marcus. He warned me that Carter needed me and that we needed him." His gaze drops to my belly and he squeezes my hand. "I would never let anything happen to you, Chlo, and I wouldn't have brought you here if I didn't think we needed to be."

"Marcus said we needed Carter?" I clarify, feeling a wave of anxiety run through me.

"If it was only about Carter, we never would have come here. You know it had to be about you."

His words sink in slowly. Even after so much time, there's still a mark on my husband, a mark on me in return. "Can you trust Marcus?" I ask him, focusing on the fact that we're here; we're safe. And that Bastian will never let anything happen to me or our child.

"No," he says, and the answer is simple. He leans forward, pulling me into him and giving me a comfort I didn't realize I needed this badly. "But he was right about Carter and he's the reason why Romano's men never came back. I should listen to his warning rather than regret not doing everything I can. If anything ever happened to you, or our little one, I wouldn't be able to survive, Chlo."

I have to keep my breath steady; I have to keep telling myself that we're safe now.

"No one is going to hurt us here. This place is changing. Carter and his brothers are taking it over. We can't let it stay what it was, Chlo; you know what happened to us, what it was like living here."

"I know," I whisper, hearing the pain etched in his words, but also the fight. To fight what's wrong in the lowest and most depraved ways. To use violence and force in a world that's nothing but merciless.

"It's not our fight anymore, but that doesn't mean we should stand back and do nothing."

"Leaving this place wasn't doing nothing," I tell him and remember the pain, the fear, the courage it took to leave everything behind. But even as they leave my lips, I doubt the truth of the words I've spoken, because they were said out of fear.

"I didn't say that it was. But now, I know we can do more. I can feel it, Chlo. I'm supposed to be here right now." Taking my hands into his, the rough pads of his thumbs rub soothing circles on the back of my knuckles. Staring deep into his eyes and knowing that I see him for who he is and he sees me just the same, knowing that settles the harsh memories that creep up at the reminder of what used to be.

"I just don't want you ...." He pauses to lick his lower lip and exhale a heavy breath. "I don't want you to think I'm..." His words are lost in the air in between us. "That I'm-"

"All you will ever be, Bastian, is mine. You are mine. Just like I'm yours. I made my life knowing that's who I was, and who I wanted to be." It takes more than I realized to admit the words out loud. "I don't want to be anything else and as long as you are mine, that is exactly who you will be to me." Pulling my right hand from his grasp, I cup the side of his jaw in my palm and feel the rough stubble as my thumb runs along his chin. "You're okay with being mine still, aren't you?" I whisper the question. It's so soft, it's nearly drowned out by the sounds around us.

"You're too good for me, Chlo." His hand covers mine and I can see in the depths of his eyes he doesn't believe that something so simple is all I need.

"It's all I've ever needed," I speak without thinking, without processing anything at all. "I wasn't whole until I had you, and I don't want to be anything but yours. I don't care if you believe the truth or not, it's still true."

"It's the truth that worries me."

"The truth is you're a good man who does bad, bad things." As Bastian pulls my hand away from his jaw, I can hear him swallow. I can practically feel it myself— the hard, aching truth that I do think what he does is wrong. And I do. On some level. But there's so much wrong in this world, I can't be bothered to let it destroy what I value most of all. "And you're mine. The only truth I just said that matters at all, is the last one."

"You still love me?" he asks as if it's a real question.

Letting a playful smile show, I tease him, staring at his lips as I say, "I love the way you kiss me." For the first time in so long, my heartbeat slows when I look back up at Bastian; it pitter-patters, it dances, it's desperately finding a new beat. It's when his eyes glance at my own lips that I realize it's been trying to beat in tandem with his.

The kiss he plants on my lips, with his hands barely holding on to mine, is soft and sweet. Everything turns to white noise and I know for a fact, this moment will last forever. To me, to anyone who ever steps foot here. They will feel it. They must. Because the world moves around us differently, refusing to let this moment go on as if it's meant to blend in, or meant to be forgotten.

My eyes are still closed when he pulls away. With a deep breath in and then out, I finally open them.

"I love falling in love with you," I whisper and barely notice how the world moves again around us.

I swear a blush colors my husband's face. It looks good on him; for all his tough exterior, a hint of vulnerability looks damn good.

He reaches up for the beer on the bar, but doesn't let go of my left hand and I don't move my right from his lap.

With an asymmetric grin he asks me casually, "You weren't already in love with me?" He can try to hide it all he wants, but I know there's a hint of fear beneath his words. How could this man ever think I didn't love him?

"I've loved you every day since that kiss," I confess to him as he lifts up the beer. When my words hit his ears, he sets the glass back down onto the bar. Staring at it, and listening as I tell him, "I love you every day and in every moment, but falling in love is something you can do over and over again."

"I want to fall in love with you every chance I get," he tells me and his voice is deep and rough, laced with a sinful desire and something else. Something pure and good. The need to be loved and to feel worthy of being loved.

Even as I bite down on my bottom lip, I smile genuinely. Snaking my ankle behind his muscular leg, I lean into him and whisper, "Then let's do it every day."

He takes a swallow of his beer before kissing me again, teasing me and I love it. He tastes like wheat IPA and something dangerous, something too tempting to ever resist.

I don't lean back as I catch a glimpse of Carter from the corner of my eye. Sebastian follows my gaze and we both watch him enter a locked door, guarded by two men who open it for him.

"I haven't said hi to Carter yet," I admit and wonder what that will be like. He's changed. We all have.

"That's his brother Jase," Bastian corrects me and I huff out a breath. "They did all used to look alike," I muster up the excuse, but Bastian doesn't seem to care. He takes my hand and my attention with it.

"Just don't stop loving me."

"I'll always love you." I speak clearly, very aware of the moment and where we are. "But don't hide anything from me. I can't live like that again. And I don't want to keep anything from you like I kept that secret."

"I have a lot to tell you then." He exhales the words. "Are you sure you want to know this?" he asks again and I just barely nod, giving him my consent to bring me into this place.

"It's not an easy story to tell," he admits to me and I already know he's telling the truth. This world is cruel and unforgiving, just as lawless as it is tragic.

"I want to know."

"Then let's start with Carter's story. Just promise me you'll still love me after this?"

"You're crazy to think I could ever not love you, Bastian. Today, tomorrow, forever."

I stare into his eyes when I speak to him, making him feel the depths of my conviction. I love this man and all he is. All that matters is that he loves me the same and that we'll be together.

SEDUCTIVE

CHAPTER 1

ADDISON

I knew when I came back here that I was making a choice. I was choosing Daniel over everything. Over the life I'd live without him and where I'd live it — far away from here and these memories.

Men like him come with those kinds of complications.

Men like him are... There are many words I could use to describe him. The most fundamental statement, though, is so easily admitted and it's the very reason I chose him.

Men like him need to be loved or the damage will consume them. More than anything. In this cruel world he's cemented into, with a tragic past and ruthless tasks ahead, he needed to be loved. He still does…

My gaze lingers on what looks like carrots or sweet potatoes, some sort of orange mush in tiny little glass jars. The packs are stacked high on the shelf. The black and white silhouette of a smiling baby stares back at me and I have to push my cart forward, listening to the quiet squeaks of the turning wheels as I think about how I ended up here.

I was reckless, that's how.

Grocery shopping with Daniel wasn't one of the things I was considering when I returned to where I grew up. I was thinking of the drugs, the violence, his brothers, and how powerful they've become. It wasn't like this back then. Not at all. It wasn't this bad. Back then, I thought they'd grow out of it one day. At least that's what I'd hoped. I didn't think they'd eventually come to rule this merciless world.

It's all surreal. Every day since I've been back has brought a fear and tension that's seeping into my every waking moment.

He knows. That's why I'm here.

Shopping for milk and orange juice feels like a sham. Like for a moment, I can maybe pretend this past week didn't happen. As if the white noise from the man on the intercom can drown out the sounds of the last six months.

"Feel like you're playing house, now?" Daniel quips as I stop and watch him settle a jar of salsa, two bags of tortillas, and a case of something else into the half-full cart. His tone is optimistic.

"I didn't say 'playing house,'" I correct him and note how cold it feels along with how dull my heart beats.

I wish I could fix my face right now; I wish I could smile and pretend like it's all fine, like they all do, but it's not and I'm finding it difficult to hide it from him. Especially after what just happened. I could deal with it; I was dealing with it. But things change. And the past month changed everything.

He doesn't hide a damn thing from me anymore, so it'd be unfair to hide from him. But what's left for him to see isn't what I want to be there.

I'm still staring blankly at the case beneath the bags of chips when his muscular forearm cuts off my vision. His strong hand wraps over mine on the handle of the cart and his other grips my chin, lifting it up. I have to look away from his rolled-up sleeve and into his dark eyes. With his rough stubble in need of a shave, and his hair messy on top, he looks as rough as I feel. Rough looks damn sexy on Daniel Cross though. It always has; it's who he's meant to be.

"I know it's been hard," he says, and his voice is low and calm, his gaze soft and comforting.

"Hard?" I force a smile to my lips as the bottom one wobbles and he looks past me, dropping his grip on my chin. I'm quick to reach out and take his hand though. I just need to feel him. "I'm sorry," I tell him quickly. That's what I am: sorry, pathetic, weak. The list goes on. I knew what he had become. What *they* had become. And I still chose to come back. I did this. It was my fault. But a lie slips out instead. It's easier to deal with it if I lie to myself the way he lies to me. "I didn't know what I was coming back to and it's been..."

"Hard," he answers for me.

"Stressful," I correct him and the tension grows tenfold between us. I look up to my right when I notice motionless figures and feel their eyes on us. My own are pricking, distraught from what's happened and how much I'm losing.

I can hear the harsh swallow Daniel makes and I watch the cords in his neck tighten as he holds my hand in his. He lifts my hand to his lips and then kisses my knuckles. One by one.

"It'll be okay," he whispers against my skin, and all the warmth from those words travels through me, calming me. Making me feel lighter, as if I believe him wholeheartedly.

It doesn't change what happened.

Nothing can ever change what happened, but we

have a choice about how we handle it. I'm starting to think I made the wrong one.

That's why I hold his hand longer than he holds mine. That's why I stand there watching him leave when he tells me he's getting the rest of what's on the list and says for me to just get the bread. I don't miss the depth in his eyes, the distance that lingers. Every day, he's farther away from me. He knows. He can feel it too. It's like the slow unraveling of thick twine. It's obvious and torturous to watch.

It wasn't this way when we were just teenagers. It wasn't like this at all.

The power he and his brothers now have comes with violence I've never seen before and a harshness that's required to survive. Shopping for fucking groceries is his way of showing me it's normal, it's okay, that life is more than that brutal side of the Cross brothers and what they do.

I can't look past the darkness though. It's never going to feel "okay." This sense of danger that lingers in my blood is always going to be there.

I have to find my place with it. That's not something he can help me with. I have tried. I thought I was there. I was wrong.

It's caused damage I can't take back. That's what hurts the most. I can't take this last month back.

"You all right?" A deep baritone voice from behind me startles me. With a quick intake of breath and my hand reaching up to my rapidly beating heart, I turn around to see a man standing there. He's older, maybe in his late forties. Kind eyes with gentle lines surrounding them meet mine.

It takes me a moment to realize when he arches his brow that he's waiting for my response.

With a few blinks to bring my mind back to the present and a shake of my head, I tell him, "Fine, sorry."

I push my cart forward thinking I'm blocking his path, but he doesn't have a cart and he doesn't seem to have any intention to move either. His boot-clad feet are firmly planted and my eyes move from them, up his dark-wash jeans and button-down white shirt to his questioning gaze.

"I'm fine." My voice is stern and carries a harshness I don't like to use with strangers when I repeat myself; this guy needs to stay the hell out of my business.

When he crosses his arms, I can tell he has some muscle to him. The cotton fabric tightens around his biceps, just as my hands do on the handle of the cart. There's an air to him that changes, a knowingness about him that sends a chill down my spine.

It's a look I recognize. It's a look I don't like. The type of look that makes me want to run.

"I don't think you are fine," he challenges and the bitterness of having this man judge me creeps into the snide response I'm ready to spit out at him. He continues, stopping my words and any breath I was daring to take. "I know he's a murderer. I know he killed your foster father. And it looks like you're having a difficult time dealing with things... just from my perspective, Miss Fawn."

That prick that has crawled slowly down my spine flows over my body in a single wave, nearly buckling my knees. I can feel the color drain from my face. Slowly, just like the twine fraying and unraveling. I don't know who this man is, but I know damn well I shouldn't be talking to him.

I have to concentrate on keeping my breathing steady — in and out — and focus on not reacting.

Murderer.

My foster father.

Daniel didn't kill him.

My eyes dart to the man and I try to hold his prying gaze.

My head wants to shake just slightly, it wants to deny what he's saying, but it can't. I can't react. I can't show him a damn thing.

Daniel didn't murder him though. That happened years ago. Before I ever even thought of leaving this place, before everything else happened. I want to speak the words, the need to defend Daniel pushing the words toward the tip of my tongue.

I bite down on the inside of my cheek instead, screaming in my head to stay silent. But silence brings questions. Not just mine but also this man's.

I've never questioned my foster father's death. It was a burglary. That's what the news said.

The Cross brothers are good at covering things up. I've heard and seen things though. Especially recently.

I know what Daniel's capable of and what he'll do out of anger. I know he loved me back then. What my foster father did... That's the second reason I stay bitterly quiet, even as the questions choke me. I hate even thinking of that man. I was only a child and he was a predator. I'd rather spit on his gravestone than mention his name.

The third reason I keep biting the inside of my cheek until I taste a tinge of blood is the most important. The man who stands silent in front of me knows more than I do. I may be the sorry excuse for a woman Daniel's chosen to be his wife, but I'm not stupid. I'm smart enough to know when to keep my mouth shut. So I do. I stand there, waiting to see if a threat comes.

Near silence reigns with only the steady hum of the coolers behind us as I stare back at him.

After a moment, his lips kick up into an asymmetric

smile. "Did you not know?" he questions but doesn't wait for a response. "Maybe you didn't know then, but you know now." His eyes narrow as he nods, persuading me to believe him.

"Who are you?" It's the first question I imagine Daniel asking when I tell him what happened.

"Cody Walsh. Your boyfriend knows who I am."

"Fiancé," I correct him.

His forehead scrunches when he stares down at my hand, the one lacking a ring, and subconsciously, my thumb runs over my ring finger.

"Congratulations," he comments. His demeanor has completely changed with every passing minute that he scrutinizes me, trying to determine where my place is in this world.

Truth be told, I have no idea what he'll find; I'm still trying to figure that out myself.

"Addison Fawn … soon-to-be Addison Cross," he says but doesn't infuse any type of emotion into the statement. It's only matter-of-fact. "Any relation to Bethany Fawn?"

Confusion travels over my face as I try to recall a Bethany of any sort.

"Oh, you don't know that either? She's the woman Jase, your fiancé's brother, has been seeing." Again, I don't answer, and I try to keep from giving him any response in my expression. He only smirks as he walks past me, letting me know to tell Daniel he said hi.

"Will do," I manage to bite out without an ounce of resentment as I accept his challenge.

I didn't know Daniel's brother was seeing anyone. I sure as hell don't know a Bethany *Fawn*. Apparently, I don't know a lot of things.

What I do know is already destroying me.

CHAPTER 2

DANIEL

A hint of lemon in the wood polish invades my lungs as I breathe in deep, gripping the armrests of the wingback chair.

I can't look at my brothers, neither of them. I'm breaking down. The farther away Addison is, the worse I crumble. If they look too closely, if I speak too loudly, they'll see every fucking crack.

Too bad I can't help myself during this bitch of a conversation.

"We have a soft truce." Carter's voice is calm, but he knows my reaction will be anything but.

"Fuck that," I say, letting the darkly spoken words

fall without looking at either him or Jase. I stare past my brother and into the woods that line the property through the paned window behind him. The shades of green blur as my blood heats with anger.

"He stays out of our way and we give him details. That was the truce." Carter speaks in time with the tapping of the pen in his hand on the desk.

"Going up to Addison and scaring her isn't exactly staying out of our way."

"He scared her?" he questions me and I don't have time to push out the snide remark: *How the fuck else should she feel?*

"Maybe we pissed him off with the last deal? We didn't exactly keep our word," Jase says carefully, and I can feel him watching me, gauging my reaction with every syllable, but I use everything in me to stay still and not give them any more than I already have.

Leaning forward, my throat is dry as I speak clearly to both of them. "He walked up to my soon-to-be wife. He tried to get to her, to get in her head." My back hits the chair as I force myself to stay seated and not turn over every piece of furniture in my brother's office. "He left like a coward before I could get my hands on him. I want his fucking head!" My pulse races as I lose control with the last sentence.

We own this town. We own the cops.

Cody Walsh is supposed to be easy. He's supposed to be predictable. All that went to shit last month. Just like everything else.

Carter ignores me, or at least he ignores my anger to instead direct his comments to Jase. "If Walsh is pissed about what we did, he'll get over it. We do what we have to." Facing me and hardening his voice, he asks me, "What exactly did he say to her?"

"That we killed that prick. That he knows I'm a murderer and he knows she's not okay."

"That's how he said it?"

Carter's constant questioning makes me inhale sharply as I straighten my shoulders and stare him down, not giving him a single word in response. Not trusting myself to speak.

"He still needs us." Carter speaks first.

"And we still need him," Jase reminds us all. It's his ass on the line. This is all his fault. His sloppy choices made us take the deal with Walsh.

Although Carter's talking to Jase, the statement is directed at me. "Until we find the footage he's blackmailing you with, his head stays on."

My blunt nails tap along the polished wood in a soothing rhythm, so at odds with what I feel. "And what am I supposed to do in the meantime? Let him scare her? Let him get to her?"

"No," both Jase and Carter say at the same time. My eyes dart between the two of them, judging their response for sincerity until I can nod.

With my thumb brushing against the fleshy tips of my fingers, I ask Carter, my older brother and the one I rely on in order to move forward every day in this shit of a mess we've gotten ourselves into with a dirty cop, "What can I do?" I feel weak asking them rather than acting. I hate this and I know they can feel the turmoil rolling off of me in waves as I close my eyes and try to loosen my tight throat. "I need something to give her. Something to make all this better." *There's nothing to make it better*, a voice hisses inside my head and I lean forward, burying my face in my hands. I grit out the words between my clenched teeth as I add, "I fucking hate this."

"For now, I'll remind Walsh that our women will be respected and they stay out of it—"

"She said..." I have to swallow the hard lump in my throat before continuing as I stare past him again at the ambers and emeralds of the trees. "She said he seemed concerned, then he was... gauging her. He's trying to flip her."

"Concerned?"

"She isn't handling the recent events well." I can barely get out the words. Each syllable claws the back of my throat before it's spoken. "He approached her, she said, because she didn't look like she was doing well."

The leather behind Carter groans and protests as he readjusts in his chair opposite the desk from me.

"If he thinks she's a weak spot, he's wrong," I tell him and there's more defensiveness in my cadence than I wanted. "She would never tell anyone anything."

"No one thinks she would."

"That's why he brought up the foster fuck? You think he was gauging her to see if it was true? To see if she knows anything?" Jase asks.

"That's what she thinks," I answer him. "If he's trying to get more dirt on us, we need to end this now. Finish him."

"He can't know for sure about her foster father, how many fucking years ago was it? And Addison would never give anything up."

"How did he know?" I question them. It happened a decade ago. No one ever knew. It was only us.

"Forensics, maybe evidence." Jase sounds suspicious but shakes his head at the thought and shrugs as he adds, "Maybe word on the street, but I don't see how."

"He's bluffing. He had a hunch and he's testing us to see if we'll play into his hands."

It's quiet as the information is digested. This balancing act is getting harder and harder. What was once planks of wood feels like a thin tightrope now.

Carter takes a deep inhale before speaking. "Let's make him feel comfortable. That's the only way we can use him until we're safe to get rid of him."

Make him feel comfortable... I'm seething inside. This isn't the way things used to be. It's complicated and every move we make only gets us deeper and deeper into bed with the devil.

"Did you tell Addison about her father—" Carter starts to ask, but stops and corrects himself. "Foster father?"

I simply nod before replying, "Last night when she told me."

I remember the way she couldn't look me in the eyes before I told her. The way she turned her back to me to go to the bathroom. The way her knuckles turned white as she stood there gripping the doorknob, not moving but not asking. She wanted to know, but she knows better than to ask. That's what we decided. I tell if she asks, but she never asks. She doesn't want to know. "I told her because I thought she'd want to know the truth."

"It's been years."

"A decade."

"She never even considered it was us back then." I repeat my thoughts, but out loud now. "No one did."

"What did she say?" Jase questions, concern clearly written on his face.

The vision returns to me of her eyes closing slowly, her chin dropping as she took in a shuddering breath. Her response came out as nothing but a whisper and then she closed the door to the bathroom, leaving me sitting there, watching the glass knob and wishing it had been my hand she was holding when I confessed.

"She said, 'thank you,'" I tell them.

"Do you think she gave anything away to Walsh?"

"No," I say and my answer is hard as I glare at Jase. He stares back, unmoving, but there's sympathy in his expression.

"He can't prove anything," Carter says between us, cutting through the thinly veiled tension.

"Since when do we let someone make us feel threatened?"

"Since he has evidence that will put me away for life," Jase answers me. "We tread carefully until Declan can find something on him and get rid of every shred of proof Walsh has."

"He's digging into everything he can so we'll work with him," Carter says, then clears his throat and sits back farther in his chair. "I'll send him a message, letting him know not to go near Addison and that his concern is unwarranted."

"A message?"

"It's the safe—"

Anger forces me to rise from my seat. "A fucking message?"

"Calm down."

"You aren't the one who lost a baby! I lost my child." The strength in my voice is all but forgotten as I voice it for the first time. They already know, but I haven't said it yet. I haven't had the audacity to breathe that truth to life. "Your wife is still pregnant. Mine isn't." Everything cracks. The air, my voice, my damn insides shatter to brittle shards.

They sit there in silence as I slowly retake my seat. *Just breathe. Calm down.* How can I do either when everything is falling apart?

Jase's firm hand squeezes my forearm as he tells me, "I know it's difficult on her; we need to keep her safe and protected."

"It was stress. That's what the doctor said. She lost the baby and this bullshit isn't stopping. It's getting worse."

All that surrounds me is silence. All that lingers inside of me is guilt. I don't know how to fix this, and I don't think anyone else knows either.

"She isn't supposed to know anything. That was our deal. But she sees how tense everyone is. She knows how much danger we've been in. She's witnessed shit firsthand... I don't think she can handle this. She wasn't supposed to know any details. That's what she wanted." The admission flows from me like a Catholic at church. Safe in the confessional, waiting to hear my penance, praying for it all to be okay. *Just tell me what to do to make it all right.*

"Maybe that's the problem," Carter suggests, and I lift my blurred gaze to his dark one.

"What?" At least my question is presentable.

"Maybe she should know," Jase says before Carter. "Maybe if she knew details, she'd feel like she has more control. Control is a damn good way to deal with stress. Even if it's only in details and not action."

I don't have time to answer; a knock at the door interrupts the conversation. It's a soft rap, quick but firm.

Before Carter can tell whoever it is to come in, the heavy door creaks open, bringing with it the light from the hall, and Addison's shadow spills into the room before she does. Her hand stays on the edge of the door when she asks, "Is it all right if I come in?"

My brothers don't answer for me, but I nod once.

The room's so quiet I can practically hear her swallow as she steps into it, not shutting the door for privacy. "I just remembered something. Something I didn't tell you." Our eyes lock as she wrings her fingers around one another. Her hair's still damp from the shower, making it look darker than her dirty-blonde should be. Her lack of sleep is just as evident. Still, she's beautiful.

She clears her throat, staring at the intricately woven rug beneath the desk and stopping a small distance from me in her bare feet.

Her small form clothed in loose pajamas is at odds with the three of us. She belongs here though. She is my counterpart in every way. I only wish I didn't hurt her like I do.

"He brought up my last name," she finally says clearly. Her admission makes a deep crease settle in my forehead.

"Fawn?" I question and that gets Jase's attention.

She nods, glancing between Jase and me. "He asked if I was related to Bethany." She speaks directly to Jase as if he'd have an answer, but he wears the same expression I do.

"I never really knew my family, so... I don't know." The insecurity in her tone is undeniable, as is her curiosity.

"You should ask her," Jase comments. "We can have dinner tomorrow night."

"That would be good for us," Carter agrees. "I'll ask Aria if she's up for cooking." All the while I stare at Addison, waiting for her to give me some sign that she's all right.

Anything. I need something from her.

"I'll ask her," Addison quickly speaks up, then adds, "I'd like to talk to her anyway." A weak smile lingers on her lips as my brothers nod in agreement. It's quiet for a moment and I can see the questions in her eyes.

"Anything else?" I prod.

"Were you talking about Walsh?"

My brothers stay quiet. They handle their relationships the way they want and I do the same. I seem to be the only one failing though. "Do you want in on the details?" I always ask. She knows when something's wrong, when I'm worried. When things have gone to shit. I'd never make her an accessory, but I'll give her what I can if she wants it.

"No," she answers, and her smile turns tight, forming a straight line before she drops her hands to her sides and says she'll head out to talk to Aria.

"How are you doing, Addie?" Jase asks her before she can leave.

"Better. I think I just needed a hot shower." Time passes with a click of the clock, a second that waits for what else is on her mind. A piece of me is dying to scream for her to speak up. To ask. The piece that wants to tell her everything. The other part of me, the bigger part, wants to shield her.

She leaves as quickly as she came, which is probably

for the best.

The less she knows, the less stress she'll have. She doesn't need to worry about this shit. It's our mess. Not hers.

I need to fix this. I just don't know how.

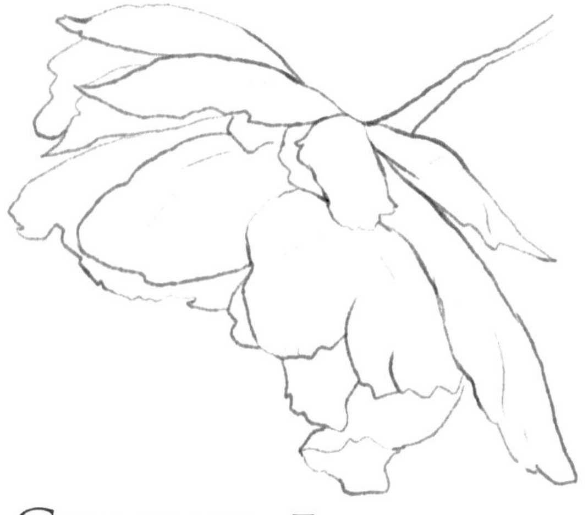

CHAPTER 3

ADDISON

Cody Walsh. A million questions linger in my mind after looking up his name online all last night. More questions scream in my head when I think about what Daniel confessed. They killed a man years ago who deserved to be hurt. They killed him because of what he did to me. They *killed* him.

How many moments have gone by where I've mentioned my childhood in passing? Or lack thereof, rather. We talked about how I was in home after home. When we found out I was pregnant, it was all I could think about. All I could talk about.

I was worried I wouldn't know how to be a good

mother, because I never had one. It opened the floodgates for all those memories. When I was young, I didn't even think I'd ever be able to get pregnant. Just the thought makes my stomach churn; it's because of what he did to me. The doctors said the scar tissue on my cervix could make it harder to open. I had problems and complications. All the aftermath of the man who was supposed to take care of me.

I brought it up maybe three or four times in the last two months when we found out I was pregnant. I couldn't *not* talk about it. No matter how much I hate to go back to those times in my life.

Daniel had so many opportunities to tell me, but he never did.

I never asked, but how would I have even known to question it? Fear has been replaced by something else. Something larger than it. A dying need to know.

"Hey." Aria's tone is already consoling when she greets me, ripping me from my thoughts as I place the heavy porcelain plates on the counter.

I didn't expect to feel this way toward her. There's a gap between us now, when only weeks ago, nothing separated us. Now I'm careful with what I say and how I say it. I'm careful I don't put this sadness on her. Just like she's careful with me now.

"How's it going?" she asks.

I can hear the emotions in her voice just as easily as the clank of the dishes. The sympathy, the guilt I know she feels because she's still pregnant when I'm not. She and Chloe, Sebastian's wife, are carrying so well. *Glowing* is the correct term. And then there's me, dull with a forced smile as I turn to her, leaning the small of my back against the granite counter.

"Hey, yourself," I answer her with enough pep in my voice to lighten the tension. I don't want anyone to feel sorry for me. It's life. It's death. It's whatever fate has in store. I don't want her to look at me and feel pity. I'd rather she look at me and see how happy I am for her.

That's one shining light in all this darkness.

"We're cooking for everyone tonight, if you're up for that?" I ask her.

"Family dinner tonight?" Aria eyes me curiously as one perfectly plucked eyebrow arches. She knows something's up, but she doesn't ask. She used to always ask.

"Does that mean something's going on?" Chloe asks as she enters, the faint sound of bags rustling carrying through the kitchen with her. Her husband is best friends with Carter and his right-hand man, but she doesn't live in the main house of the estate like the rest of us. She and Sebastian have a place deeper in the woods; it's still protected though. At first, I thought it was sweet for all of us to live so close. But the more I think about it, the fact that we need to be protected, the more it startles me.

I watch as she sets a large brown paper bag down on the table, her belly protruding, round and an obvious sign that she's in her second trimester.

Taking off her light jacket, she lays it across the chair and then smooths her flowing cream blouse down her front.

"Carter told Sebastian and he told me," Chloe says, answering the unspoken question. "I brought everything for cheesecake," she adds easily with a genuine smile. She doesn't look at me like I'm broken, but that's because she doesn't know me well. She doesn't see how off I am like Aria does. She can't tell that I'm damaged goods because she doesn't know what I was like before. It's comforting, really.

"So?" she questions. "Is something going on?"

"What do you mean?" I have no idea what she's referring to. "Something is always going on."

"Well, have you guys been doing family dinners where this is normal, or is this a way for the guys to keep us in line?"

"I never thought about it like that." The murmured words are accompanied by a deep line settling into my forehead as I consider it.

"If something's up, Bastian better tell me," Chloe

comments as she unloads the contents of her bag on the table.

"No, nothing's up. It's a little tense right now. But no more than usual. The only thing eating at Carter is a cop who's getting to Jase. He caused a little stir yesterday."

"How do you know for sure?" I ask her.

"Carter keeps me updated. We have a little ritual. It calms him and keeps his head clear to talk things out."

"I can't imagine how that could be calming." I don't realize I've spoken until the words are out there and the room goes quiet.

Chloe's huff is amused when I look at her with wide eyes. "You'd be surprised how much a conversation is worth." Her gaze falls for just a moment, but I see it happen. The haze of a smile falls along with it. "How have you been?"

Aria's been popping grapes in her mouth, but she pauses when Chloe ventures into *that* territory. Her bump isn't so visible. Our babies would have been about a month apart.

It's hard to contain the deluge of emotions.

"You can say it sucks. Or that it hurts. Or that you're better or worse... You can tell me to shut my mouth too and mind my own damn business," she offers after rattling off a list of appropriate responses.

I feel like it's my fault. Like I should have known better. I say the words in my head, because I can't admit them.

Not to Aria and Chloe. Not to Daniel. I don't even want to know that's how I feel. But I do.

"We should make dinner," I suggest in a whisper. "Just because I'm suffering a loss doesn't mean I can't be happy for all we have," I add and Chloe gives me a small smile that doesn't reach her eyes.

"The dinner for the non-worrying mob wives," Chloe jokes.

"We are not the mob." Aria hisses the admonishment before eating another grape. "It's been hectic and there's always something to worry about, but—"

I don't want the tears to fall, but I can't hide them. My face is hot and my breath comes in short pants. The next inhale is harsh, and with it, both women come to me. "I'm sorry," I say, and my words are strangled as I rush past them for a napkin on the table so I can stop it all.

"Don't say that. Don't be sorry for crying. I've always thought that was the silliest of things."

"It's good to cry." Aria's voice is so soothing. She is my rock in all of this. She's steady and we share so much in common. She grew up in this life though. She didn't run away from it all. "Sometimes crying — showing mourning, showing vulnerability — leads to the best things."

I respond with the one truth the last six months has taught me and say, "You can't be vulnerable in this world."

She counters my statement as I swipe the napkin

under my eyes, drying them, calming my breathing and feeling foolish all over again.

"Of course you can," Aria corrects me. "We all are. Trying to hide that isn't going to fool anyone." She emphasizes, "We're all vulnerable."

All I have in response is a sniffle and then I rest my head on her shoulder. "I didn't mean to cry though; I don't want you to think seeing you guys makes me sad." I can barely get the statement out, because it's not entirely true. Still, I don't want them to think it.

We hide truths like that, don't we?

"So, weird thing," I blurt out, cutting off Chloe, who no doubt has something sweet to say, and instead I help her move all the items on the table to the counter as I speak. It's back to business, back to cooking for this non-worrying dinner. "Did you know Jase has a girlfriend?" I ask them and my tone is so much peppier than I feel. I heard once though, if you speak like you're happy, you'll start to feel like it.

"Carter told me a couple of days ago. She's funny but with a dry sense of humor and she's very blunt."

"Sounds delightful," Chloe jokes.

"She's also coming to dinner, I think."

Aria eyes me before grabbing a large bowl from the lower cabinet and I take that as my cue to unwrap Chloe's cream cheese.

Looks like the dessert will be done before the actual meal at this rate.

"Bastian also mentioned she's a nurse. Should be good to have one of those in the family."

"Family," Aria says and rolls her eyes.

"I didn't mean in a mob way."

"Her last name is Fawn," I comment to no one in particular and unwrap the next bar of cream cheese. "I wonder if she knows if we're related."

"Like biologically? Or from... Is your last name your mother's or did you get that from a...?" Aria stops mid-thought and it's then that I realize from the look on her face that she was going to say *foster family* but stopped herself because she thought it would hurt me to hear it. She stopped herself because she knows about the fresh wounds.

She knows because Carter told her.

Or maybe she's known since I came back. I wonder if Carter told her everything all the way back then.

"You know I still love you, right?" I question Aria and quickly add, "And that I'm happy for you, both of you?" I look between them both, hoping they know it's true. I may be held together by glue and tape and questioning my decisions, but I know I'm happy for them.

"I know," Aria answers with kind eyes. She repeats, "I know."

CHAPTER 4

DANIEL

Tyler always hid it from her. He was good at it though.

Tyler's all I can think about as we sit down at the table. Three brothers and a friend. One brother late, as per usual. Another never coming to a family dinner again.

He didn't have this problem with Addison. He was good at hiding it. He hid so much from her; I just don't know how he could do it.

"The candles are a nice touch," Addison says and smiles warmly at Aria, who does a small curtsy and the three girls let out a peal of feminine laughter.

Addison's is short, genuine. But it disappears

quickly. It's like the warm water of the ocean, splashing on the tips of your toes before retreating all too soon. I miss it already. I find myself staying still, wanting it to come back.

The day must've gone well for her. With a glass of wine in her hand and a beautiful flush in her cheeks, she's unwinding with the help of the alcohol.

"Just let me smell one more time," Aria says and inhales close to the large goblet at the same time Carter wraps his arm around her waist and pulls her into his lap. Another wave of giggling leaves the women and then is replaced by soft hums as the other two women are kissed and kiss back, falling into their seats for dinner.

Mine's already seated, and when I look to her, her lips are on the wineglass. So instead of kissing her, I place my hand over hers on her lap. My fingers slip into the spaces between hers, feeling her soft skin, her warmth. Before she places the glass back on the table, her fingers close around mine, bringing them closer together, and she doesn't let go. Not until the large bowl of antipasto salad is passed.

"Looks delicious, ladies." Sebastian's compliment is rewarded with a story from Aria about how she learned a new recipe for the main dish.

Lasagna, candlelight, and delicate dishes, the hum of chatter and constant smiles. Everything in the room is full of life, but that's not how I feel. It's not the reality I'm living in.

If Tyler were here though, he'd fit right in, and that would help Addison. He was good at hiding. He would have been good for her.

I wash the thought away with a single swig of the bourbon in front of me. I try to tell myself he's on my mind because of what happened recently. And not because I truly think Addison would be better off if he were still here.

It's not like before. Nothing is. I have to remind myself of that sometimes. The memories of what used to be, the reminder of Tyler and what life was like back then...it's an ebb and flow of past and present. We're better now. So long as we're together. I won't let anything change that.

Reaching up onto the table, Addison's grasp is small and comforting when she lays her hand on my wrist. It's a shock to my system to feel her touch in this moment.

"You okay?" Her question is soft and murmured so no one else can hear.

"Fine," I answer her because it's automatic. I don't tell her more because she doesn't ask. She doesn't let go like I expect her to though. She eats with her left hand, leaving her right on mine. And I leave my hand just where it is, needing to feel that warmth, needing to feel her to make all this regret go away.

So long as I have her, it's all okay. I just need to know I still have her.

ADDISON

He's supposed to be the strong one.

The man is supposed to be the rock. That's what the world leads you to believe, but I think it's bullshit. Why else would I feel more complete, more grounded when I'm trying to hold Daniel together?

Aria and Chloe put a Band-Aid over my pain. They make me forget temporarily, and that's worth something. They make me feel like it's normal to be down right now, and that's worth even more.

But holding on to Daniel, holding him together, that feels like purpose. It feels like belonging and worthiness. One small touch, and it's like the pieces have been soldered back together, making them stronger than they ever were before.

Even if it is just holding his hand and smiling with his family, *my* family.

"Where's Bethany?" Aria asks and my eyes dart to hers

although she's slipping her fork into her mouth with her focus on Jase. I know she's asking for my benefit though.

"She couldn't come tonight, but she'll be here tomorrow. She's getting some things adjusted."

"Adjusted?"

"She went through a hard time."

His answer quiets the room for a moment until I speak up. "I'd like to meet her."

Daniel's hand shifts under mine until the back of it is to the table and his palm is against mine.

"I bet you would," Carter comments with the hint of a smile.

"You'll like her," Jase says after a quick drink from his tumbler. The ice clinks as he sets it down on the table. "I don't know anything about what Walsh said, but she may know. If not, you'll still find plenty to talk about."

"Walsh." I roll my eyes as I say his name and take a sip of wine as I feel everyone's eyes on me. The nervousness in the room creeps up a notch. The dark red is sweet, with a hint of lingering decadence. I bring my gaze to Carter's at the head of the table and tell him simply, "He doesn't like me much, I don't think."

"He doesn't like me much either." Jase's response comes with a huff of a laugh from Sebastian as he sits back into his chair with ease, resting an arm over Chloe's chair behind her shoulders.

"He has poor taste then," I offer Jase and that gets me a small laugh from Chloe and her husband. Daniel only observes and half of all my senses are focused on him, focused on me. Everyone's waiting to see if I'm going to break down again. I can feel it. They're waiting to see if I'm okay. And I'm not, I know I'm not. But isn't it okay if I'm not all right?

It sounds like a paradox, but I think it's more real than anything.

Carter takes a deep breath, then says, "He's not going anywhere soon, but he'll get on board. Or I'll take care of it." His darkly spoken words are overshadowed by Jase's.

"He will," Jase adds and then tells me he's sorry that I felt uncomfortable yesterday. That it never should have happened. He tells me he'd never let anything happen to me. None of them would.

They say we're family, and I know we are.

There's a pit in my gut though when Aria speaks. "Don't worry, Addie, we're in this together."

"Right," I say and nod in agreement, then thank God when I bring the glass up to finish the small pool of wine in it when she tells me, "Nothing bad can happen if we're in it together."

The glass hides my immediate reaction.

I don't know why she says it when she knows that's not true. Bad things happen regardless. Bad things have already happened.

When I set my glass down, I smile at her instead of saying just that. The words still exist though. I can feel them in the tense air. I think everyone can.

Until Chloe stands up abruptly and remembers the cheesecake. She's sweet enough to bring the rest of the bottle in for me too.

"I can't get tipsy with both of you out of commission," I tell her, not wanting to keep drinking in front of them.

"Please, have a glass for me," Aria requests with a yawn.

"I already did," I remind her. The wine was her idea, and not a bad one.

"Then have another one for me." Chloe's cheerful with her pleading eyes and faux pout as she holds out the bottle.

"Well, how can I say no to that?" I jokingly respond to cut the tension in the room more than anything else.

Another round, a plate of sweets, and the story of how Chloe and Sebastian came to be a couple turns the night around. That and the fact that Daniel pulls me into his embrace. My right side is pressed to his hard, toned body, and his stubble gently scratches my hair as he sets his chin on my head and then kisses my crown.

Maybe it works both ways. Back and forth. The rock thing. That makes it difficult, though, when both people are breaking apart.

CHAPTER 5

DANIEL

Her laugh is addictive. It's my drug. The way her cheeks flush, the way her back arches just slightly and her shoulders shake so gently—it all soothes something inside of me that I don't even know is broken until that sweet sound seeps into the crevices and calms the hurt that follows me every day.

That's how I knew I loved her.

The sad, pretty girl who was always around when we were kids smiled easily enough. It wasn't real though. It was a smile that wanted to be more. She wanted to laugh.

And everything inside of me wanted to hear it. I *needed* to hear it.

Just like I needed to hear it tonight. Everyone else's laugh turns to white noise, just like the clinking of the silverware on empty plates and the dull hum of Aria saying something to Carter. All I can hear is Addison's laugh. All I can watch is how her shoulders curl in, and instinctively, her hand finds my lap.

I'm quick to catch it with my own, to squeeze it gently. When she leans into me, humming a small good night to Chloe as she leaves, I kiss her hair and try to memorize everything about this moment.

It's perfect like this. This is how it should be all the time. She should laugh every day. She should smile and reach out to me while she catches her breath with the soft murmur of happiness lingering on her lips.

Every day.

It's easy to say we're broken. It's easy to feel the pain. To hold on to this though — the moments I feel what's really between us — to let ourselves feel it, that's the easiest thing I can do, and the hardest just the same.

"Night." Carter's voice is accompanied by a tight squeeze of my shoulder as they walk behind us.

Addison makes a move to clean up the dishes but Jase reaches for them first, clearing the table and collecting the few remaining dishes in one stack balanced in his left hand. "I got this," he says with a smirk and winks at her. "You cook, we clean."

"Thanks," she tells him and he tells us good night, exiting the room, leaving us to head to bed.

The sound of an empty room is the worst sound. I've spent too much of my life in quiet spaces.

"You had a good time tonight." I hold Addison's hand as we walk, not wanting to let her go just yet. There were good moments and bad ones too, but I don't mention the tense ones.

Carter or Jase...whoever it was who thought to have the dinner tonight, was right. We never had dinners growing up, not like this. Not after our mom died and everything happened. I could hardly stand to walk into the eat-in kitchen, let alone sit at the table with hope like I did tonight. "We should do it more often."

"Yeah. It was fun," she tells me as we walk down the quiet hall to our wing. The walls are decorated with her photographs. Moments she thought were worthy of capturing on film. Before we get to the bedroom, she stops, lifting her hand from my grasp to touch the edge of a carved black frame mounted against the walls, which are painted a pale dusty blue.

"This one's my favorite of the ones I took while we were away," she says softly.

Her fingertips trace over the glass and down the alley that led to the bar where she first saw me again after so many years had passed.

While we were away. Is that the way she thinks of it?

"I think I like the others better."

"What others?" she says and turns to me quickly, her hair swirling from her shoulder to tumble down her back. Her genuine curiosity makes her eyes widen slightly and it forces my lips to curve up.

"The ones of you in my bed," I answer her and then quickly nip her lower lip as lust just barely reaches her eyes. My blood simmers with desire for her and the need to touch her always.

"You're bad, Daniel Cross," she whispers playfully with passion in her voice as I open the door behind her while letting my lips caress the crook of her neck.

Her eyes are still closed when I pull back. She swallows with a gentle hum and lets her head fall back to rest against the molding that lines the bedroom door.

I find myself trapped in her words. *You're bad, Daniel Cross.*

She knew it all along. She can live with that. She can love me still, even knowing all the wretched things I've done. It's this world though, the world she fled and the world I dragged her back to, that's doing the harm.

I want so badly to blame it on that when I brush the loose strands of her hair off her collarbone with the backs of my fingers so I can kiss her there. I wish I could blame it all on this place. It's only when I stop touching her that she opens her eyes.

A hint of a smile plays at her lips when she finally looks back at me.

"Come to bed with me." I give her the command when we get into the bedroom. With the curtains parted, there's no need to turn on the light. It's dimly lit, but enough so that I can see her perfectly when my eyes adjust. I can see her standing in the doorway, slow to follow me and hesitant to do what I told her.

Hesitant to come to bed with me.

All she's thinking about is the sex. It's not because she's uncertain if it's safe; the doctor said it was last week. Our first time getting pregnant was an accident. She's questioning if we should try for a baby on purpose.

Whether or not we should try again. Whether we should use protection.

Whether she wants this like I do.

Whether she wants me still... I know that's a question that drifts into her mind when she looks at me like that.

That part of me that doesn't know it's broken until she heals me... it's screaming in pain right now.

"I think I just need to sleep. There's so much on my mind." Her excuse falters in the air as she heads to the dresser, taking off her earrings. I can hear them clink in the small ceramic trinket bowl.

"Tell me," I insist and then clear my throat, pretending

like I haven't been devastated every night she's looked at me like that and made some kind of excuse. "Tell me what's on your mind."

"I haven't processed everything."

"You can talk it out with me." I ignore the thump in my chest as I speak. The battering of something hard against my rib cage aches with every small movement.

"Like you talk things out with me?" She turns from the dresser, tense and on the angry side. She seems to realize her quick temper before I can react, crossing her arms over her chest. "Sorry," she apologizes in a hushed murmur. When did it get to be like this? Where we can't talk. The start of a conversation turns into a fight, even if we know we need each other.

Tucking her hair behind her ear, she looks me in the eyes and says, "I know you would… if…"

I close the distance between us and make my way over to finish the thought for her and say, "If that's what you wanted."

"Right," she breathes, the tension leaving her, her arms falling to her side the moment I place my hand on her hip. "It's my fault," she tells me with a harsh swallow.

"Come here," I tell her and my words come out low and rough. There's an edge that's demanding, I know there is. It's a part of me that I'm trying to soften for her. It's still a part of me though.

Falling into my chest and pressing her body as close to mine as she can, she breathes so softly I almost don't hear the admission just under my chin, "I don't know what I want anymore." I tighten my hold on her, wishing I could go back to moments ago. When she was laughing and reaching for me. She confesses, "I'm scared."

It's the first time she's shown me this raw sincerity since we lost the baby.

"It's all right to be scared." With my arm wrapped around her lower back, I splay my hand against her shoulder and rock her slightly, just slightly. She pulls back a tiny bit, only to see me, her chest to mine. I watch as the moonlight filters in from the subtle movement of the curtains, reflecting in her gaze. There's so much vulnerability there. Even now. Even after all we've been through. How much more can she take?

"Kiss me." I give her the command and her posture relaxes, her composure softening the instant her eyes close, and she stands on her tiptoes to bring her lips closer to mine. I keep my eyes open. I watch as she reaches up with both hands, twining her fingers behind my neck as she pushes her lips against mine. She doesn't hesitate this time.

"I love you," she whispers against my lips, peeking up at me through her thick lashes. The curtains sway and bring with them a sudden gust of late-night air, carrying the faint smells of early spring with them.

"I love you too," I tell her, but it's not enough. They're only words that don't compare to what I feel inside.

I'm sorry I put her through all of this. I don't admit it though, because more than sorry, I'm selfish and I wouldn't change it. That's the most fucked-up part. I can't live without her. Even knowing how it breaks her.

"Get ready for bed," she tells me with a weak smile. The smile that's not a smile. The fake one she's always had.

I'm still fully clothed, shoes and all.

The wooden floor creaks in time with her deep inhale as she turns from me and I do as she wishes, letting her take the lead although I don't know how long she'll want it.

"Tell me something and I will," I barter with her.

"I feel lonely," she tells me with her back to me and I can only watch as she pulls the sheets back, sitting on the edge of the bed.

Lonely. Lonely like the quiet halls I hate. Even though I'm right here, it's still lonely. I know she's right.

"Lonely?" I repeat as I drop my watch to the dresser, letting it fall where it may with my gaze still pinned on Addison as she strips down slowly, leaving a puddle of clothes at the side of the bed. She does it every night. She has for the longest time. In the morning, she'll gather them and drop them in the basket. When she has energy;

that's the excuse she gave me when I teased her about it before. The memory kicks my lips up into a small smirk, but it fades when I catch her profile in the dark room, the pale light showing me the lack of playfulness, the lack of happiness she's always held on to.

The months we've been back here have worn her down.

"There are moments when I'm okay but they're so fleeting. Recently," she adds quickly. "It's been a lot to take in."

"You don't like being back here, do you?" I question her and that gets her attention.

Turning to face me fully, she doesn't even bother to grab the sheets to cover herself as she answers me with shock clear in her cadence. "Of course I do." She swallows before adding, "I love your family. I've always loved them."

"Things are different now."

"We're all different," she comments without sparing a second between my statement and hers. Her gaze is bold, challenging even. "Just because things are different doesn't mean the pieces I love aren't the same."

I take my time pulling my undershirt over my head and dropping it to the dark wood floor. I strip down to nothing but my boxer briefs before climbing into bed. All the while she watches and waits.

Taking her hand in both of mine, the hand that still doesn't have a ring on it, I run my thumb across its barren finger and ask her, "Did you feel lonely before we lost the baby?"

"No," she answers me quickly and with a slight shake of her head. "It was after. Even with everyone around us... even with you, I just feel lonely sometimes. Like glimpses of loneliness. And I don't know what to do to shake it."

"You aren't alone, and this will pass."

"I know," she admits. "I know. It will pass, but I just don't know what to do in between. I don't know if I'm able to handle it all."

"Do you still want to marry me? You still want to stay here with me?"

"Yes," she answers quickly although she's just as hasty to look down at our hands. Like she spoke without thinking. Like there's a but.

"Then why no ring?" I ask her quietly and then clear my throat. "Why don't you want to wear it? I asked you to marry me weeks ago. You picked out the ring, but you don't wear it."

"Are you going to wear a ring?" she rebuts.

"An engagement ring?" She nods at the clarification. "Is that what you want? For me to wear a ring?"

Looking past me and out of the cracked window still

bringing a gentle breeze, she admits, "No."

"You have to help me understand, Addison." The frustration in my voice is clear as I run a hand down my face and reposition on the bed as I pull my hands away. "It feels like...you aren't completely here with me anymore." Admitting the words makes my chest feel tighter, makes my hands feel colder and numb.

"I'm trying to be," she admits with a single harsh swallow.

"I get wanting to wait to try again," I say, and she tries to interrupt me but I stop her with a finger over her soft lips. "I understand that. It hurts, but I get it. I get that you feel lonely, because I do too. That's what happens when you lose someone. And we did. But I don't understand not wearing my ring. I can wait for you to come back to me and deal with this together; I just need to know that you will or what to do to help you. Losing the baby... I know it's because of everything else. I know it has to do with being here and that you don't love it."

"I never said that."

"You didn't have to."

"I just don't know my place."

"It's next to me. That's your place, with me." My words are rushed and full of frustration.

She starts to speak again, but she has to close her eyes

and swallow thickly first, reaching out to me. A moment passes with an uncomfortable pang in my chest. The soft tips of her fingers run down my rough knuckles, tracing scars before she kisses them.

"I want you to wear the ring I got you." She nods once but she still doesn't speak, and she doesn't take her gaze off my knuckles. "I know it's harder, being around my family when the last time you saw them you weren't with me." My words make her still. Every piece of her is frozen as I speak the truth she doesn't say out loud. That's why she's not wearing the ring. It has to be because of that. We came back to the place where she didn't belong to me.

"You're mine now. You're going to find your place and I'll figure out how to help you. We're going to get married. We're going to have a baby one day."

The mention of a baby breaks her composure and I hold her tighter when her face crumples. Kissing her hair, I breathe the words, "I love you and you love me; there's no reason the world shouldn't know that. There's nothing to hide."

"It's not about hiding, it's...it's just everything is..." She trails off as she struggles to voice another word and attempts to move away from me, but I put my hand over hers.

"Just tell me," I say.

"It's never going to just be us. Our past...even right now. It's more than just us and I am struggling."

"Because of Tyler—"

She cuts me off before I can say more. "No. Your other brothers. Your life. *This* life." Breathing in deeper, heavier, she focuses on keeping her breathing steady as she looks me in the eyes to state, "You come with a lot of baggage, Daniel Cross. Some of it, I carry too."

"If this isn't what you want, you shouldn't have come back." I can't describe the way my blood chills and everything hardens. My jaw, my stiff back, the thump in my chest that quiets to a dull ache.

"I know, it's all my fault." The hurt in her voice reflects in her gaze.

"Stop saying that. We're in this together. None of this is your fault."

She looks like she'll say something, but all she does is nod slightly, refusing to open up and tell me what's going on in that beautiful head of hers.

"Don't keep it from me."

"I'm struggling to handle it; I need help."

"Tell me how."

"I just can't wear your ring," she confesses weakly.

"What part of not wearing my ring is supposed to help you?"

"Are you so dense, Daniel?" The contempt is

unexpected. "You gave it to me after I found out. You gave me a ring because I was pregnant. That's the only reason. And we never should have gotten pregnant. It was an accident. I wasn't ready. It's my fault!"

"Addison—"

"I'm doing my best and I'm highly aware that it's not good enough. I couldn't even carry our baby," she says, and the last two words are a strangled mess between the shuddering sob she holds back.

"Don't say that… You are more than enough." I stress my words, grasping both of her hands in mine firmly and holding her gaze with mine to steady her. "Not a damn thing is your fault. Nothing but keeping all of this from me and letting it tear us apart. You have to talk to me."

"You have to talk to me too." She whimpers the plea as her watery eyes look up to mine.

"I can do that." I'm quick to acquiesce to her request. "I can talk to you, but you have to tell me if it's too much."

"It's all too much," she admits, "but I still want it. I still want you."

The relief that blooms inside of me is instant. It's everything I needed.

"One thing at a time." I wait for her to nod at my words, to know she's listening. "You are more than good enough. You're too good for me, but I'm keeping you anyway."

"Daniel—"

"No." I don't let her interrupt me. "You got to tell me, now it's my turn to tell you."

"Okay," she whispers, her grip getting tighter as she waits.

"You are with me and I am with you. We can't let each other be lonely. I'm right here," I whisper against the shell of her ear and then plant a gentle kiss against the tender skin beneath her ear. "We're going to be okay. You're going to find your place...so long as it's right next to me. We have to talk. We can't hold it in." I'm careful with my next suggestion. "You don't know your place, because you don't know what's going on. I want to tell you. I want you to know."

"The stress..." The words leave her sounding more like a helpless question than a statement.

"I think it will help, not hurt to know. It's the not knowing that's stressful."

She doesn't respond even though I give her time to.

"Do you think you'd be all right with that? Instead of you asking, I just tell and if it's too much, you tell me to stop and I will."

"Will that help you?" she questions me. The hope in her voice is there, but it's surprising that it comes with this particular question.

I almost tell her I'm fine. I'm so close to saying just

that. Which would defeat the purpose of all of this. "Yes. It fucking kills me that I can't tell you what's eating at me."

"Okay then. New rules. You tell me everything unless I say stop." Fear and hope swirl in her glossy gaze.

"The loss is something we have to go through together and maybe we'll have moments where we feel alone, because we were wishing those moments were with the little life we never got to hold. But if you can try to remember I'm here, I hope it will help."

She swallows her words rather than responding. I keep going though. I'll take the lead and she'll follow. She has to. I don't know how this can work otherwise.

"I gave you the ring because I love you. The only reason I didn't give it to you sooner was because I wasn't sure you'd say yes. I thought I had a little anchor knowing you were pregnant. It wasn't an obligation because you were pregnant. It wasn't that, Addison. Don't think that."

She searches my expression, maybe in an attempt to determine if I'm sincere or not. It's what I deserve. Years ago, I kept everything from her, for a very long time. Our relationship started with lies, and it's carried on with secrets. She'll learn to trust me though. She has to. I won't give her any reason not to.

"I want you to wear my ring. I want you to come to bed with me, be with me again, even if you want to be safe and wait to try again. I need you, Addison."

It feels like I've emptied everything out. Leaving me hollow and waiting with nothing but the hope that she'll know this is all I've got. It's everything, every bit of me, and I don't know if it's enough but I'm damn sure going to try.

"I need you too," she finally whispers in the warm air between us, making it feel even hotter than it already is. I'm still on edge, waiting and needing more of her.

"Tell me we're going to be all right. That you're going to be all right." It's a command.

"I'm going to try," she answers, and I know it's because she wants to be honest and that she doesn't actually believe it. She doesn't know deep in her bones that it'll work. It never has before.

"You're going to succeed. You are meant to be with me, Addison. There's no way this ends otherwise. I need you and I need my family." I suck in a breath, ready to tell her if we have to, we'll leave. We did it before; we can do it again. It'll kill me, but for her, I'd do it.

"I need them too," she says, quick to cut me off. "I want this to work. Not just us; we work, and I love you, but this place. I just...I don't know."

"You don't know, that's exactly it. You don't know anything and that's the problem. I'll fix it. We'll fix this."

"I don't know that I can handle it," she confesses with

a quivering bottom lip. "I've never felt so insignificant and weak." As she speaks, her voice goes dry and cracks at the words.

"I've put you through hell, and you survived."

"They've gone through worse. Aria—"

"Don't compare your story to hers; it doesn't change your pain." She's unraveling in front of me. Six months of being here and I've never seen her like this. How did I let it get this bad? "Get on the bed. In the center."

"Daniel—"

"The bed. Get in the middle, now." I emphasize my words and slowly pull away from her, keeping my gaze pinned to hers. "You can handle it, Addison. You can take everything."

Her shoulders drop heavily as she swallows, and her chest rises faster with every breath as she stares back at me. Not moving.

"I need you, Addison, and you need me. That's why we're off, why everything feels wrong. Get on the bed."

I've never had to repeat myself. She's always listened before, and staring at her now, not knowing what she'll do, I can't breathe. I can't lose her.

"On the bed, Addison. Don't make me tell you again."

ADDISON

I've loved this man since before I knew what love was.

I've craved him, adored him, fucking worshipped him.

But never like this. An intense heat ignites inside of me, a spark hotter and brighter than the sun dances on every nerve ending in my body.

I'm paralyzed, needing to feel him take me, own me, and devour me exactly how he wants.

I need it more than he'll ever know.

Slowly, I obey, although I don't know how. Every movement is gentle and meticulous. My hands reach the center first and immediately my fingers dig into the mattress.

It's so slow. Time moves so slowly. A part of me knows it's because I'm trying to remember this moment. Remember it all and hold on to it forever. I need it in the good times and the bad. In the horrible moments, I need this. What we have right now. I wish I could just stay here forever. Being his and him being so completely mine.

Bared to him, I wait and watch. His cock is hard and ready as he strokes himself in front of me, pacing, debating what he wants me to do, what he needs from me.

All the while, those sparks tingle up and down my body in waves of want.

Instead of climbing on the bed, pinning me down,

and ravaging me, he asks me, "Why do I love you?"

His words are hoarse and at first I hear him wrong. I hear, "Why do you love me?" but I catch myself before the answer can leave me.

"I don't know," I answer him.

Instead of answering me, he tells me to spread my legs wide so he can see me.

"Fuck, I can see how wet you are from here," he breathes out deep with frustration as my fingertips run along the length of my pussy and then rub my swollen clit so he can see. A shiver of desire runs down my body from my shoulders to the tips of my toes. It's cold compared to the heat that burns between my thighs for him to enter me.

"Why do I love you?"

I close my eyes, pushing my head back into the mattress, and move my hand away, hating that I don't know what to tell him.

I don't know why people fall in love. I know why I love him though; I want to answer him that. *Ask me something I know.*

"Eyes on me. Don't you dare close your eyes." His steps are hard as he rounds the bed, getting close enough to backhand the inside of my thigh as punishment. The sting is fierce, but the touch is so needed, all I feel is a spike of desire shoot through me.

My breath is stolen from his admonishment, seething through my teeth and desperate.

"Put your fingers back on that pretty cunt of yours and look me in the eyes when you tell me you don't know why I love you." There's no hurt in his eyes, no pain in his voice, even though I feel it, deep down inside of me. Past everything physical, I feel it.

Tears prick at the back of my eyes as I let my fingers touch my warmth. His gaze parts from mine, only to watch me.

I have to give him something, so I tell him what I know. I tell him why I love him, praying he loves me the same.

"You know I've wanted you for as long as we've known each other. You know I'd risk it all to be with you."

My fingers slip just inside my entrance as I start to say the next reason, and a soft moan spills from my lips in its place.

"Fuck," he mutters. The word is a groan on Daniel's lips and hearing it makes my body heat.

"Touch me please," I beg him, but he shakes his head.

"Why else?" he asks huskily, the need showing through his intended words.

"You know that I would die without you. Whatever makes a person a person—I'd die if you weren't here anymore."

"I don't want you to ever say that again. Don't you ever talk about that. You're not allowed to die."

A short laugh that's not humorous at all bubbles from my lips. I feel crazy, on the verge of tears, feeling the pain of a great loss at the very thought that he might die. "That's my fear. It kills me, Daniel. You can't die."

"Well, for you then, I'll do my best not to," he tells me as the bed dips with his weight while he climbs over my body.

Pinning my wrists above my head, he nearly kisses my lips, but he moves to suck the arousal off my fingertips before our lips touch. The light, warm feeling is a stark contrast to his hard cock pressed into my thigh.

I try to writhe under him, but he keeps me still as he takes his time. The second he braces his forearm beside my head and positions himself, I suck in a deep breath and stare into his dark eyes.

He enters me slowly, torturously so. Taking his time to stretch me. The gentle sting elicits an instant heated wave that forces my back to arch. He doesn't stop, he just pushes in deeper and stays there, pressing against my walls and forcing my lips to form a perfect O.

Still inside of me, he tells me, "Because I want to grow old with you. I want everything you want, whatever it is, because it'll make you happy. I want my family to love you and protect you, in case something ever happens to me.

"You don't want those things unless you love that person. I love you more than I love myself, Addison. I need you to know that."

I only know I'm crying because he bends down to kiss the tears.

When his lips finally brush against mine, I steal them, kissing him hard and with the passion I have for him, for what's between us.

With his left hand still pinning my wrists down, he ravages me, a savage taking of what's his. I scream my pleasure into his mouth, letting the strangled moans take over when my climax hits me with a force I've never felt before.

It's all consuming. It's everything I've wanted and needed and the only thing I'll ever crave for as long as I live. Because it's him.

CHAPTER 6

ADDISON

"It's a pretty ring." The timid voice carries across the large kitchen. "Blue under it; that's unique. Is it a blue diamond?"

I didn't even hear her walk in. As I stirred the sugar into my coffee, watching the white swirl of steam, I was focused on the ache between my thighs and the memory of Daniel kissing me all over last night.

He only left me to get the ring from my nightstand and to put it on my finger. If this ring ever comes off my hand, it'll be because someone took it from my grave.

"It is. It reminds me of forget-me-nots," I answer her. "That's why we went with this one."

"You picked out your ring together?"

"I know it's not traditional—"

"What is anymore?" she says and shrugs. "If you haven't guessed, I'm Bethany." The smile she gives me reaches her eyes.

I laugh, short and with a single breath. It's genuine. "I guessed as much," I answer her with a smile.

It's only us in the kitchen and as she pulls out one of the tall chairs at the island, the sound carries through the open space.

"First, I want to say hi. Second, I want to say I'm sorry. Jase told me...about the baby."

My little piece of heaven splinters, but only slightly as I take my seat.

"Thank you," I answer her.

Holding on to my mug of coffee, I pull it up to my lips to keep me from saying more. The warmth billows into my face as I take a long sip, praying for composure.

I don't want to break down. Especially not in front of her, someone I don't know. This...Bethany Fawn. I don't know that I'll ever be okay with losing our baby. Especially if we never get pregnant again, if we never have a little one to hold. I don't see how it's possible. I don't think there's anything wrong with that either.

"I heard you got a ring too," I say as I lift a brow and when her gaze catches mine, I make a note of staring down at her ring finger. She pulls her hand into her chest with a blush rising to her cheeks.

"It was a shock, to be honest," she answers but the content note in her voice and the smile on her face remain the same. "We're quite different...Jase and I," she adds when I look questioningly at her.

"Yes, they are...different. That's a word for it." We could write a book about the Cross brothers and how *different* they are. There's a time and place for that conversation though. "So Jase told me your last name is Fawn?"

"It is."

"Mother or father?" I ask her and then shake my head as I let out a sigh at my ridiculousness. "This isn't an inquisition. I'm just... I'm very curious."

"It's fine," she responds and then she leans forward on the chair to rest on the counter. Her thin cream sweater is pushed up to her elbows. Paired with her dark blue jeans, it's a simple look, but something about this woman screams that she's anything but simple.

"My father's last name, but he didn't stick around after I was born."

"My father's last name as well," I tell her and feel a chill sweep over my skin.

"You're a couple years younger than me, right?" she questions me and I nod. Daniel told me what he knew of Bethany.

"A little over a year younger."

"What's your father's first name?" I ask her as my gaze sweeps over her facial features. She doesn't look like me, nothing but her lips. My father's lips.

"Jeremy," she answers, and I tell her the middle name, "Nathanial. Jeremy Nathanial Fawn."

"This is weird." Bethany pushes out the same thought I have.

"I think your dad left your mom because my mom was pregnant with me." The years make sense. "That's why you didn't grow up with him." Not that I grew up with him either. He left my mother and my mother left me.

"So he knocked up my mom and had my sister. Married her and they had me. Then he left us when I was a baby, because your mother was pregnant with you?" Bethany fills in the blanks.

"He got around, as if I needed another reason to hate the thought of him."

"My mother had substance abuse issues; I always thought that was why he left us," Bethany muses. "He was good at leaving," she comments with a crease in her forehead, as though a bad memory is creating a groove right there. "That's what my mother used to say." She doesn't try to hide the bitterness as she turns her back to me, leaving her seat so she can go to a cabinet to get herself a mug. I note that she already knows where they're kept and where everything else in the room is too.

"If it makes you feel any better, he didn't stay long and what I knew of my mother and the men she was with, it's probably best you grew up without him." With another sip of coffee, the room's quiet except for the muffled hiss of the coffee machine. I don't comment that I was a child when I knew them. Either of them.

"Yet we both received his last name," Bethany says as she leans against the cabinet and then offers me a half smile curved with sarcasm before lifting her mug and telling me cheers. "Lucky us."

"If we hadn't, we never would have known."

"We're sisters. Same father, different mother."

"Right." I nod in understanding. Curiosity nags at the back of my mind, but I can't bring myself to ask her any questions. That part of my life is long behind me. I wish it would stay in the past. I don't want to think about my father or how many other children he had.

"Do you have any other siblings?" she asks me and I shake my head no as I reply, "All I had growing up was a rotating address until I met..." I pause and wave my hand in the air. My throat's dry but I shake it off. I'm stronger because of what I went through. But that doesn't mean I want to relive it with this woman. Biological sister or not. My curiosity can wait until I'm better prepared and in a more stable state. Everything is chaos now and it doesn't look like she's going anywhere anyway.

"The Cross brothers," she answers for me. "So you knew them before all this? Back when things weren't so..."

"Yeah, but I left. I left before a lot of things happened. I left when things got bad. What a wonderful mother I'll be." All of our past history hits me at once and the same thoughts I had before, the ones that tell me I don't deserve Daniel, I don't deserve a happily ever after, and I don't deserve to be a mother come back. Weaker than before, they're only whispers and not screams. Nonetheless, they're back.

"Don't say that. You were young and you didn't know. You'll be a great mother. I hardly know you, but I know that. We'll be better than our parents."

"How can you know?"

"One, because you're already thinking about it. Already wanting more for your children. And two, because we're loved. Love does... Love changes a person.

"The best thing you can do for a child is to love them. You can ask anyone that. It's the thing they need most. If you love Daniel and he loves you, you're already off to a better start than our parents."

"God knows one thing these men do is love hard," I comment, agreeing with her and hoping she's right. "Even with all the shit they're in."

"They do," she agrees with me, casually reaching

in the fridge for creamer. As if this is only a mundane conversation and not the turning point in my life that I feel it is in my bones.

"So you're going to try again?" she asks me.

I want to tell her I'm scared. Scared to try, scared to lose. Scared I won't be good enough. But I save those sentiments for Daniel. If I tell anyone, it should be him.

So I answer simply, "Yes." I want a baby with him. A life. I want to grow old with him and be surrounded by a loving family. To love and be loved. "We're going to try again."

CHAPTER 7

DANIEL

"I just need to know." A raw hint of emotion makes Carter's voice tight. He clears his throat as he leans back in the chair. "I would understand; I just need to be prepared and we can work something out." His voice is clearer, firmer, but he still can't look me in the eyes.

"I'm not leaving. There's nothing else for me. I can't leave."

"But Addison—" he argues, already having it in his head that we need to leave.

"She doesn't want to leave either." It's quiet for a moment, then Carter finally looks at me, letting the statement sink in. "We're staying and we'll be all right."

The ticking of the clock in his office is ever present. It fills the silence until he nods in agreement.

"A lot happened," he comments.

"It will settle down. It'll slow down."

A knock at the office door accompanies his hum of agreement.

"It will," he tells me before calling out, "Come in" to whoever it is at the door.

Addison.

"Am I interrupting?" Her question is softly spoken, but it carries through the room clearly as she stands there, not in the room, but not out of it either.

"Not at all," Carter answers. His shoulders are straighter, his expression firmer. He really thought we were going to leave. He has the look of a man who'd already accepted loss.

"I was hoping to talk to both of you..." She trails off as her gaze drops to the floor nervously before peeking back up at us. "I had a thought."

A prick of uncertainty creeps along my spine as she slowly walks into the room and stops at the chair next to mine. With her grip on the back of it, she chooses not to sit as she tells us, "I want to pay a visit to Officer Walsh."

"The hell you are." My answer is immediate. And also ignored. Addison's stare is unmoving and directed at Carter.

He doesn't answer, neither of them looking at me.

"The fuck you are," I say to emphasize my position. "There's no reason for you to be anywhere near him."

"Other than the fact that I'm with you. That my place is beside you...so yeah, there is."

Carter's still quiet and the ticking of the clock is louder, just like the rush of my blood is in my ears.

"Daniel," she says, and Addison's tone is gentle.

"No. You shouldn't be concerned with this."

"I don't want to be mixed up in this, but I don't want to be afraid of this man. I don't want him to think he can get to me."

"Are you sure you want to do that? You getting involved is more..." Carter talks to her, again, ignoring me.

The irritation grows as the two of them discuss this as though it's a casual conversation.

"Stress? No. I think the stress comes from not knowing. I need to know. And if I can do something, I need to do it."

"I don't want you to—"

"To go to a police station? Where you have plenty of men in your back pocket?" Addison cuts me off and slight desperation seeps into her cadence. "I..." She pauses and swallows thickly. "I want you to think about it. Think about what I should be doing and what it would do for me." She puts her hand over mine to tell me, "I want to do this. I want to show that man who I am and that I'm with you. With all of you," she amends, giving Carter a nod.

"Just think about it." She leaves me there, my foot subconsciously tapping against the leg of the chair. The second the office door closes, I admonish my brother, "You couldn't back me up with that one?" The sarcasm is thick and unforgiving.

"You weren't lying, were you? She does want to stay."

For the first time in a long time, my brother smiles.

"If she wants to stay, then, Daniel, for the love of God, let her. Let her do what she needs to do."

CHAPTER 8

ADDISON

"Two sets of eyes are on his office in case he shuts the door."

"I know," I answer Daniel.

"If we lose sight for even a moment, I'm coming in."

"I know," I repeat and even though I'm attempting to sound agitated, I'm anything but. "You're cute when you're worried."

His short huff is humorless, coming deep from his chest as we sit in the car.

"In and out, Addison," he tells me, leaning over the console to give me a peck on the cheek. I don't kiss him back, because I'm waiting, and sure enough, he asks again.

"You sure you want to do this?"

The way he asks it melts everything inside of me. I don't answer him with words; instead I put a hand on either side of his handsome face, feeling his stubble beneath my palms, and press a gentle kiss to his lips. His dark eyes are open and staring down at me when I pull away.

"I'll be right back," I murmur.

"And I'll be right here."

As I shut the door to the car, I hear him say he's starting the clock. I have five minutes. That's what he gave me and I'm just fine with that.

If I'm going to be here with Daniel, as his wife and as a part of his family, I'm going to make sure everyone knows exactly where I stand.

Even with that confidence, my heart hammers as I walk through the dark glass doors to the station. Officer Walsh's office is upstairs on the second floor. The elevator is empty, which doesn't ease my nerves at all. I have to shake out my clammy hands and give myself a pep talk.

I'm merely planning to apologize for being caught off guard. To thank Officer Walsh for asking if I was all right and to let him know that I'm more than all right and not to question where I stand with the Cross brothers again.

Daniel and his brothers told me where Walsh's office is. It's the back-right corner office. I'm glad I know where it is and that when I finally get close, his door is open and he's right in view. Alone, unsuspecting. Just like I was when he approached me.

It's hard to give him the benefit of the doubt. That he's only a cop looking out for a woman who's mixed up with men like the Cross brothers.

I try to keep it in mind as I raise my fist to the open door and knock gently.

Words were nearly spoken as he lifts his head, but when Cody Walsh sees me, they're silenced and instead he's slow to tap the papers in his hands on the desk. "Miss Fawn."

"Officer Walsh." I speak his name pleasantly. Forgetting the pounding of adrenaline in my blood and noting that he's only a man. Nothing more than human.

"I thought I'd see you again," he comments. "Please come in."

It's quiet for a moment as I try to get ahold of my bearings.

He speaks first, easing the tension. "You'll have to forgive my first impression. I don't know what to make of the relationships they have. Your fiancé and his brothers."

"Relationships?" I question, raising a brow and deciding to make light of it. "If Daniel has more than one of me…well, no wonder he's so stressed."

The short chuckle eases the officer slightly as he leans back in his chair, but his guard is still up. Something tells me it always is.

"Have a seat," he offers, and I shake my head, telling him I was just stopping by for a quick moment.

"I'm not the bad guy, you know?" he tells me, catching me off guard.

"I didn't say you were."

"You didn't have to," he responds solemnly. "I'm still getting a read on them and you didn't seem like you were all right," he explains although he doesn't have to.

"He's not a bad guy either." And I defend Daniel, although I don't have to.

"I didn't say he was."

It's quiet for a moment and I debate saying what's on my mind. I nearly don't but I decide I may never have another chance, so I should take it.

"You shouldn't have mentioned my past. The foster… situation. Without it, you would have seemed like less of a bad guy."

"Without it, I wouldn't have known whether or not you knew."

I hum in agreement, nodding although I don't take my eyes off of his.

"What do I owe this visit to?" he asks when I go quiet, taking him in and trying to see where he falls. It changes with every passing minute. "Did you have a message for me?" he questions.

"As if I'd do their dirty work? No, I don't have a message. I'm not privy to those conversations, Mr. Walsh. As you know, I appear to be the last to know most things around here." Lying comes easier than I thought it would. In fact, I kind of like it. There's a devilish spark that riddles its way through me as he asks me, "And you're okay with that?"

I'm not okay with it. But that's one thing that's changing. Daniel's right. I need to know. I was always meant to be a part of this. I *need* this.

Reaching into my purse, I pull out a Tupperware of fresh-baked cookies.

"For you," I say while offering the small container. "I made a larger batch, but not all of them survived."

He rises out of his seat but stops short of taking them for only a moment before accepting the gift. "Snickerdoodles?"

I shrug and say, "Cinnamon makes people happy."

"You made me cookies?"

"I was having a bad day; I was short with you and I apologize."

"I apologize as well; I sometimes forget that not every conversation is an interrogation."

Looking at the clock on the wall above his head, I see

five minutes has already passed. Half of me is surprised Daniel isn't here, waiting behind me. The other half is relieved he's given me this. I can handle this, and I want him to know it.

Patting the lid of the Tupperware, I offer him a smile and say, "I hope you like them. And I hope you know where I stand now."

His statement keeps me from turning and leaving like I'd planned. "I'm just wondering what you see in him." Officer Walsh doesn't look at me with curiosity; it's simply matter-of-fact. "From what I read, you had a hard upbringing, you fell into step with a group of brothers who took care of your problems, but then you took off. You'd gotten away, you made a new life, and then you came back... Why? Why come back to this?"

"To them, you mean." It's not a question that comes from me so easily, it's a correction. "You obviously don't know them well...yet," I add. "If you knew them, you'd know why."

His chair groans as he heaves back. It gives with the pressure of his back pushing against it and then he clicks his tongue. He seems to debate his words and then he jokes, of all things, lightening the tension, "It's because he's good-looking, isn't it?"

I let a small laugh leave me before I playfully respond, "He's handsome. He has a really charming smile...but you should hear him laugh."

My heart does a funny thing at the memory of it from just the other night.

The officer's rough chuckle doesn't compare in the least. He's a handsome man, on the right side of the law, with power and a strength that any woman would find attractive. But he's not my damaged hero. He's not a part of my family.

He's a pawn in their game and I'm content in doing my part.

"Are you sure you know what you're doing?" he asks me just as I turn my back to him, and my smile nearly falters. Nearly, but I hold it in place.

Turning back around and leaning forward, I have to lower my voice and whisper as though what I'm telling him is a secret. "I'm absolutely certain."

I leave without another word, but before the door closes to his office, I hear him say, "I really hope you are."

The ghost of a smile on my lips doesn't leave; it stays right where it is even though I feel a chill down my spine. It grows colder with every step. Among the clatter of keyboards, phones ringing, and the white noise of the officers and secretaries talking, I hear the click of heels clearly. They're in time with the beat of my heart.

It's not until I'm outside of the double-doored station and a gust of wind blows my hair over my shoulders, tickling up my neck, that the chill leaves me. With a deep breath, I search for the car, finding it quickly, with Daniel leaning against it.

He is my home. He is my person. Beside him is where I belong, and I'll do whatever it takes to stay there. Every sacrifice it demands, I'll make.

Thank you for reading these sexy novellas, intense shorts, and some of my favorite stories I've written. I usually don't write quickies, but I have to admit I love these stories and the road they paved to lead me where I am today in this writing career. Thank you for making it all possible.

Happy reading and best wishes,

Willow xx

About the Author

Thank you so much for reading my romances. I'm just a stay at home Mom and an avid reader turned Author and I couldn't be happier.

I hope you love my books as much as I do!

More by Willow Winters
www.willowwinterswrites.com/books

www.ingramcontent.com/pod-product-compliance
Lightning Source LLC
Chambersburg PA
CBHW020342010826
48973CB00005B/1241